Station Secrets

Regarding Hayworth

Book I

L. P. Suzanne Atkinson

lpsabooks
http://lpsabooks.wix.com/lpsabooks#

Cover Design by Adam Murray
Cover Photography by David Weintraub

ISBN
978-0-9949-5907-2 (Paperback)
978-0-9949-5908-9 (eBook)

1. Fiction, Contemporary Women
2. Fiction, Psychological Suspense

Distributed to the trade by the Ingram Book Company
Printed in the USA

Table of Contents

Nothing makes us so lonely as our secrets.
—Paul Tournier

Being prepared to die is one of the greatest secrets of living.
—George Lincoln Rockwell

I like characters who have strong facades and then have secrets.
They have cracks.
—Eva Green

Other works by L. P. Suzanne Atkinson

~Creative Non-Fiction~
Emily's Will Be Done

~Fiction~
Ties That Bind
Hexagon Dilemma: Regarding Hayworth Book II

For David
(in appreciation for his patience, indulgence, and photographs for the cover)

Thank-you to Pauline, Wyneth, Pat A., Kat, Marguerite,
Barb, Lesley and Jonathan A.

Chapter 1

Ben

She twists around to inspect her ass in the full-length mirror suspended on the back of the bathroom door. Her white cotton panties droop like a wet diaper. She's curious about just how much weight she's lost. Benjamine Grace Tullis is seventy-five. Her thick and white, naturally wavy hair hangs down over one eye, always poised to be dragged unceremoniously back behind her ear. She is still a beautiful woman despite her advancing age and current significant weight loss; still curvy, maintaining the enviable figure of a woman half her age.

Although she tries to temper her mood, a reluctant sigh escapes anyway. Today, she will close down her antique shop, opened in 1955. It's hard to believe she scratched out a living in this northern prairie town for twenty-five years. Most of the stock has been snatched up by faithful regulars and not-so-faithful bargain hunters, hoping to discover the crown jewels at fifty cents on the dollar. Despite all this, she is determined to have no regrets. The dregs will be loaded today and trucked to Edmonton as part of a big estate auction. Her neighbours, Patrick and Joe, volunteered to take time off from their own work to help. Good neighbours are one of the advantages of long time residency at The Station.

Sitting at the opposite edge of town from the Hayworth Diner, The Station got its name almost thirty years ago. The railway decided to build a fancy, modern facility and summarily moved the old station building to an empty lot as far away as they could, without putting it on a farm someplace. It was purchased by an outfit in Edmonton that turned it into an apartment house with six units. The building is old, built in 1920. It's now situated on a sloping lot, perched on a foundation constructed at the time of the move. It's high off the ground in the back and overlooks the creek that flows through town. The basement apartment is occupied by the building managers. There are two apartments on the main floor. Ben lives in Number Three on the right. There are two apartments on the second floor and one on the third. They call the third floor "the attic" and Patrick lives up there in Number Six.

When Ben moved to Hayworth, Alberta and opened her antique shop, she heard that everyone considered her a certifiable lunatic. Who was this woman, arriving out of nowhere and deciding she could just start a business? Well, times were tough for a while but then attitudes changed. Ben became a community fixture. She stayed. She contributed. She didn't move on, like so many easterners who come to northern Alberta to make a quick buck and then leave. She adopted the uniform of the locals and wore jeans with cowboy boots. Her favourite boots are crimson leather. She is well aware she can be spotted, when she crosses the street to the post office, from the other end of town. Her crazy white hair and those red boots have become her signature. She's honest and forthright. The locals started to like her back then. More importantly, they began to support her.

Her shop is a rented storefront on the main drag. The street is so wide that when pick-up trucks angle park on both sides there's still ample room for two lanes of traffic. She rents half of an old saloon-style building. The other side has been serially occupied over the years by a denturist, a dog groomer, an ice cream parlor, and currently, a nail salon. The smell of the lacquer bothers Ben but she doesn't complain.

The space is long and narrow. From the entry, stock and fixtures past the halfway point appear shadowed and lost. Her counter is at the front, and passersby can sometimes catch a glimpse of her through the display window. One wall is lined with shelves from front to back and floor to ceiling. The open areas were once filled to bursting with furniture. Customers could snag their pockets attempting to wedge themselves between the chests of drawers and dining room tables.

As she unlocks the back door and turns on the lights, her mind is focused on the shop in its glory days, so the appearance of the place takes her by surprise. The remaining stock sits like the picked over bones of a Thanksgiving turkey.

There won't be much to go on the truck. She makes her way to the front and the phone, when she remembers it's already been disconnected. Scheduling a doctor's appointment will have to wait until later. She'll have lots of time tomorrow.

The glass front door rattles and startles her out of her brief reverie. It's Patrick. She unlocks it, and he sidles inside. He doesn't make eye contact but merely nods to his friend as is his habit. Patrick Hollinger is twenty-five and works as a dishwasher in the kitchen of the local roadside diner located on the outskirts of Hayworth. He is scrawny and his brown hair always hangs in greasy strings. He usually smells and Ben has never seen him in any attire other than jeans, a black T-shirt, and a jean jacket. His skin is scarred by acne which still plays a significant role in defining his complexion. His obvious and serious challenges with hygiene follow him like a mongrel dog. Ben assumes he must have some kind of mental issue. He is socially crippled and associates with very few people. His loyalty to Ben is fierce, though. He's come to know her through his passion for collecting old toys. She has treated him with respect, a rare commodity for someone like Patrick. He lives in the attic apartment at The Station, and she is confident he would do whatever she asked of him.

"Good morning, Patrick." Ben closes the door behind him. "The furniture that's left will be loaded on the truck when the movers get here. Joe is coming to help, too." She gives him a big grin, perhaps employing a little too much enthusiasm. She doesn't want Patrick to hide in the back because there are too many people in the little shop.

"I can pack stuff." He gazes at the remnants of collectibles that still occupy shelf and table space. He doesn't look at Ben.

She walks to the office in the rear. "I've got boxes and paper in here. We'll make a plan before Joe shows up."

"I'm Patrick, not Pat. Pat's a girl's name." This is a familiar and repeated statement; an anxiety that pokes out on a regular basis.

"I know, Patrick. Don't worry. I'll always call you Patrick and ask other people to do the same." She turns and gives him a supportive nod as they enter her now cluttered and chaotic office. It used to be so neat and orderly but the act of liquidation has taken a toll, and she currently possesses neither the energy nor the enthusiasm to care.

Patrick focuses his gaze just above her left ear and replies with a smile, exposing his missing front tooth. "And I will call you Ben, even though that's really a boy's name."

Just as she gets Patrick settled into the rhythm of reaching, wrapping, and placing in the box, Joe Dodd strolls in. Joe is a self-employed carpenter and lives in Number Four at The Station, across the hall and up one flight from Ben. He's a tall man with a barrel chest and receding hairline. He drives one of the biggest trucks Ben has ever seen, even for the north which is renowned for big trucks. It's blue with a full crew cab, a wide box, and tandem wheels on the back—old but obviously well-maintained. He pulls a big white closed-in trailer containing all his tools when he goes on a job site. He mostly works alone and only hires help when necessary, which appears to be seldom. His voice booms as he throws out hellos and places three large coffees from the diner on the first table he encounters. The nutty, java smell wafts through the space, mingling with dust and the odour of old.

Ben appreciates the fact that he's taken the morning to lend a hand. She hopes he hasn't noticed the spur-of-the-moment nature of her decision to close. She doesn't worry that he has observed her obvious weight loss. Most men don't pay attention to such things anyway. "When's the truck showing up, Ben?" His voice echoes off the naked walls in the now-hollow space.

"They said about ten, Joe. We'll be ready to load by then. There isn't as much as I originally estimated." She takes a few steps closer and he hands her a coffee, hot and black, just the way she used to like it. She nods her thanks. "Do you want to start moving the furniture closer to the door while Patrick and I continue packing?" Joe and Patrick exchange polite nods of recognition, though neither man speaks. Ben is well aware that Patrick finds Joe intimidating, and that Joe thinks Patrick is just plain weird—and that he stinks most of the time.

"No problem," grunts Joe, as he picks up an oak side table and puts it at the beginning of what will soon be a line of furniture at the front door. They work in companionable silence for almost an hour, stopping only briefly for sips of cooling coffee. The truck pulls up. Its sudden appearance blocks the eastern sunshine spilling in through the display window and door. This permits the gloom from the back office to creep into the front of the shop. Joe loads the furniture, while Patrick lugs boxes of dishes and collectables from the office. It's over in no time. As the truck pulls out of the parking space and turns toward Edmonton, Patrick begins to sweep and Joe refocuses his attention on cleaning the bathroom. Ben tackles her office. By noon they're done, and she asks the men if she can buy them lunch at the diner. Although happy to do it, she's surprised they both accept.

The Hayworth Diner is familiar territory for Patrick, and Ben can tell by his demeanour that he likes being there. He gazes up at Nancy, their waitress, with puppy dog eyes. "What are you up to today?" She grins at Joe and Ben as she pours coffee and hands out menus.

Patrick answers, easily and without hesitation. "We helped Ben clean out the antique shop. She's retiring!" He grins widely, revealing the toothless gap in the front of his face for all to see. Nancy quickly shifts her focus toward Ben and congratulates her. Then she turns back to Patrick. "Aren't you on the schedule today?"

Patrick's pimples radiate a deeper red and his eyes drop down to his coffee cup. "Tonight," he mumbles.

Ben leans toward him. "You helped me all morning and now you intend to work a full day starting at three o'clock this afternoon?" She's suddenly sorry she recruited him. He had said he would get the day off, and she told him she'd pay so he wouldn't lose any money.

"They needed someone, so I said okay." His head is hung so low that his face almost touches the table, and Nancy is obviously uncomfortable.

"It's okay, Patrick. Just don't work too hard, that's all." Ben pats him on the shoulder. "What would you like for lunch?" They order. Ben and Joe discuss her retirement plans. She is purposely vague—just relax awhile, she guesses.

She doesn't eat very much. She has a couple of mouthfuls of scrambled eggs, and a bite of toast. The cramps start almost immediately. She excuses herself and moves as casually as she dares to the bathroom. When she returns, she puts a twenty on the table. "This will cover lunch and a tip for Nancy, you guys. I have to leave now. Thanks again for all the help." She's gone before anyone can argue.

Hayworth is a sight to behold in the spring. The poplar leaves are just starting to unfurl. The roads aren't terribly dusty yet. If it weren't for the oftentimes swarming black flies, it would be a great place. At one time everyone believed Hayworth would grow and develop into the gateway to the north, sitting as it does at the intersection of north, south, and western roadways. With the gas and oil industries beginning to boom, the Northern Alberta Railway Station plunked in the middle of it all, and companies hauling timber and crude south as fast as they can get it on the train, it only seems logical. For whatever reason it hasn't happened, yet everyone keeps waiting for "something". Hayworth remains a fledgling town of about three thousand with a ten-bed hospital, a set of schools, a post office, a grain elevator, a couple of churches, and a few small shops. There's no mall, no drive-through chicken take-out, no burger joints, and no coffee shops. It hasn't changed much since the day Ben first arrived.

As she drives her dark blue 1975 Datsun pick-up down Main Street from the diner to The Station, she can see beyond the two parallel streets of houses, out on to fields of wheat and canola. It has been a good spring, with just the right amount of rain and sun. Most of the fields are seeded. Later in the spring and summer, the canola will produce a blanket of yellow blossoms that will emit a scent that settles in the nostrils somewhere between sweat and musk. To the uninitiated, it can be disgusting, but for those who appreciate the true nature of the product, it's simply the sweet smell of success.

After she parks in The Station front lot, she unloads a box containing the remnants of her office paperwork, as well as a few odds and ends she has set aside as gifts for her neighbours, into her apartment. Her body says it should be eight at night and it's only a little after two in the afternoon. She wishes she could have a nap, as she hastily piles shop remnants on the counter and hustles to the bathroom. Diarrhea again! This has been happening pretty much every day for a long while now. The last time she went to her doctor he said she had a nervous condition and perhaps she needed to explore the option of retiring and relaxing a bit. She's wrung out as she returns to the kitchen, weak and shaky. Sorting the paperwork will wait for another day. Exhausted, she surveys her apartment and finds herself longing for the comfort of her couch. There should be more to this day than coming home, feeling sick, and taking a nap; such an anticlimax after being in business for so long.

So she stretches out on the navy blue leather down-filled sofa, its soft and familiar folds cupping her bony behind as she wiggles to get comfortable. This sofa has always reminded her of Hollywood movies from the forties. She lets her tired eyes rest on the space around her; on all the familiar objects. When she moved into the apartment, it shrieked newly renovated and sterile. It consists of a huge room with two bedrooms off to one side. Both bedrooms have a door to the bathroom located between the two of them. The kitchen is along one wall—sink, stove, and fridge with cupboards separating them.

Sparse and devoid of personality would not come close to describing it in the beginning.

Ben had no possessions, except for what fit in her car, when she first arrived in Hayworth. She bought a bed and a do-it-yourself spruce picnic table in a box. They delivered both and left the table in the middle of the floor. She asked the fellow who lived across the hall at the time if he could put it together and he happily obliged. Unsurprisingly, he was more than a little curious to know why this woman wanted a picnic table in her apartment. "You do know you won't be able to get it out without taking it apart?" She understood. It had been a door crasher special for fifteen bucks. Where could you get a table and chairs for fifteen bucks? Other furniture came in time, as she went to estate sales and gradually built up the business over that first year. It seems so long ago now.

She found the primitive coffee table, made from old barn boards, behind a family's shed. They planned to throw it out and gave it to Ben for being fair with them when they wanted to sell many of their possessions. It's round, the size of a wagon wheel, and the most delicious shade of chestnut imaginable. On it sits one of her most prized possessions—a pottery bowl that dates from the 1850s. Shaped like a helmet turned upside down and supported by a narrow foot, it's endowed with a perfectly crimped and symmetrical rim. The salt glaze and hand-painted brushed flowers reflect the chestnut hues of the table. She could swim in the beauty of these two objects forever.

The kitchen was never big enough. Shortly after Joe moved into The Station and found himself between jobs, she got him to build her a pine peninsula. It starts at the wall just past the window and stretches across the kitchen to the other end, to create a corridor that leads to the low window at the front of the building. Joe still talks about how much fun he had making it for her. The unit has two levels of open shelves and a heavy marble top. It took Joe and two big guys from a nearby job site to get that top into the apartment. The marble had to come from Edmonton and she has never told anyone how much it cost. To her eyes, the whole unit is a work of art.

As she starts to relax, sleep rolls in like an intimate fog. Her hand slips down and just touches the grey shag carpet trimmed in navy leather. The flaccid loops surround her fingertips with prickly softness. It seems like only seconds before she's awake, vaguely aware of urgency and a sense of panic. This can't be happening. She jumps up and propels her still only half awake self across the carpet, through the bedroom, and toward the toilet. Her pants are around her legs, but she isn't fast enough, as rank and disgusting liquid stool dribbles through her underwear and down her leg. She cries out as she sits, and the mess just runs out of her in a river of grey muck. She thinks that there isn't a bathroom fan strong enough to get rid of the stench. Tears stream down her cheeks. No more excuses. She will have to call the doctor.

Chapter 2

Amanda

Amanda watches her husband's dilapidated pick-up truck make the turn around the side of The Station. She stoops to put Mason back down in his playpen for the time being. He's fed and changed; contented with a teething ring so she can tidy up, take a shower, and start her day. She will probably drop in and see Ben for a minute to congratulate her on her retirement.

She surveys her space. The manager's apartment isn't particularly stylish. It consists of a huge open room, painted fawn beige, with two bedrooms off to one side and a bathroom in between—just like the apartments upstairs. The windows are across the back and on the bedroom side. Facing the creek and the open field, they're big and let in lots of light for a basement unit. It's almost as if you're in the middle of the countryside. Amanda worries that the constantly bubbling creek might overflow and they'll be flooded out, but it hasn't ever happened so perhaps, like other issues in her life, she worries for no reason.

Her mind unavoidably wanders to Chester. Born and brought up on a ranch just north of Hayworth, he's still young—twenty-eight, to be precise. Since he's the third oldest boy, he knew early on in life that he would likely not be running his father's grain ranch one day. As a consequence, he went to community college and got his mechanic's licence. Tall and good-looking in a boy-face kind of way with wavy dark hair that never seems to stay in place, he could probably land a TV commercial for shaving cream or shampoo. He always wears blue jeans and a plaid shirt to work. She knows the guys tease him because he covers up with a blue mechanic's coat. There will be no grease on Chester's clothes when he returns home at night. They call him The Professor and tell him he should work in a laboratory somewhere. He laughs. He takes it in stride.

Chester is very sure of himself but Amanda worries that he might have moments when he thinks he's gotten in over his head with too many responsibilities too fast. All of their burdens seem to have crept up on him over the last couple of years. He often says he's surprised at where he is in life. The job and the handyman combination are a lot. Amanda helps with rent collection and messages, but now that Mason has come along, she can't clean empty apartments or do painting and yardwork to the same degree she did a year ago. Chester doesn't seem unhappy, just overwhelmed lots of days. There's no more time to hang out at the diner after work or go to the Creek Tavern on the weekend. Babies are expensive. She pictures his square, heavy hands gripping the steering wheel as he negotiates the old pick-up into the gravel lot next door to the dealership; of him grabbing his lunch bucket off the seat and strolling in through the service entrance at the side of the building.

Amanda gives her head an almost imperceptible shake. Right now, instead of Chester's life goals, her biggest concern should be getting rid of this baby fat. Mason is six months old and she's still fifty pounds heavier than when she got married. Her long and liberally tinted red hair rests on shoulders that seem closer to her ears now that her neck is so wide. What the hell happened? Today she will pack Mason in the stroller and go for a walk; although, on second thought, the extra weight is one way to keep from being recognized. Amanda often silently frets that with all the comings and goings in a town like Hayworth, someone from out east might just turn up and know who she is. She'll go for a walk but it will be for Mason. To hell with weight loss! Chester doesn't seem to care. She grins as she turns toward the shower. She glances over at her chubby baby boy as he drifts off to sleep holding tight to the blanket made for him by Rose Woodward, up in Number Two. Rose has been a big help to Amanda as has mostly everyone in the building, for that matter. Lots of people offer to babysit but Chester and Amanda don't go out that often. It costs too much money and Amanda always searches for excuses to stay home.

The couple met purely by chance. Amanda came to Hayworth two-and-a-half years ago. She worked as a camp cook out in the bush and turned up in the small town when she got laid off all of a sudden. Jobs fluctuate with the price of oil and a downward turn changed the status of many camp workers. She landed a job at the Hayworth Diner as a short order cook, but she would never have met Chester if not for her Ford Bronco—a pain-in-the-ass truck if ever there was one. When she took it in to the dealership for the umpteenth time, Chester offered to drive her back to work. Chester came and got her, and Chester fixed that godforsaken rattletrap some might still refer to as a truck. They dated for months. She lived in a boarding house and spent all her waking hours at the diner. He had an apartment at The Station. Life fell into place when The Station needed a building superintendent and they could have the basement apartment for free. They'd been dating for almost a year by this time. Amanda stayed on at the diner for another six months, until she discovered her pregnancy. Chester really wanted to get married. Her eyes twinkle when she thinks about how sweet he was about their predicament; first came the proposal, then the ring, and finally the trip to Edmonton to get a fancy dress. Throughout the process, Amanda looked for ways out, but no plausible escape route presented itself. Soon they were Mr. and Mrs. Chester Wolski. She took on building management chores full-time so she could stay home with the baby. One would think their life was perfect. They were saving for a house and hoped, one day, to be able to live in their own place with Chester working his mechanics job and Amanda running a small cafe of her own. Everyone should be entitled to dreams regardless of their past.

By ten o'clock, she's organized. Mason is awake again. The apartment is tidied. She will take him into the front foyer in his stroller while she sweeps the stairs. Maybe Ben will pop out and keep them company. Mason gurgles and wiggles as she dresses him up in little bibbed overalls and a red undershirt. He knows he's going somewhere and the little guy is always ready for a ride—typical boy. Amanda wears the blue jeans she wore when she was pregnant, and a baggy yellow polka dot blouse that could pass for a maternity top if she happened to be having another baby. She gives herself a wry glance in the kitchen mirror as she ties her hair with a big elastic and plops a black Hayworth Diner ball cap on her head. She digs the pony tail out the hole in the back. Sweeping and then walking. At least she'll accomplish a task or two today.

She manoeuvres the bulky stroller, along with the broom and dustpan, around to the front of the building. She hauls her burden up across the big granite slab step and into the main hall. She gives Mason his soother and runs up the two flights so she can sweep down from the attic. It isn't that bad—just dust from roads and parking lots not paved, along with dirt from tenants' boots. They're all pretty good, seeming to treat the place as their own. It isn't unusual to see weird Patrick sweeping or Joe shovelling the front walk in the winter. Just when she starts down the stairs to the main entrance, Mason lets out a chirp as Number Three opens up to reveal Ben, still in her pyjamas.

"What have we got here, little man?" Ben enters the open space and her big blue eyes dart around quickly before she spies Amanda making her way down the steps. "Are you helping your mama today?" She bends over, and as she reaches out to touch the little boy, he grabs her finger and chirps again. He kicks his feet out from under his blanket, revealing little red sneakers. Amanda doesn't miss the indulgent smile that crosses Ben's face. Known for her red boots, she told Amanda she came across the sneakers at the thrift store and nabbed them for the baby long before his birth.

"Hey, Ben. Happy retirement. Aren't you the lazy-daisy, still in your pjs and the morning half gone?" Amanda grins down on Ben and finishes the stairs to the bottom in no time. "Mason and I are about to go for a little walk. We hoped maybe you might like to come." Quickly observing the anxiety in Ben's eyes, she adds that it won't be a long walk; she's too out of shape and it isn't horribly warm yet this spring.

Ben declines but adds, with out-of-character haste, that Amanda and Mason are more than welcome to stop in for tea and an Arrowroot biscuit on their way back. "I have a couple of calls to make; some loose ends to tie up this morning, but you two come back later." She retreats into her apartment with more abruptness than seems necessary. Amanda and Mason, left to their own devices in the foyer, set out for their walk.

Amanda is ashamed of herself. They didn't travel far. She excuses her negligence since she thinks the wind might be too brisk for her baby. She huffs a little with the effort but drags the stroller back up over the stone step and taps on Number Three. It takes almost a minute but Ben eventually appears. As good as her word, she invites the twosome in for tea and a cookie.

Amanda, always alert and observant after years of keeping a low profile, takes particular note today. Ben's skin has a grey cast. She seems to have lost considerable weight. Her voice sounds tearful and anxious. They won't stay long. "Big plans for your retirement? I must admit I was surprised to hear you were closing your shop. I thought you would run that place forever." She watches the older woman try to get comfortable at the end of the sofa.

"An antique selling antiques." Ben laughs, but without any enthusiasm. "I just couldn't do it anymore. Got tired. The doctor said I should pack it in." Her beautiful white hair falls across her eye as she shakes her head. "I don't have any particular plans, except I'd really like my health to improve a bit. I've been under the weather."

Amanda nods with sympathy. Pyjamas in the middle of the day, a distinctly unpleasant odor in the apartment, and a diet of rosehip tea and Arrowroot cookies all point to a lady with tummy trouble of one sort or another. You don't have to be a doctor to figure that out. "Might you be allergic to a food? I had an aunt allergic to milk and it was terrible. She had cramps all the time. Milk's in everything!"

Ben lifts her hand like a stop sign. She obviously doesn't want suggestions from the peanut gallery. "The doctor thinks I have a nervous stomach. He said I should get rid of the work and retire."

Amanda knows when to stop asking questions. She turns her attention to Mason who has been busy destroying his cookie and trimming every part of his body and the stroller with crumbs and sticky little blobs of Arrowroot. He tilts his sweet face up toward her and produces a toothless grin. "Look at this mess." She laughs as she turns back to Ben. She silently acknowledges the conversation about the older woman's health has come to an end.

"He is such a good-natured baby; so contented. You are an excellent mother, Amanda." She leans over and pats the girl's hand.

Amanda takes advantage of this moment of connection. "I know this is personal, Ben, but do you have any family? I don't believe I remember anybody visiting."

There is no mistaking the expression of profound sadness that moves across Ben's beautiful face. "I had a daughter once. She's dead." The words fall with force between them. Amanda doesn't know quite how to respond. She simply sits quietly and returns the soft touch to the hand that just touched her. "I used to have a grandson but I don't anymore." At this point, Ben rises from her seat and asks Amanda if she would like another cup of tea, thereby slamming the door to any more personal revelations.

Amanda accepts more tea because she's afraid that she would appear insensitive, somehow, if she left after what she just heard. They eat more

Arrowroot, which is just what she needs, and drink more tea. They play with Mason and talk about Hayworth, about Chester, and about The Station— all safe topics given the circumstances. Amanda is happy she stopped by and sadly surprised in the knowledge that she's not the only one with a burdensome past. Perhaps now that Ben's retired and will be around more often, they will get to know one another better and she'll be able to confide her secret. It would be a relief to share with someone she instinctively knows she can trust.

Chapter 3

Ben

As Chester Wolski made his way out to the street and off to the Ford dealership where he works as a mechanic, he most likely was unaware of the tenant perched on a stool at the end of her galley kitchen. With one long flannelette pajama-clad leg crossed over the other, she listened to rather than saw his old Ford 150 truck make the turn. She was up all night running back and forth to the can, throwing up mostly. She held a mug of recently brewed rose hip tea close to her nose and inhaled a smell it appeared she could actually tolerate.

Ben got up early as her primary goal is to secure an appointment with Dr. Gunton for today, if possible. She fears she'll lose her nerve. She tried really early and hoped to leave a message but the answering machine only says the office hours. She paced the floor for an hour and tried again. The line was busy at first. Then Rose put her on hold. Then she came on the line and said they were busy so could she call Ben back. Ben doesn't want to get in the shower for fear the phone will ring, so she waits.

Brushing a stray silver lock of hair across her forehead, she wanders into the spare room and stares at the box of papers and stack of offerings still sitting where she placed them yesterday. She really needs to sort through her paperwork and then call the accountant. Her stomach rolls. She takes a Tums and makes some more rosehip tea. It's almost noon when Rose calls back. Ben's just returned from another trip to the bathroom. She's a wreck and feels weepy, shaky, and more than a little bit sorry for herself.

She answers the telephone's bleat on the third ring. "Yes, Rose. I need an appointment. I really need to talk to the doctor again."

She hears Rose's huff of impatience. "Same problem, Ben? Back pain? Weight loss? Diarrhea and vomiting?"

"Yes. Yes. I must be sick. He told me to retire, so I've retired. If I have a nervous gut, the damned thing is still nervous. Can I get in today?"

"No. Not today. If you want to come over early tomorrow morning, I'll try and fit you in but it could be a long wait. It could take all morning."

Ben is resigned. "I guess that'll have to do. As long as I can find a seat close to the can."

"I'll pop by tonight after work, Ben. Shall I bring some chicken soup from the diner?"

Ben, with limited success, attempts to control the wobble in her voice; the shadows of tears lie on top of each word. "I'll try the soup, Rose. It's always good. I have trouble keeping down anything but Arrowroot, though. Mason likes them so it's not all bad." She gives the receiver a watery smile, thinking back to her visit with Amanda and Mason earlier in the morning. She still can't fathom why she decided to share information about her dead daughter and her phantom grandson. Hopefully, the girl isn't a blabbermouth. For some reason, the words just fell out of her face and she instinctively trusted Amanda not to repeat them. She must be getting soft in her old age.

She knows Rose sympathizes and agrees that she must be sick. Over the last six months, she's mentioned more than once that Ben appears to be fading away. Alexander Gunton will have no patience. He'll tell her to relax, take Tums, take a vacation, or find a hobby. He's more than likely to mumble, under his breath, about coping with menopause—at her age! He can be obtuse sometimes!

****

After a long day of not going any great distance from the bathroom, Rose's unmistakable knock sounds at the door.

Ben trudges over, reluctant at this point to even pretend to have a conversation. She opens the door a crack and then widens it slightly when she sees Rose, who has taken the time to go over to the diner after a long day of work in that zoo of an office. She holds a Styrofoam tub of soup in one hand and her purse in the other. She hasn't even opened her own apartment door yet.

"Hi, Ben." Her voice is too cheery. It's annoying. "Are you any better?" Perhaps if Rose actually uses her powers of observation, and Ben is fully aware of how she comes across, Rose will figure it out for herself.

"I look like shit and that's exactly how I feel." Her words are flat, without emotion. "Thanks for bringing me the soup. Very kind." The smell makes her queasy. She can't stand here much longer. "I intend to go to bed soon. I'll have the soup first," she lies.

Rose hands over her gift, while summarily ignoring the money in Ben's outstretched hand. She then rifles around for her keys, which she probably tucked in her pocket when she got out of her car. "Do you want me to pop over and check on you later?"

"God, no! I'll be fine. Just a little wrung out is all. You enjoy your evening after that long day at work." Ben attempts a smile, with limited success, as she slowly moves the door toward closed.

Rose tilts her head sideways in order to continue connecting with Ben, nods, waves, and turns to her own apartment. Ben glances quickly at the back of her, spits out another hopefully appreciative thank-you, and mercifully closes the door. Ben throws the soup out. Even the smell of it makes her want to hurl.

****

After drinking half a bottle of Pepto-Bismol before leaving home, she now sits in Dr. Gunton's office prepared for a long wait. She has chosen a red stackable vinyl chair close to the bathroom but the pink stuff seems to have done the trick. Maybe she should just drink it every day and all this would go away. Rose glances over at her often, from behind the counter. The room is filling up with cranky toddlers, workmen in muddy boots, and other old ladies. Ben hopes she doesn't come across as decrepit and miserable as some of them do. Funeral music plays in the background. Couldn't Rose find better radio than that? Even the local country and western station would be an improvement. At least they read the news and weather every half hour.

It's past eleven when Rose finally calls her name. She is settled in a little room with an exam table and a sink. The overhead fluorescent is very bright. It makes the cuticles of her nails look purple. With this type of light, it would be hard to appear the picture of health regardless of your condition. After another half hour, in sprints the man.

Dr. Alex Gunton is a male chauvinist pig. Ben firmly believes he both knows it and is proud of it. Everyone assumes he thinks most women have too much time on their hands and create their own health problems. As for him, he's slim, trim, and cocky. His wife stays home like any proper wife. She makes sure his meals are ready, his kids are managed, and his social calendar is properly administered. At forty-two years old, he obviously thinks he is in his prime and is the best person to tell his patients how to live their lives. That's why he became a doctor, he hastens to tell anyone who will listen and even many who couldn't care less—to help people be better versions of themselves. What he's coming to discover, much to his often expressed annoyance, is that not everyone is anxious to cooperate. He avoids eye contact. He makes little attempt to hide the fact that he isn't particularly fond of the elderly, especially women. He acts like they're all a little sullied or something. If there were more doctors in town, he would likely lose a large measure of his practice. He opens her file and scratches a few notes.

Ben has chills. Her hands are clammy. *Listen to what he's saying.* She imagines herself immersed in a well, hearing his voice float over the top barely discernible. Her head aches from trying to concentrate. She must frustrate him somehow. She knows she's expected to recite her symptoms and has little doubt he will manage to get through the appointment without ever examining her.

"We might as well send you for some blood work. How much weight have you lost?"

"I don't know. I don't have a scale but my clothes don't fit anymore. Even my boots are loose." Her attempt at a joke fails. He pays no attention.

"Hop up on the scale and tell me what you weigh."

Ben does as she's told and moves the weights. She figures she should be about one hundred and forty, shocked as she reports one hundred and fifteen to Dr. Gunton.

"Lots of women would be thrilled to be that weight," he responds to her report without turning around. "Try an elimination diet. You know what that is?" He shoves a pamphlet across the desk. "Start with brown rice and then add other foods gradually. It's all in this. You might have a food allergy. Keep a diary. No smoking. You don't smoke, do you? No coffee or alcohol. Once I get your blood work back, Rose will call you and let you know if you need to come in. Do you want an x-ray? Who knows? Maybe you have an ulcer.

I'll order an x-ray, too. There. Satisfied?" He closes the file with a thud and stands up to leave. There are two orders that remain on the table. They must be intended for her.

Ben nods to Rose as she leaves the office. Although anxious to get home and rest her aching bones across her bed, she will make a trip to the grocery store first. It feels like it should be the middle of the night. She'll get the blood work tomorrow and make an appointment with Hayworth Community Hospital for an x-ray. She sits in her truck as the warm midday sun falls across the brochure she holds in her lap. She reads the information about elimination diets before she pulls out of the parking lot. Basically, she needs to eat brown rice with herbal tea, water and no additives. No sugar, no dairy, and no wheat. Only rice flour or rice milk. Now, who on earth would think you could find rice flour in a small town in the north? The nearest health food store is hours away. No spices, no red meat. Only chicken or fish. Nothing fried. No citrus fruit. Nothing canned or boxed. No soy products of any kind. She mutters to herself. Wouldn't life be great if she was just allergic to some kind of food? Deep in her heart of hearts she suspects this will not be the answer. She will try.

Ben shops as best she can. Although not relishing the prospect of eating and the inevitable aftermath, she makes brown rice and bakes a chicken breast when she gets home. She takes her time, assembles the ingredients, and prepares a plate. She sets the table and uses pretty dishes. She makes more rosehip tea, in a teapot, not just in a mug. Her mind is famished. Her body may well have other ideas. The food tastes good. She wants this to be okay. She sits at her picnic table, listens to the radio, and eats slowly, chewing every bite. She wills herself to keep the food down. She concentrates on trying to enjoy the moment although images of her daughter and grandson cloud her focus—a situation she has tried to control without much success over the years. She is desperate to be fine.

Chapter 4

Rose

Rose navigates her faded red 1975 Chevy Nova sedan into the front parking lot at The Station. She leans back into the seat and stares out the dusty windshield with exhausted eyes. The office was wall to wall people all day. She managed to stop at Stedman's Variety on the way home to pick up some more wool. There was no mail. She drags her purchase and her tattered navy blue shoulder bag from the passenger seat, locks her car, and enters the building as she thinks about Ben. She'll check on her later. The smell of chicken wafts from Number Three and answers the question of whether she prepared herself some food to eat besides Arrowroot and tea. It remains to be seen if she actually ate it.

Rose Woodward has worked for Dr. Alex Gunton almost ten years now. It can be a challenge but she's learned how to manage his chronically idiosyncratic behaviour. In some ways, she thinks she might be the one woman he genuinely respects. Today was merciless. He pushed people through like a madman. She thinks he has lost patience with Ben and hopes her long-time neighbour isn't really sick.

Rose unlocks the door and enters what she considers her private sanctuary "far from the maddening, or was that madding, crowd"? Didn't she read that in a book somewhere? Perhaps a Thomas Hardy title. She can't remember. She smiles as her tired eyes rest on the turquoise walls and yellow accessories throughout the main apartment. Caesar comes to greet her. He rubs his sleek tortoiseshell furriness around her legs as she wiggles in the door and drops her bags and keys on the seven-foot-long harvest table employed as an island in the middle of the kitchen. He's a good cat. They have been roommates for five years now. She picked him up at the shelter when a big cry went out that older cats were all to be euthanized. He is very regal. He often sits on top of the refrigerator and observes Rose as she works. His head tilts just slightly as his slanted green eyes with golden flecks watch her every move. She sometimes thinks she's living with him instead of the other way around.

No meetings tonight. She sighs with relief, as she reaches over to fill the kettle with water and gives some serious consideration to the topic of supper. She must try to go for a walk tonight. The idea of leftover casserole does not stimulate her appetite but that's probably good. Too much sitting at the office is adding pounds to her already frumpy physique. Rose is almost five foot four. She has straight blond hair that requires the expertise of professional curling augmentation about four times a year. Rose hates to get her hair permed but it's the only way to manage straight, fine, wispy strands that she is horrified to admit are starting to turn grey in the right light. With a little bit of curl she can employ a hair band with teeth and keep the wisps under control. Rose mostly wears gathered skirts and sweater sets, or blouses she makes herself and pairs with a cardigan. She sews her clothes and knits her sweaters. She is a crafting queen. She fills her spare hours with knitting, sewing, or crocheting for herself, her friends, and local charities. There isn't a baby born in Hayworth that doesn't have a newborn hat and a baby blanket made by Rose. The hospital has started to expect them and she tries to have a few on hand. For a little hospital, they deliver a lot of babies. Of course, working in one of the doctors' offices gives her an inside track.

Rose putters away in her kitchen, makes a pot of Earl Grey tea, and turns on the oven to heat up the hamburger and macaroni casserole that has probably occupied too much real estate inside her fridge for too long. Perhaps, if it's good and hot, it will serve the purpose of nourishment for tonight.

She feeds Caesar and tunes in the news. Rose is a television junkie and a news hound. The squawk box, as many call it, is on at Rose's as long as she's awake. It doesn't really matter what's scheduled. She loves her TV. It has become her company over the years, the other voice in the house, and her window to the world. When she first left her husband, she bought a TV before she got a couch. She knew she needed company. She was the first tenant at

The Station to get cable. American news always makes her happy to be living in Canada. A twenty-four hour news station will start in the summer. It will be called the Cable News Network. Rose can hardly wait. Live television all the time! Canada is all over the news right now because of what Canadians did for Americans in Iran. Rose was so proud. The world is changing. Canada has its first female governor general. Who would have believed that would happen in her lifetime? She watches all the reports she can about Mt. St. Helens erupting. When the winds blow a certain way it seems darker here in the north, like there are forest fires burning in the distance. The dust plume is moving across North America. The pictures are unbelievable and they haven't even gotten up the mountain yet. How many people must be dead? Some towns have a foot of ash in the streets. It's hard to believe. Rose marvels at how much you can learn from just watching TV.

She settles into the floral upholstered wing-backed rocker. If you squint in the right light, carefully, you may actually discover some of the turquoise colour mirroring the paint on the walls. It matches the extra long sofa positioned with precision facing the kitchen. She purchased them at an auction when she first came to town. She added a coffee table, the harvest table she uses as a kitchen island, and the art deco dining room set from the 1930s, all over the next couple of years. She got the dining room set from Ben for a steal because the Bakelite hardware was damaged and there were only three chairs instead of four. Rose didn't care. She loved the curvy lines, the slight hint of orange in the finish, and the doors with the glass panes that resemble church windows. Ben gave her the distinct impression Rose was doing the antique dealer a favour by taking it off her hands. The little shop was crowded and Ben was trying to weed out any stock that wasn't in mint condition. Rose gazes over at the suite. Even though she rarely has dinner guests, she holds meetings at her apartment and the furniture definitely comes in handy. She, on the other hand, always eats in front of the TV.

With her supper ready, Rose repositions her ample bum and settles in to watch the seven o'clock version of the US news out of Seattle. She munches away on casserole, sips her tea, and promises Caesar he may chair-share once she's finished eating.

****

Rose is thirty-five years old. She came to Hayworth ten years ago after she left her husband of six months. Marriage just did not prove to be a viable option for the young woman she was at the time. She simply could not cope with the idea of some guy telling her what to do and when to do it. She feared she would accidentally get pregnant and then be stuck for life so she left. Leaving had worked in the past and it worked again. Eventually he divorced her. No big deal. Rose likes to be involved in the lives of others so her work in the doctor's office is a good fit. She managed to get a high school equivalency and then a medical receptionist certificate on her own, after she left school and home at sixteen.

Jobs were hard to come by when she first arrived so, like the many others both before and after her, she waited tables at the Hayworth Diner and rented a room until she landed the position with Alex Gunton. She figures no one else would tolerate his attitude. He can be such a pig. She just made up her mind she had suffered through a lot worse and her life experiences had prepared her well for dealing with an asshole like him. It's worked out fine.

Rose's social life consists mainly of her charity work now. She is on the hospital auxiliary and the library board. She has her crafts to keep her company on the long northern winter nights, and the tenants at The Station have proved themselves to be tolerable. Everyone respects each other's privacy. They all came from away, just sort of turned up in Hayworth, started to make a living, and stayed. Odd.

****

The phone jangles and jogs Rose out of her comfort zone of casserole, chair, and TV. She balances her plate on the end table as she struggles to get up. She crosses the kitchen to attend to the disruption. Amanda is on the other end. Rose can hear Mason gurgling.

"Hi. Amanda? What can I do for you tonight?" Rose checks her kitchen clock. It's already past seven-thirty. That baby should be asleep. She watches Caesar to make sure he doesn't try to help himself to her supper. He is most certainly not above such behaviour.

"Hi, Rose. Do you know if Ben's okay? I wanted to have a little building get-together for her this weekend to celebrate her retirement but I'm worried she isn't well. When I swept the stairs yesterday mid-morning, she came to the door still in her pyjamas. Then just before lunch we went back for tea and a cookie. She was still dressed for bed."

Rose, ever mindful of confidentiality and small towns, replies with caution. "Well, she's retired. She should take advantage of sleeping in. Did you wake her up?" Rose laughs and tries to sound casual. "Have you called her to see if she wants a party?"

Amanda's obviously readjusting Mason on her knee. She grunts a little with all the effort as she replies. "I won't phone her this late but I guess I can touch base with her in the morning. I just assumed you had talked to her." Rose is pretty sure Amanda isn't just nosey and wanting information from the doctor's office. "Would you come to a little Station gathering, Rose?"

"Of course I'll come, Amanda. Can I help? I'll contribute chips and some of my homemade dip. How about some cocktail weenies and sauce? What else do you need?" She hears Amanda sigh. Maybe she thinks that chips and weenies aren't fancy enough and she'd prefer an offer more along the lines of mini quiche and summer salad. Amanda fancies herself as some kind of chef. Too bad! It is what it is—probably a barbecue at the back of the building.

"That's a great start, Rose. I'll call everyone and then get back to you. We'll try for Saturday afternoon and have a barbecue if the weather holds. See you later. Bye for now."

Rose gathers up her dinner plate, tidies her kitchen, and returns to her chair but stops before she settles in for the evening. Maybe she'll just pop over to Ben's and see how she is. It's still light out so she's probably up. She opens her door situated straight across the hall from Ben's. She leaves it ajar, tiptoes over, and knocks softly. She can't hear Ben. She tries again with a little more determination this time.

"I'm coming! Just give me a second, already!" The grouchy voice gets closer with each word hurled against the still-closed door. Ben slides it open just a crack and peers out at her neighbour. "Rose! Is there a problem?"

"Not at all." Rose just now starts to feel uncomfortable for some reason. "Were you asleep? I'm sorry if I woke you up. I just wanted to see if you got what you needed at the grocery store or if I could help somehow." The words fall out of her mouth like water out of an overflowing bucket. Ben just stands there and stares at her. "Are you okay?"

The older woman exhales audibly and her shoulders heave with the effort. "Do you want to come in? You left your door open. Here comes Caesar."

She bends over and pats the cat, like she has to be polite. Caesar accepts her attention and then promptly returns to familiar surroundings, his curiosity obviously satisfied.

Rose hesitates. Her comfy chair and a quiet evening with some fresh wool for knitting beckon her back across the hall. She thinks about the plans she has to start to make for her annual pilgrimage to Forest Hills Institute in southern Ontario. Her car might make it one more time but she'll probably need new tires. "I'll just close my door and come in for a minute."

The apartment is hot, cluttered, and smells bad. It smells a bit like a barn, if the truth be known and it's too late in the evening to open windows with a seventy-five year old frail lady occupying the space inside. Rose tries to breathe through her mouth. "I ate some chicken and brown rice for supper." Ben's voice sounds defeatist, as if eating failed somehow. "At any rate, I've spent the last hour on the toilet, so chicken and rice aren't the answer to my problems. I'm beginning to think I will be eating Arrowroot for the rest of my life." Seeming to sense Rose's discomfort, she continues. "I suppose I should apologize for the smell. I imagine it stinks to high heaven in here. I can't tell anymore." She scuffs over to her big blue leather sofa. Her flannelette pyjama bottoms drag on the honey buffed floorboards. She curls up into a little ball in the corner. Her shrunken frame reveals itself through her open dressing gown. Her pyjamas appear three sizes too big. "To answer your question and a kind gesture it is, there is not one thing you can do to help. I went to the store and got what I needed. I took the time to cook and eat. I actually enjoyed doing both but I've been miserable ever since. I guess I'll stick to the Arrowroot until after the blood tests and X-rays are back. Any other suggestions?"

Rose decides to change the subject. She stays attached to the brown mat that proclaims welcome and determines she won't sit. "Amanda called. She wants to have a potluck on Saturday for your retirement. You think you might be up for that?" She has doubts.

"Do I look ready to party?" Ben's shoulders shudder. She emits a stifled moan as she attempts to smile. "I think my party days are behind me."

"Maybe I can tell her we can plan a tenant barbecue and you'll pop down if you're up to it. Would that work?" *Did Alex actually examine the woman at all? He probably didn't lay a hand on her. God!*

Ben relents as Rose graciously lets her off the hook, reaches for the knob, and takes her leave. "I'll check on you tomorrow," she says as she crosses the threshold. She turns around just in time to notice the older woman clutch her side and grimace as another wave of cramps obviously envelopes her.

Rose experiences guilty relief as she removes herself from the olfactory influences across the hall. With gratitude she returns to her casserole-scented apartment with the slight undertones of lavender from a potpourri sachet that she must remember to refresh. Once again ensconced in her wing-back, she reaches for her knitting after turning the television back on just in time to watch *Dallas*. Rose is convinced Ben is sick. She's lost a remarkable amount of weight and this whole vomiting and diarrhea situation has gotten out of hand. She wishes she could talk it over with her boss but Dr. Alexander Gunton would never listen to information from his receptionist. He's a lost cause. She makes a mental note to keep a special eye out for the reports on Ben. The familiar music begins and Rose permits herself to be transported into the world of the Ewing family and their oil empire. Her knitting needles clatter to the rhythm of the series theme song as Caesar perches on the back of the chair.

Chapter 5

Joe

Joe pulls his truck into the back lot behind The Station. He never parks out front. He leaves those spaces for visitors and little vehicles. The sun continues to blaze although it's after eight at night. He's hungry, sweaty, and bone-tired. Since he took more than half a day to help Ben on Monday, he expects to be under the gun all this week. Gail Willford insists that her kitchen installation be complete by Friday and that will mean some long days. Mrs. Willford is part of Hayworth's top tier, as it were. Her husband has made a lot of money in the oil field maintenance business and she figures she can have whatever she wants, whenever she wants it. Anyone who works for Gail is treated like a servant, and a "piss-poor" one at that by the time she's done with them. She picked out a dark pine kitchen in Edmonton. She refused to deal with the Hayworth or Carter River lumber yards and their choices although they've always seemed more than adequate for most locals. She got a dozen quotes for installation and then picked Joe even though he was sure he wasn't the cheapest. She said she wanted someone who knew what they were doing and he had a good reputation. Fair enough, but she is a ball-buster nonetheless. When one of her husband's trucks arrived with the cabinets last Saturday she called Joe and expected him to drop whatever he was doing, come out to her house, and supervise the unloading of the lot to ensure all the shipment arrived safely and in one piece. Joe argued for a couple of minutes. He wasn't hired to supply the kitchen—just install it. If there were problems she would have to deal with the company in Edmonton. She knew all that. Mr. Willford was away and she wanted someone besides the truck driver to do an inspection. So he went but made it abundantly clear that installation could not start until Monday afternoon. He wanted time to help Ben.

Gail finally relented, under protest, and he knew she wouldn't go easy on him when he finally started the job. She was obviously not the least bit pleased.

So on his first full day at the site her attitude hadn't improved. He smiles as he makes his way up the granite step, into the foyer, and on to Number Four on the second floor while he thinks about his client. She is tall and thin. She met him at the door, in pink capris and little heeled sandals. Her curly hair was tied into a knot on the top of her head with a pink candy-striped ribbon. She sashayed around, smoked her extra long Benson and Hedges, asked useless questions, and was generally an annoying pain in the arse. By noon he was fed up to the teeth with tripping over her in his workspace, so he assigned her chores—like fetching screws, holding the level, discarding cardboard wrapping—whatever he could find to keep her busy. It worked. Before day's end she'd changed into coveralls and sneakers and proved herself to be a decent helper, although she complained about missing supper. Who knows? With her assistance he might actually get the damned cupboards installed by the end of the week.

Joe is met at the door by Blanche. She would have heard the truck when he turned into the yard. Blanche is a blind, white, long haired cat weighing at least fifteen pounds. She was abandoned at a job site a few years ago, starved and confused. Joe is sure someone threw a toxic chemical of some sort into her face. He brought her home and that was that. He never considered himself a pet-person, but Blanche obviously did not know that and it has apparently worked out. He bends over, croons her name, and picks her up as he turns to close the door. "Now, little girl, you and I need to get ourselves some supper," Joe continues to croon. He refers to her as "little" to spare her sensibilities about her waistline.

It's in the kitchen where the real Joe is revealed. Just like his meticulousness on the job site, Joe has gradually and with determination fully equipped his adequate kitchen so that he can turn out healthy and interesting meals in short order. After feeding Blanche, he reaches for cooked chicken sliced precisely and frozen weeks ago in a meal-sized portion, then left to thaw in the fridge this morning. He adds a bowl of vegetables, already prepared before he left for work. He boils water for the rice and quickly throws together a ginger sauce that would rival any good restaurant. Coupled with a generous glass of chilled white German wine, he sits down at the chrome set in the middle of the room to listen to *As It Happens* on CBC. Although he has a TV, his preference is most often the radio.

His eyes travel lazily around his apartment as he thinks about Ben. She didn't seem too good yesterday. He remembers the week or so he spent making her kitchen peninsula and that God-forsaken marble top she insisted she have. Of course there was no one in Hayworth, back then, who could supply a top like that so she got one out of Edmonton. Only Benjamine could pull that off! That's when they became friends and he has enjoyed their relationship ever since.

Joe's apartment tastes are simple. A guy has to make a living so any extra money is spent on his truck and tools. The apartment has the basics: a good double bed for a forty-five-year-old with few prospects and a temperamental back, a thrift store dresser, the chrome kitchen set he bought at a yard sale—Ben says it's collectible, but Joe thinks it's serviceable—and a living room set including the end tables and lamps he bought at a furniture warehouse in a town nearby. It's plaid. It's manly. It came with a matching recliner. He likes simplicity and long ago determined he deserves no more. He doesn't have cable.

****

As he washes his supper dishes while Blanche weaves her way in and out around his ankles, his mind drifts back to those early days in Nova Scotia when he lived with Leslie. She was a party girl, tall and thin like a model, with naturally curly hair that had a mind of its own. She insisted on growing it long and then complained that it would never do what she wanted. She was always reduced to snarling it up in a big elastic or clawing it behind her ears in order to see out through the masses. She wore really tight jeans and blouses with frilly fronts. She liked chunky jewellery. She worked in the clerical department for an outfit that manufactured fishing equipment. It wasn't as glamorous as Leslie but it paid well. She drank a lot and he was pretty sure she smoked pot, too, but never around him. He started to do the house chores because she simply had no use for activities other than having a good time.

That was fun while they dated, but after they moved in together he wanted them to knuckle down, save some money, and maybe buy a house. She said she wanted a family but Joe couldn't cope with the idea of kids, especially with someone so irresponsible. God, they were young then! Two people like that shouldn't have kids. They'd never be able to take care of them. He left Leslie just like he left his family. He listened to a show on the radio once that said that people try to outrun their family history. It sounded familiar.

He actually married Mona and it lasted for two years—a whole six months longer than his relationship with Leslie. Mona became the antithesis of Leslie in Joe's mind. Short and kind of dumpy, she had straight dark hair cut every six weeks in the same style she referred to as "Pixie". She didn't like Joe's help around the house and acted like she could do it all. Joe often felt in the way. By this time, he figured his penance in life would be to work really hard and not have a great deal of fun. He worked even harder and spent more time on the job site. She made noises about wanting to start a family and from that point on their relationship disintegrated pretty fast. He and Mona got divorced. It wasn't complicated. They didn't have much to speak of. Joe jumped in his truck and started to drive. He followed a well-honed pattern and found himself in Hayworth in 1966 at the ripe old age of thirty-one. He had to try and make a living with little to go on but a work ethic, limited construction skills, and a determination few could understand.

He worked for a long time with an old guy who had needed a helper. When he retired, Joe took over his work and has been in Hayworth ever since. He doesn't go back to the Maritimes although he could. He has two sisters there and his mother is still living in the scruffy backwoods town near the South Shore of Nova Scotia where he grew up. She lives in a village farmhouse. It's a big old rundown affair that used to be a farm, but the land gradually got sold off and the village developed around it. It badly needed a paint job when he left and probably still does. His mother isn't well according to the annual letter he got last Christmas from one of his sisters—the forgiving one. Christine is just one year older than Joe. She's always taken the initiative and maintained contact. He isn't sure if anyone else even knows. Anita is older and absorbed the emotions of their parents all those years ago. She has never spoken to him since it happened. His father died without any semblance of reconciliation. Joe didn't go to his funeral. He never hears from his mother, but Chrissie says she's pretty sick.

He tries to imagine what they're all like now. When they were kids, Anita was prim and proper—a holier-than-thou type. She bugged everybody with her bossiness. Her mannerisms screamed severe. She tied her mousy brown hair back from her face so tight it seemed like her eyebrows stretched toward her ears. Maybe that contributed to her attitude. Chrissie was a tomboy. You couldn't pay her to wear anything but overalls. His mother tried to bribe her into a dress just to go to church but God forbid the idea of a ribbon in that long blond hair. Joe's mother was always old to him—in house dresses and aprons, pushing wisps of grey hair off her damp face with the back of a chapped hand as she hovered over the ancient wood stove in the kitchen. It was the singular source of heat back then.

****

Just as he's about to jump into the shower before going to bed, his phone propels him back to reality. The thought crosses his mind that this might be Gail calling to torment him one more time before he can call it a day. He's surprised to hear Amanda on the other end.

"Hi. I saw your truck come into the lot. Is it too late to call?" The perkiness of her voice serves to emphasize how exhausted he feels.

"Not at all, Amanda. What can I do for you?" He drops into his recliner and drags the long phone cord with him. Blanche, pleased with his decision, springs into the centre of his lap, immediately starts to purr, and snuggles in. As he balances the phone on the arm of the chair, Joe is curious if Chester needs some help with a maintenance issue. It wouldn't be the first time. He likes the young couple and Mason is a cutie, but he sometimes thinks the building might be a bit too much for them.

"I'm planning a barbecue for the tenants this Saturday. Can you come? It started off as a retirement party for Ben but at this point I'm not totally sure Ben will even show up, so I decided we would have a spring potluck and she'll make it if she's able."

Joe knows Ben was having a bad day when they vacated her antique shop. Is she sick? What about her family? She's never talked about relatives and no one's ever visited, at least not since he's been living here, which is almost as long as Ben. He makes a mental note to ask her if she needs any help. "I'll come, Amanda. Sure, no problem, but I'm working with a lady who will probably find a way to keep me on the job site all day Saturday, so how about I bring the beer?" He would prefer to contribute coleslaw and probably will, but doesn't want to make promises he can't keep.

"That's great. I knew I could count on you, Joe. We're all worried about Ben, you know."

Joe is pretty sure "all" means Amanda and Rose. He can't imagine them talking about Ben around weird "Call-me-Patrick-Pat's-a-girl's-name," and Cheryl Nadler, across the hall, barely says hello to anyone just on principle. It must be because she's a social worker. You never know what other people know. "Well," he adds, not wanting to share any observations at this point, "she seemed tired after she got the stuff at the store all wrapped up. I hope she isn't sick."

Amanda thanks him for his offer to bring the beer and signs off. As Joe continues to sit in his recliner, balancing the phone on the arm of the chair and rubbing his hand with absent tenderness down Blanche's broad and silky back, he lets his mind wander through the apartments of The Station. His thoughts settle momentarily on each resident in the little community. They all get along. It's like a village, no doubt about it. Then again, Chester is the only resident he knows much about. He was born and brought up in the area. Everyone else is a bit of a mystery. Where did Patrick come from, anyway? He moved in about five years ago and has worked in the kitchen at the diner ever since. What brought Ben here back in 1955? Rose has been here over ten years. Why Hayworth for her? Amanda seemed to turn up out of nowhere three years ago.

And then there's the mysterious Cheryl. He shakes his head. He wishes he could ask Cheryl out but she's like the ice queen. She responds to a greeting, but that's about it. He half hopes she might see Ben's kitchen peninsula and want one of her own. At least that would get him a foot in the door. Maybe Ben could recommend him. Then he remembers Gail Willford.

Into the shower and off to bed. Tomorrow will be another day focused on the complicated, yet somehow rewarding, management of the lovely Mrs. Willford who reminds him of Leslie in many ways. He decides to teach her how to install the cabinet hardware so she'll have a productive task to perform while he gets the oven wall unit and the pantry assembled. The upper cabinet hardware should keep her busy for a few hours.

He gently lifts Blanche off his knee and places her down on the floor. He hauls himself out of the chair, where he knows he could sleep the night away if inclined to give himself permission, and drags the phone cord back to the kitchen. Blanche pops up into his seat and takes over the warm spot. No wonder he always has white cat hair on his ass.

Just before he turns in for the night, Joe takes the time to compose a note to Ben. He'll slip it under her door on his way out in the morning.

> *Hey, Ben, hope you're all rested up after Monday. If there's any other help you need, just let me know. Happy to be of assistance, or visit for tea. Call anytime. Joe.*

Joe's sleep is fitful. Blanche sits as sentry on the night table and watches with empty eyes, ears pricked as he tosses and turns. Plaster angels perch on crooked branches of giant fir trees that reach high into a sky of mahogany slats. He is afraid. Everyone stares at him. No one touches him. There is no hand of comfort on a small boy's shoulder; no mother's hug. All he sees is the unsympathetic back of an uncle in an ill-fitted suit jacket that needs the attention of a dry cleaner. He stands alone. The wind blows hard and he is cold from the inside out.

Chapter 6

Patrick

The streets of Hayworth are quiet in the subdued twilight late Wednesday evening as Patrick Hollinger, returning home after his shift at the diner, walks the length of the small town on foot. It's been a long day. They were busy for a mid-week in May. His hands are raw from the hot water. Gloves suffocate his skin and constrict him in a way he can't explain even to himself. His lanky frame rolls, like an overloaded hay cart, down the darkened street where only pick-up trucks parked in front of the Creek Tavern serve to break up the wide expanse of the main drag. He had some supper before he left and now he'll be able to go back to the attic at The Station and listen to all the information the television is sure to share. He'll watch TV until just about dawn. He won't go to bed until he determines all the instructions he needs to know have been disseminated.

He wears his standard garb of black jeans, one of his few T-shirts, and a deep navy jean jacket he bought at a thrift store almost four years ago. Ben told him he needs to change his clothes more and wash more. He tries to do as she says but he really doesn't understand the point. Unless he falls in the mud or gets garbage spilled on him at work, then he doesn't have any dirt to wash away. She uses the word "hygiene" a lot but he's never been sure exactly what that means and doesn't want to seem stupid by asking.

When he finally approaches The Station he notices a few lights still on so the front door is probably open. Everyone knows he'll lock it after he gets home. Last winter Rose left early to go to work and found a guy curled up in the hall sleeping off a bender. Granted, it must have been thirty below outside but no one in the building expected the front hall to be used as a flop house. As a result, Amanda and Chester called a meeting. They all got keys to the front door and bells with their name. They mostly leave the door open and the last one in locks up. Sometimes the door is locked before Patrick gets home but he always has his key. He opens the big old black door, still glossy from a fresh coat of paint Chester applied a few weeks ago, and closes it quietly behind him. He turns the bolt before he ascends the two flights to the attic. He walks on tiptoe as he tries to be considerate of his neighbours.

There's no light creeping out from under Ben's door. He hopes she's feeling better than she was on Monday. Rose is still up. He could tell before he came in. Joe and Cheryl are probably asleep. They work early. You never know with the Wolskis, but Mason probably gets them up at night so they would turn in early. He likes living here. Everyone is friendly although he knows Joe thinks he's weird. Cheryl helped him find this apartment and helped him get out of that rat hole of a boarding house. Then she moved in, too, but he never lets on he knows her in front of anybody. Rose works for Dr. Gunton but he tries not to go near doctors. Ben has been really good to him. Does she know?

****

In his mind, the tenants of The Station have become his family. They have replaced his mother, long dead now, his two sisters, both younger than him, and a father he could never fully understand. Patrick's mother was not quite right. She would sit in her room for days on end while three children ran amok, and she never seemed to care. She gazed into space and said she felt like she wore a gauze veil so the world looked kind of faded and fuzzy. The nurses from the mental health office would come once a month to give her a shot. Sometimes they had to hold her down. That's why they always came in pairs. A couple of days after they left his mother would clean the house, make cookies, do laundry, and most importantly, cut her nails and take off the red polish. As the weeks would pass she did less and less. She sat in her room more and more. She let her nails grow and every week she painted them a different shade of red until the nurses came to visit again and the cycle would start all over. The nurses were very interested in his sisters. They watched them closely, asked a lot of questions, and kept track of how they did in school. When he was little he would spy on the nurses from behind a kitchen chair. He never said much. Later on he avoided them by staying in the room in the basement where he kept his favourite toys. He would go down there right after school and remain there until his father hollered that supper was ready. His father spent a lot of time with the girls. He gave them whatever they wanted. They even went to see their own mental health counsellor because everyone was so afraid they would get whatever was wrong with their mother.

Patrick was content in the basement and happy with the friends in his head. He learned, at a very young age, to keep his mouth shut and not talk about himself. Besides, everybody knew it was the girls who might get sick. He watched his mother like a hawk. He knew her patterns and was thankful the nurses arrived like clockwork. He was always happy to see her cutting those red nails and scraping off the polish. He often wished there was a way for him to scrape away the commotion that rattled around inside his brain most of the time.

He didn't do well in school. The teachers told his father he didn't concentrate and his father said it was because his mother was sick and he was often upset. They never brought friends home so his isolation went virtually unnoticed. The girls had each other. They actually did quite well in school and in any activity they laid a hand to—piano, acting, basketball—it didn't seem to matter. One of them always got pats on the back for one accomplishment or another. Patrick spent his time in the basement. He asked his father for a TV down there and after that, his fate determined itself.

****

Patrick, his spirit most often turned inward like his posture, runs his tongue over the sides of two teeth, open to the elements and no longer bordering or supporting the left front incisor once snuggled between them. This is a habit he's developed when deep in thought. His missing front tooth seems to make people uncomfortable; the reason why he doesn't get to bus tables very often at the diner. Ben offered to pay for him to get a false tooth but he just can't bring himself to face the idea of a mouth full of wires. It would be too dangerous. Aliens would probably try to contact him. He has enough problems and has learned to live without his front tooth, thank you very much. He can't blame Ben though. She only tried to be generous and to help. He simply told her he was saving for the dental work himself and how important it would be for him to pay for it personally. That was what she wanted to hear. She was happy and never offered again.

He carefully unlocks the three dead bolts on his door. One is courtesy of the building but the other two were installed by Chester after Patrick pleaded for the extra security. Patrick's apartment is different from the rest. The ceilings slope and the windows are dormers. He often imagines them as gun ports in his castle walls. There are four of them, two on the front of the building and two on the back. When you walk in the door, you enter a wide expanse. The only break is the bathroom on the left, swallowing one back dormer inside. The kitchen is along the wall like in the other units, but there are no separate bedrooms. His single cot, rumpled and grubby, stretches like an abandoned corpse in the far corner. He has an old couch that Ben found for him. His biggest expense other than rent is for his television, which he got from the Rent to Own store downtown. It will be his in another five months. He has cable which he loves. Patrick lives in his world of television. The kitchen is bereft of groceries since he eats dry cereal in the morning and then goes to the diner early so they will feed him lunch as well as supper. He owns two plates, a glass, a cup (with a small chip), a knife, fork, spoon, and a paring knife. They all came from the thrift store and sit on one shelf in the cupboard by the fridge that smells slightly and contains milk and apple juice, as well as a handful of ketchup packets from the diner.

Occupying pride of place on a high bookshelf just to the left of his television, are his toys. Patrick collects toys from the 1930s to the 1960s. It's his passion and the reason he initially became friends with Ben. Most of his collection relates to old television series and movies, so he has lots of James Bond memorabilia snuggled in beside Roy Rogers six-guns and a Lone Ranger mask. All of his extra money goes toward his collection. He saves and pays cash. He can spend hours reviewing his pieces, dusting them off, and reorganizing them on the shelves. Original packaging is never, ever removed or tampered with in any way. Items in their original packaging are the holy grail of toy collecting. Sometimes Patrick will go months without ever finding an old toy to buy. He might search every yard sale and every auction to no avail and then Ben calls to tell him she's found guns, or robots, or a Hopalong Cassidy lunch box. Once she had a 1952 Gene Autry movie poster. How will he ever find a piece for his collection now that Ben's shop is closed? Troubled by the prospect, he emits a sigh that sounds somewhere between annoyance and despair as he throws himself down on the dilapidated old dirt-brown couch. It groans for mercy as the springs scrape the floor. The television snaps to life following the jab to the button Patrick inflicted on his way past.

It's late but *Mary Tyler Moore* reruns will be on and she always has important information to provide to him. He relaxes, able to relish the anticipation of the information he's about to receive. Mary is Patrick's adviser. He watches her carefully and listens to every word she says so he's able to decipher her code and interpret her messages. Tonight the messages relate to his health. Patrick often worries that he may be sick or that he will lose control and hurt himself. Mary understands his fears. She tells him he will be fine even though the antique shop is gone. She explains how he can still be friends with Ben even if he can't buy antiques from her. Patrick has never considered that. He always assumed they were friends only because he was a customer. Mary tells him to go see Ben and make sure she's okay. Mary says Ben needs a friend and so does Patrick.

The show ends. The audience laughs but Patrick isn't sure why. His concerns are no laughing matter and he wishes the other people watching it with him didn't laugh so much. Maybe it's just Rhoda. He doesn't pay any attention to Rhoda so he never notices if she's funny or not. That must be it. What's on next? *Gunsmoke.* Patrick stretches out, ready to listen as carefully to Marshal Dillon as he did to Mary a few minutes ago. The marshal is wise and speaks directly to Patrick's soul. He settles into the worn couch cushions as he allows himself to be absorbed by the sermon-like pronouncements of the lawman.

When he wakes up, it's past four in the morning and he has a crick in his neck. He hauls himself up, turns off the TV that's projecting snow as well as any blizzard, and collapses on his cot in the corner. The one piece of clothing he's removed is the jean jacket when he first came in the door. The lights remain on. Patrick never sleeps with the lights out. He simply can't. They're his lights. They stay on. The marshal told him to be his own man and not to depend on anyone else. The marshal told him to be nice to women. So Mary and the marshal both agree. It's okay to be friends with Ben. He drifts off to sleep believing he's blessed to have such good advisers. His television helps him organize the voices. What would he do if the voices on the television told him to do wrong? Well, it would have to be important. Patrick doesn't think of himself as a bad person so he's sure he could defy the voices if he felt he had to. He can't worry about that. Marshal Dillon and Mary Richards are both good people and wouldn't steer him down wrongful paths.

He sleeps late as is always the case. He goes to the diner at lunchtime and starts his shift at two so there will be just enough time to stop in and see Ben before he takes his familiar walk back through the little prairie town and out to work. He pours cornflakes into his bowl. He munches away with a contentment only truly felt for the first couple of hours after he wakes. There are no voices and his world is a quiet place. With the windows closed and his location three stories up, he can hear little more than vague rumblings from the building either inside or out. He swims through the quiet in his brain, exploring every corner usually occupied by disturbance, annoyance, instructions, observations, and generalized chaos. His mind is like a well-cleaned and spartan room. He yearns for it to stay that way but knows full-well that the landscape of his consciousness will heat up momentarily and another circus will be in full swing soon. He carefully washes his bowl and spoon in the sink with cold water and his finger rubbing it around. No soap. No sponge. He wipes them dry with a stained and soiled dishrag hanging from the front of the stove and places them both carefully back where he found them.

After he locks up, he clomps down the stairs and stops in front of Number Three. He knocks, perhaps with a bit more aggression than necessary. Ben doesn't answer. He knocks again and hears her. "I'm coming". She sounds happy.

Ben opens the door and blinks a couple of times. She must be a bit surprised as this is the first time he has ever pounded on her door. "Well, neighbour! What brings you to my threshold this morning?" Her voice is kind. He knows she likes him despite his challenges.

Patrick shuffles a little and examines the floor. "Just thought I'd stop and say hi on my way out to the diner. Wanted to know if you needed any more help. You seemed sick the other day." He still hasn't met her eyes.

"I'm a lot better, Patrick." She grins at him, tilts her head, and peeks up into his face. Her white hair falls away from her eyes with the movement. "Did you hear about the barbecue on Saturday? Do you have the day off? Are you going to come?"

Patrick is confused now. There are too many questions. They compete with ideas relating to people being sick and not saying so rattling around in his mind. Ben continues to talk only she mercifully slows down. "Amanda is organizing a potluck for Saturday to celebrate my retirement or just because it's spring, in case I'm having a bad day and can't come. Right now, I seem to be good. She probably hasn't talked to you yet because you worked the evening shift last night. So, are you working Saturday?"

"Only until five on Saturday. I can come if they invite me. I could bring a pie from the diner."

"Great!" Ben is all business. "I'll speak to Amanda and tell her I invited you. Don't worry. It's fine. If she's calling this a retirement party for me, I guess I can make sure my friends are there." She pats Patrick on the arm. "Try to get a pecan pie for Saturday, okay? The diner makes the best pecan pie."

Patrick gallops down the front steps and off to work. Ben is his friend even though he won't be buying stuff from her anymore. As he struts along he feels quite good about life in general—a rarity in Patrick's world. Just then up pulls a big blue pick-up. Joe leans over and yells out the open passenger window. "Need a lift to the diner? I'm off to get coffee before I go back to the job site."

Patrick lifts his head, surprised. "I guess so." His voice is quiet. Joe doesn't like him.

"Haul it up here, then. Time's a wastin'."

Chapter 7

Cheryl

Cheryl Nadler employs her signature brisk and no-nonsense step. The walk home from the "Hexagon", the pet name given the building housing most of the government social support services offices in Hayworth, is just under thirty minutes so she enters her apartment no later than five o'clock.

Cheryl would exaggerate to say she is five foot three inches tall. Her petite body is perfectly proportioned with a narrow waist, dropped and flaring hips, and what she considers to be an adequate bust line. She would tip the scale at one hundred and ten pounds, but rarely checks her weight thinking it's a better use of her time to carefully watch her diet instead. She wears her thick dark hair short with brushed over bangs. Tiny curls tease the edges of her ears and the nape of her neck. She has a standing appointment with her hairdresser for once every four weeks on Friday, immediately following work, for a trim. Her hair is always exactly the same and that's the way Cheryl wants it. Today she is wearing a flowered A-line dress that safely hides her curves. Over the peach and pink hues she sports a navy blazer which she rarely takes off in public, even in the office, as she would be reluctant to expose her bare arms for unrestricted viewing. She wears her Nike Cortez sneakers, originally designed for the 1972 Olympics in Munich, and carries her dark blue flats in a bag. She is twenty-nine and a social worker at Adoption Services. She lives in Number Five, right above Ben Tullis.

She's anxious to get home, have a hot shower, and go for her run. She always runs before supper. As she enters The Station's front parking lot

Amanda seems to appear out of nowhere, and as is typical, she has Mason in her arms. Cheryl has no doubt she's a good mother but the poor girl never seems to get much of a break. She flutters her hand in a recognition, yet dismissive, wave. It does not impede Amanda's steady progress toward her. Cheryl thinks about her schedule being disrupted if Amanda proves to be particularly needy.

"Hi," comes the greeting. "I'm trying to organize a barbecue on Saturday for the whole building. Can you come?" She jostles Mason on her hip and brushes that unruly dyed red hair out of her eyes as she reaches Cheryl

"A barbecue?" Cheryl is cautious. "What's the occasion?" She smiles down at Mason. He is a sweet little boy and her heart twitches a bit.

"Well," Amanda grunts as she repositions Mason yet again. "Ben's retired. She closed her shop the first of the week. You probably knew that." Cheryl nods in her knowing social work way although she knew nothing of the sort, and Amanda continues. "She hasn't been well. You probably knew that too, but I wanted to have a little party for her. I guess, if she can't come because she's having a bad day, well, we'll just have the barbecue anyway and celebrate spring!" She ends her gushy speech with a flourish as Cheryl attempts to sidle closer to the building. "So, will you come?"

It's a simple request and Cheryl knows she'll say yes, but still struggles to make the commitment. Finally, forced into a corner she created for herself, she nods and produces her indulgent but nonetheless practised professional facade. "Would you like me to bring pasta salad, Amanda? Would that help?" She knows she won't eat anyone else's food but her own so she might as well contribute a substantial side dish.

Amanda's thankful reaction seems inspired by relief. They part ways as the building manager continues around the corner to her outside entrance. Cheryl hauls open the shiny, black front door on her way to her apartment. Finally home, she takes a quick glance at her watch. Now she's about five minutes behind schedule but her supper is already prepared on a plate in the fridge so she'll be able to have her second shower of the day, run, and still be back by six-thirty to watch the national evening news and have supper. No harm done.

Cheryl's apartment is a lesson in minimalism and meticulous housekeeping. She cleans twice a week which enables her to ensure all corners are examined and every surface is wiped down. Placement is perfect. Her table and chairs are chrome and glass—very modern. She polishes them daily, whether she uses the table or not. Her couch and chair are Danish. The frames are Teak. The fabric is brushed leather and virtually indestructible. They are a sandy brown colour. When she bought them, the clerk said a cat would not even be able to scratch the fabric it is so strong. As if Cheryl would ever allow an animal in her apartment! She didn't respond to the clerk—she just smiled a social work smile. There are no items on her kitchen counter, not even a bowl for fruit or a basket for decoration. It all must be undercover. The cupboards are a sight to behold. All food is arranged according to size and with labels facing out. Her fridge is the same. She cleans her fridge every week. Her second bedroom has been converted to a laundry room since she convinced Chester Wolski to permit a washer and dryer installation. Her ironing board is always up and ready to go. She carefully removes her blazer and hangs it on a wooden hanger where it can be refreshed with her steam-iron. She folds her dress and places it in the laundry hamper. She removes her pantyhose and underpants. She carefully inserts them into a mesh bag used to protect delicates in the washer. She takes off her bra and places it in a separate bag that contains items to be hand washed. Laundry is done twice weekly on Sundays and Wednesdays.

After she takes a shower that would sear the skin off a normal woman, Cheryl hangs her wet towel with precision behind the door on a rod installed specifically to dry a towel before it is folded and placed in the hamper. She then proceeds into her bedroom. She stretches a perfectly manicured hand into her closet for a gray sweatshirt and fleece pants. Clean socks are in the top drawer of her bureau where they're lined up like little sleeping white mice, side by side. Panties and bras are in the next drawer down. With her Nikes tied up to snug perfection and her apartment key safely tucked into the zippered pocket of her pants, she is off down the stairs, past Ben's door, and out into the still brilliant northern sunshine.

Her run takes about an hour. She follows the perimeter of town, along the creek and over the bridge at the far end, up to a residential street just behind and parallel to the main drag, and then back around to The Station. As her Nikes pound the sidewalk, her thoughts run to the group support class she held today for the handful of pregnant teenage girls on her caseload—those who intend to surrender their babies for adoption. Sometimes she worries certain girls are more likely to change their minds. Other days she worries that they won't. Her job is to support them no matter what. What would have happened if she had been offered the same support? He would be fourteen now.

As she turns from the bridge and trots along Poplar Street, thoughts of her mother creep into her consciousness. Cheryl's mother was, and presumably still is, an unapologetic drunk who picked up men, drifted from one lousy waitressing job to another, and ran out on her bills every chance she got. Cheryl knows that anyone who is especially observant, and is watching her on her late afternoon run, would notice her head give a little shake every so often as she has these philosophical conversations with herself. She easily justifies the estrangement from her mother who didn't so much raise her as share living accommodations with her until she was sixteen. Cheryl came to the conclusion, after the death of her boyfriend from an overdose, that she would never have a life if she didn't make it for herself. Her destiny would be to become increasingly submersed in a culture of drugs, alcohol, and men who would hurt her.

****

At sixteen and abandoned by her mother, Cheryl worked as a waitress and crashed wherever she could find a place. She made her way west and finally ended up just south of Hayworth. Somebody at a shelter for teens suggested she apply to go to the community college and get a social work certificate. She barely understood what that meant except that it would be a career and she wouldn't have to waitress any more. She got a special government welfare grant where you could be on the dole as long as you went to school. It took her four years but she finally got her GED and then the social work certificate. She graduated. Then the dole stopped.

She got part-time contracts where her clients were mostly welfare recipients. She finally landed the position in Hayworth in 1975. The primary focus of her job is teenage mothers and mothers-to-be, as well as adoptions. While covering for a colleague one week, she managed to meet Patrick Hollinger. Now, he's a weird one, but she helped him find his apartment. She liked the place so much that she signed a lease for the next one available, hot water and all. Patrick never speaks to her when anyone else is around but Cheryl's used to that. People who have crossed paths with social services of one stripe or another usually don't want to be seen associating with the staff. That's just the name of the game.

As Cheryl remembers it now, she thinks of life with her mother as an episode neatly tucked away in a box underneath a bed in her mind. She drags it out for examination on occasion but it's really just another item that takes up unnecessary space. Too bad she couldn't throw it out on garbage day.

****

She senses the familiar face flush as she gets closer to home. She speeds up just a little, so the burn is a tiny bit more intense. No point in doing a task if you don't benefit from it. She stops just short of the granite stair to bend at the waist for a moment and catch her breath. Before going inside she does a couple of lunges as she starts to cool down.

She enters her apartment, closes the door carefully so as not to disturb any of her neighbours who might be home, and checks her watch. Right on time! Back in her laundry room, she peels off her sweatshirt and pants, folds each carefully, and places them in the hamper. She removes her socks, sports bra, and panties, adds them to the mesh bag, and steps into the shower once again. This time, when she emerges into the living room, she's clad in cotton pants with a string tie waist, a long sleeved T-shirt tucked in, and soft leather mules that cradle her feet. Five minutes until the national news. She reaches for her salad supper, already made and chilled in the fridge. She pours herself a tall glass of water, adds four ice cubes, and sits at her glass-topped table to watch her program.

Cheryl is distracted. She hates distraction. What could be the matter with Ben? Amanda says she might be sick. Cheryl doesn't know Ben all that well. She calls herself an antique dealer and that may well be true, but Cheryl cannot even fathom the idea of using someone else's old dishes, sofa, or, God forbid, clothes. She couldn't stomach ever entering Ben's store. All that old stuff just smelled like rubbish to Cheryl. Maybe it affected the woman's health somehow. She must stop by and see if she needs any assistance. Maybe tomorrow after work. She'll just tell her about the invitation to the party. That could be her excuse. Yes, yes. Pasta salad. She places her plate on the counter and opens a kitchen drawer. Inside there's a notepad, ruler, and a pen. This is Cheryl's running grocery list. She adds the ingredients necessary for the pasta salad. She prints by holding the ruler as a gauge so every line is perfect. She shops on Friday after work. Once a month, this activity occurs after she gets her hair cut. She doesn't run on Fridays in the winter, because it would be dark. She only runs on Fridays once it's light until six o'clock or later.

She loves the hot water in this building. It never runs out. This is the reason she moved. Her old place didn't have adequate hot water. She runs a scalding and soapy sink full for her plate, glass, and fork. They soak for exactly five minutes while she brushes her teeth. Then she pours boiling water from the kettle over each dish in order to rinse and sterilize them. She pulls a clean cup towel out of the drawer, dries the dishes, returns them to their respective places, folds the towel, and places it in the hamper. There will be lots of laundry on Sunday. Her face glows with pleasure.

Cheryl goes to bed relatively early mainly because she likes to be at work by about seven-thirty every day. She finds she can accomplish a lot in that hour before the phones start to ring. She takes off her clothes and follows the familiar ritual of folding, hamper, and mesh bag for the underwear. She pulls a clean nightgown out of the third of four drawers in her bureau. That drawer holds ten almost identical white cotton gowns. She turns down her bed and runs the palm of her hand over the bottom sheet so wrinkles are kept to a bare minimum. She changes her bed twice a week when she does laundry. Cheryl would be much happier if she could change her bed every day but time just does not permit such an indulgence. If Cheryl won the lottery she would employ someone to change her bed and iron her sheets daily. She crawls in and lies on her side facing the door. She is a light sleeper and is confident she would wake up if anyone tried to disturb her. She has extensive experience. She never moves when she sleeps. She remains in a ball, curled into the foetal position. She does not get up to pee or get a drink. One does not court disaster. Cheryl has experience with this as well.

Cheryl's mornings are much like her evenings—filled with ritual. She chooses her clothes from a closet organized in sections according to garment and then colour. She wears mostly shapeless dresses to work. For variety, she has slightly baggy sweaters paired with gathered skirts or pleated trousers. Her choices are designed to camouflage her rather striking figure. Today she reaches for a navy blue shirt dress and pairs it with an ivory jacket. She looks taller until she adds the jacket which has the effect of cutting her nicely in half. Breakfast consists of orange juice, one slice of toast with strawberry jam, and a boiled egg. While the egg cooks, she tosses a salad to take for her lunch. She pairs it with a whole-wheat bun she removes from the freezer. At the same time, she places a small salmon filet to thaw in the fridge. She will have this with rice and another salad for supper. She eats breakfast while she stands at the counter and looks out on the front parking lot of The Station. After washing her dishes and brushing her teeth, she puts on her sneakers, places her lunch and her shoes in separate bags, checks her hair one last time in the mirror, grabs her purse and keys from the shelf by the door, and begins her walk to the office.

On the way down past Ben's door she makes a mental note to stop in for a visit after work. She'll get a fruit basket when she shops for groceries. Perhaps she can help the old girl in some way. As she leaves the parking lot, Chester, all bright-eyed and bushy-tailed for first thing in the morning, pulls up beside her and leans over to crank down the window of the old Ford pick-up. "Going my way? Can I give a lady a lift?"

God, what a charmer, with his movie star hair hanging down and his plaid shirt lighting up the front seat of the old truck. He honestly thinks everybody will say yes. "No thanks, Chester. I leave early for the walk. It defeats the purpose if I hitch a ride." She makes a conscious effort to sound casual and comfortable, but he is so attractive.

"No problem, Cheryl. See you later." Off he goes, kicking up more dust than Cheryl will ever get used to. She should probably have another shower when she gets to work. If only that were an option. Today she will finalize an adoption and a couple will meet their new baby daughter for the first time. It is, by far, her favourite part of the job. How many of these adoptions will she have to facilitate to atone for her own poor choices? After fourteen years and a life turned around, one would think it might get easier but it doesn't seem to work that way. She picks up the pace a little. It will be good to do the adoption today.

Chapter 8

Ben

Saturday proves to be the perfect day for a spring barbecue. For the first time in a couple of weeks, Ben feels well when she wakes up. She lies in her bed. The open window catches a cool breeze that just barely moves the curtains. She stares at the ceiling, takes stock of her internal workings, and can't for the moment find any issues. She almost laughs out loud. She'll make potato salad for the party. She'll go. She'll have fun. Maybe the worst has passed and she's on the mend.

As she trundles about the apartment, she basks in the glow of a perfect spring morning and enjoys the cocoon of quiet that often hovers over The Station on the weekend. She recalls Cheryl's rather surprising visit Friday afternoon. She turned up at the door, all nervous and funny, with a basket of fruit and a book she seemed to think Ben might like. Titled *...And Ladies of the Club* by Helen Hooven Santmyer, Ben thinks it's the single biggest pocket novel she's ever seen. It has more than fourteen hundred pages of infinitesimal print. The girl must think the only activity she has to do now is read. It wasn't a good time but, compelled to be polite, Ben invited the social worker in even though she actually thinks that social workers are busybodies, and Cheryl would never become her friend no matter how much the girl reached out. Ben wore her pyjamas and housecoat. It was almost six. Cheryl still looked like she was all fresh and on her way to work early in the morning. The girl always appears plastic. She did not have a hair out of place. The collar on her blouse lay on her neck like it just came out of a package. Her shoes had no scuffs.

Ben imagined Cheryl standing up all day at work because the ass of her skirt wasn't even wrinkled.

Brushing back her own white mop which was hanging as per usual down over one eye, she minded her manners, accepted the gifts, and offered her neighbour a seat. Cheryl surveyed the place—probably doing some sort of governmental inspection—and declined.

"Congratulations on your retirement, Ben. Amanda's planning a little soiree for Saturday night. Are you going to come? Are you up to it?"

So everyone knew she hadn't been well. Small towns. Small buildings. Love 'em; hate 'em. She nodded quickly to the girl. "Oh, I told Amanda I would come if I felt up to it. I'll probably be there. Don't want to miss a party." She smiled and tried her best to sound casual, but this one would not be easily brushed off.

"I won't keep you. You must have been getting ready for bed." Cheryl eyed the pyjamas with what appeared to Ben to be disdain. She turned for the door and was out in the hall before Ben had time to explain about how she feels cozy in her pjs any time of day.

"Thanks for the fruit. I'll be sure to return the book." Ben imagined her voice floating up the stairs behind the retreating rhythm of clicking heels.

At the time of the visit, Ben hadn't been sure if she would be able to attend the barbecue or not; but today, as she prepares to have a nice hot shower and some rice toast and tea, she's pretty certain she will go. As she continues about her morning routine, she reflects on her neighbours. It really is quite special that they are investing a Saturday evening to celebrate her retirement. She realizes with a surprising suddenness, that she has no friends her own age. She could be mother, grandmother, or even great grandmother to each of them in turn. She has no contemporaries that she would call friends. How did that happen?

She takes stock. She is friends with a couple who have a baby. The fellow is a local and the girl has no history of which she is aware. She will have to make an effort to find out more about Amanda. Rose, her neighbour across the hall, seems to have a sister down east somewhere but she never talks about her or any other family. She will have to find out about Rose's family. Doesn't she drive to Ontario every summer? Maybe she'd like company this year—someone to share the expenses. Cheryl is a social worker—that much she knows but virtually nothing else. She's not very old, likely not thirty. Where did she come from? And then there's Joe—good old Joe. She thinks he's been married at least once and assumes he has no kids, but she doesn't know his history either. Patrick, don't-call-me-Pat, has his own issues. He must have a mental problem of some sort or another. In any event, he's definitely odd. Of course, if she starts to poke around in their lives asking questions and wanting to get to know them better, they are likely to follow suit with her. Ben isn't sure she's prepared to reveal her life story to these people even if they did become real friends. Nevertheless, 1953 was a long time ago. Perhaps people don't care about ancient history.

At the appointed time, Ben checks out her bedroom window. Because it faces the back, she can just make out a part of the Wolski's patio peeking out from under the overhang. She hears voices and can tell Chester has lit the barbecue as smoke trails across the back field. She reaches for the over-sized antique cranberry glass bowl filled to the brim with potato salad, balances a thermos of her tea, and starts out. Just as she reaches the big front door, Patrick appears out of nowhere. She hadn't heard him clatter down the stairs as he usually does. "I can help, Ben." He balances a pie in one hand and opens the door with the other. "This is going to be fun!" He eyeballs the potatoes and grins, exposing the cavern that replaces his missing front tooth.

As the two of them round the corner of the building, Ben can hear chatter just above the strains of Kenny Rogers singing. Chester has managed to haul a speaker from their stereo out through the apartment window. Very creative. Patrick doesn't seem so impressed. His eyes dart around for a second as if he's trying to locate the person with the guitar. Amanda, all gussied up in a tie-dyed dress and a crocheted shawl, looks like a throwback to the sixties. She sits on a kitchen stool and chats with Rose who happily bounces Mason on her knee. They both acknowledge Ben and she cannot miss the appearance of relief and pleasure she sees reflected in their eyes.

Rose has donned a long denim skirt and her standard sweater set, this one in a soft yellow. She seems particularly happy to see Ben who can't help but be suspicious that the obvious enthusiasm might reflect her, as yet not revealed, test results.

"Come on around. Find a seat. Amanda, grab that bowl from Ben. The potatoes look good, Ben, but that bowl must be worth a fortune. Careful, Amanda." Chester waves a spatula and acts like a master of ceremonies. Patrick puts the pie down beside the cranberry bowl. He accepts a soda while

Ben opts for some of the tea from her party-sized thermos. Mason gurgles away on Rose's knee while Amanda goes inside to bring out paper plates and more utensils. The music is suddenly a little less overwhelming and Ben now believes she can talk in a normal voice.

"Is Joe coming?" she asks no one in particular.

Amanda responds out the open doorway. "Joe is likely working late. He said he would be here, though. Cheryl has gone for her pre-dinner run—like she needs a run," she adds. Her tone reflects a mixture of envy and annoyance. "I expect them both anytime now."

Just on cue, Joe lumbers around the corner surprising everyone by not putting his truck in the back lot. "Wanted to spare everybody the dust," he says in explanation before questioning eyes. He has a case of beer in one hand and a glass salad bowl, impressed with a leaf design in the side and filled with coleslaw, in the other. "Finished the kitchen earlier than I expected," he notes as he adds his offering to the collection already on the table. The red and white checked cloth flutters in the late afternoon breeze. Joe proceeds to flip the top on one of the beer he just brought and sits down on an upturned stump near Ben, perched upright in a chair meant for lounging. "How are you, old thing?" He chuckles as he leans over and touches her just slightly with his shoulder. "You're looking pretty good this afternoon."

Ben responds with sudden shyness to the attention. Joe could be her son but it's nice to get a compliment. For the first time in days, she actually paid attention to what she put on and sports soft grey linen pants with a black T-shirt tucked in. She chose the pants because they have a tie waist and other pairs no longer fit. She has a multi-coloured cardigan, designed to resemble a patchwork quilt, draped over her shoulders. Her thick white hair is held back from her face with an antique tortoiseshell clip that she bought years ago and just could never manage to price and leave in the shop. She knows that for someone seventy-five she has maintained her looks—if you didn't know how much weight she's actually lost. "Stop your flirting, mister. I could be your mother!" Ben laughs. She sips her tea and listens to the buzz of conversation that floats around her. Joe and Chester get into some discussion about trucks. Patrick plays peek-a-boo with Mason, still held by Rose. Amanda fusses with the table and keeps an eye out for Cheryl.

She appears, standing at the corner of the building seemingly unsure if she should make the turn without an invitation. Chester spies her first. "Come on. Come on." He motions with the spatula, caught between burger turns and wiener rolls. "Whatcha' got there?"

Cheryl nods ever so slightly as she moves forward on awkward little sandals more suitable for walking around the mall. "I brought a pasta salad—lots of veggies. Hope you like it." She carefully places the pottery bowl on the table.

"We like it all," says Amanda.

Ben watches Cheryl. Funny, she seems so thin and in really good shape but the only physical feature she really shows off is her feet and her perfectly manicured toes. Today, after her run she changed into clean sweat pants and a hoodie. She could be a professional runner if it weren't for the footwear. Strange girl. She says she would prefer water to drink and sits down on a kitchen stool near Rose.

"So, the gang's all here," announces Chester. "Has everybody got a drink?" He responds to the collective nods, holds up his beer, and focuses his attention on Ben. "Here's to a grand lady and a great neighbour. We congratulate you on your retirement and hope you don't move away somewhere else. Here's to Ben and here's to our wonderful little community at The Station." He finishes with a flurry and takes a sip of his beer in an attempt, without much success, to disguise the tremor that developed in his voice just before he completed the toast.

Ben senses an obligation to stand up and respond. "Without too much formality thank you, Chester." She nods at the building manager. "Thank you, Amanda, for putting all this together despite the demands of managing motherhood for the first time." She nods her appreciation at Amanda and lifts her mug in a small salute. "Thanks to everyone for coming. I have no particular plans to move anywhere so will always be available for tea and a chat. Now, the food smells and looks fabulous. How about we eat?"

Much later, back in her apartment, as she rinses out the cranberry bowl and hopes against hope she will avoid sitting up all night with cramps, Ben reviews the knowledge she has gained about her neighbours. The evening went on longer than she expected it would. Conversation seemed to flow easily. Everybody interacted, even Joe and Patrick for a few minutes. Ben also watched Joe talk to Cheryl and observed how motherly Rose seemed to Chester and Amanda. Rose would probably call in sick to Dr. Gunton if it meant she could spend a day with Mason. Ben's ultimate goal is to get to know each of them a little better so she tries to review exactly what she learned.

Cheryl is twenty-nine. It seems the young social worker put herself through college and doesn't have much in the way of family. Ben suspects she is a clean freak of some sort. She mentioned she had a shower after her run and said she would go home after the party to have a shower. Who does that? She's very petite and wears bulky clothes. She ate only her own pasta dish and drank water. Ruefully, Ben thinks that she didn't uncover much information about this young woman who might have been born under a cabbage leaf for all the family history she could get out of her.

Joe proved to be a slightly easier nut to crack. He's forty-five and has actually experienced two serious relationships although he was only married and divorced once. He told Ben a little bit about the two women, saying they were pretty nice in their own ways but both times they just grew apart. He didn't really say why or how. He mentioned a sister he corresponds with but no other family.

Patrick acted funny in his normally weird way. Ben tried to ask him about his family and how he ended up in Hayworth. He got quite paranoid. Why did she want to know? Was there a problem? He finally told her about his deceased mother, and how he has two sisters but lost touch with them years ago. Well, at least that's progress. They discussed his toy collection and he responded with significantly more openness about that subject. He told Ben he remembered to change his T-shirt before the party so he wouldn't smell like kitchen grease. He obviously expected her to be pleased.

Ben jumped right in with Rose about her trip east. Did she visit family? Rose's answer seemed vague. When Ben suggested Rose might like some company this year, the younger woman appeared almost panicky as she tried to find a polite way to decline. Ben could see the anxiety on her face and backed off. Obviously, everyone in this building has their secrets.

Finally, her least successful attempt was in pinning Amanda down for a chat. She used the excuse of hosting duties but Ben could guess she didn't want anyone to delve too deeply into her past. Amanda likes to leave the impression that she simply appeared in Hayworth one day and after she met Chester, all was right with the world. Ben is quite sure there is more to her story.

****

Early the following Tuesday morning the phone rings. It's Rose calling from Dr. Gunton's office. Could Ben come in that afternoon? Ben, startled by the tendrils of Rose's anxiety creeping through the phone line, wants to know the results of her tests. Rose obviously has been thoroughly schooled in the art of avoidance when it comes to revealing health issues over the phone. Ben is to see the doctor at three o'clock.

As she drives down to the office, Ben can't imagine what the urgency could be. She hasn't been sick since last Friday morning and has been particularly good since Saturday. She continues to follow her diet such as it is, and rests a lot. Rose spies her the minute she walks in the door and ushers her down to an exam room. The place is oddly quiet and, instead of smelling old people and sweaty children, all she can smell is antiseptic. Her footfalls echo in the hallway. Rose tells her that normally Dr. Gunton plays golf on Tuesdays at this time but he will see her first today. This little tidbit of information scares Ben more than all the rest. Dr. Gunton is not the type to do an old lady a favour. Before Rose leaves, she tells Ben the doctor may want to examine her. Even more strange.

In comes Alex Gunton staring at her chart and avoiding her eyes—his typical demeanour. "Ben, I have a couple of questions and I want honest answers, okay?"

"Of course, Dr. Gunton. What would you like to know?" Her voice sounds wobbly to her own ears and she hopes he hasn't heard it.

"Do you get bad cramps?"

"Sometimes. No bad ones since last Thursday." She tries to anticipate his questions out of nervousness, and more than a little fear.

"Is your poop white?"

"No. Maybe beige?" She isn't sure what this means.

"I need to palpate your belly. Hop up on the table and lay down. No need to take your clothes off."

Ben does as she's told although hopping might be a stretch. Dr. Gunton lifts up her T-shirt and attempts to pull down on the waist band of her pants. She unties the drawstring so they'll move. He presses his hands into her side and she squeals. Tears spring into her eyes. She's shocked at how much it hurts.

"I'm sending you down to the hospital for an ultrasound, Ben, but I'm pretty sure I know your problem. Tell me again how long has this been going on?"

Ben stands up, tucks in her T-shirt, and reties her pants. She swipes at a tear running down her cheek. "I think I came in and complained about not being able to keep food down and about having diarrhea and cramps about a year ago." She says this with no expression in her voice. "So what do you think the problem is, Doctor?"

He never takes his eyes from the chart as he says, like he's asking her to remember to use hand cream, "I think you have pancreatic cancer, specifically pancreatic adenocarcinoma. One never knows for sure with this issue, but the ultrasound might help." He could probably hear Ben's intake of breath as he adds, "There's a tumour, Ben. I may not have the greatest bedside manner, but I know what I feel. Have the ultrasound and then we'll talk again."

Chapter 9

Amanda

So...it's come to this. Amanda smirks as she fills her blender with cooked carrots and glances over at Mason, gurgling away to himself in his playpen. He's teething now and can get cranky but today seems to be off to a good start. She's taking advantage by making baby food. The task saves her money at the grocery store but she contemplates how her dreams of being a chef in a restaurant have been so compromised. It's not bad, just different.

Amanda can't remember a time she didn't want to be a cook, to work in a restaurant, and become a chef. Her dreams have expanded and contracted based on her life circumstances. Her mom and dad told her she could be whatever she wanted. They were young when she was born. They ran away to get married and would have moved the world for her, had they lived. Her mother loved to be in the kitchen and Amanda always helped from the time she could balance on a chair.

****

The car crash happened when she was nine and asleep in the back seat of her father's 1950 yellow Chevrolet Impala. He always said that car was special because it was made the year she was born. She remembers peeking into the front seat after the car stopped rolling. She reached out to her mother, who took her hand, smiled, and then closed her eyes. She never saw her father's face at all.

She was the little girl nobody wanted, it seemed. At just nine years old she had no idea why grandparents, or some other family member, didn't step up to take her in but no one did. She was carted off to a foster home. She remembers the Tallard family well. They were a good family—nice people. She could have done a lot worse. They had two teenage daughters and took her in right after the accident. Mrs. Tallard let her cook, teaching her how to bake and make bread. Amanda was careful to behave herself, work hard in school, do all her chores, and get along. She felt fear every day for nine years—a crippling fear that the Tallards would decide they didn't want to keep her anymore.

Then she turned eighteen and graduated from high school. The social worker from Children's Services came for a visit and told Amanda she was on her own now. The Tallards would no longer be paid to keep her. She could get a job and that would be the end of her relationship with the government, or she could get a trade. If she chose the latter, they would pay her an allowance and tuition for two years and then call it quits. Amanda enrolled in the cooking school at the local community college. Although she wanted to stay at the Tallards and pay them room and board from her allowance, they had already accepted another little girl and she was out. She tried not to wallow in thoughts of abandonment but it was hard. She got a room in a big old rattletrap boarding house for girls next to the school, and heard from the Tallards at Christmas for the next two years.

Amanda loved community college. Although not particularly social, she made friends and did well. She had her own room in the boarding house, prepared her own meals, and paid her own way, albeit with a social welfare cheque. It made her feel independent—like a woman with a future, not a little girl without a family. On Saturday night she would cook dinner for the nine other residents. She usually baked cookies or made a cake, too. She felt liked. By this time, she began to have trouble remembering she'd ever been loved.

She did her practicum at the Long Point Lodge located about ten miles outside the town. It was a lovely old rustic place and reminded her of Somerset Maugham stories she had read in high school. The main lodge was made of logs, outfitted with a huge stone fireplace, a bar, and a dining room. The lodge was surrounded by individual cottages and duplex cottages, most with easy access to the lake. Families came to Long Point Lodge all year round. In the fall, the place was alive with hunters. Amanda worked in the kitchen.

She worked hard three days a week after she spent four days in classes at the college. They paid her minimum wage but it didn't matter. Whatever she made was deducted from her welfare cheque.

At the end of her apprenticeship, the chef at the lodge offered her a job. She could live on site if she wanted to and for the first time since her parents died so suddenly, she felt like she had a future.

After she worked for about a year, Amanda met Jeremy Bradway. It was just a chance encounter. She was walking back to the staff residence from the kitchen after finishing a lunch shift. Jeremy was sitting on a red Adirondack lawn chair smoking a cigarette. She recalls the day like it was yesterday and allows the memories to collide. Man, what a handsome guy!

"Hi! I haven't seen you here before. Are you hanging around for this wedding, too?" Amanda knew there were a number of families booked in for this July long weekend because of a wedding. It always caused a big buzz in the kitchen as well as the reception rooms, when they were planning a shindig.

"No. No. I'm on staff." She produced a polite smile for the guest and kept on walking.

"So, you got a name?" He stood up at this point; swaggering just a little on long legs topped by broad shoulders and chiseled cheekbones.

This guy could be a model. "Yes, sir. I'm Amanda. On the kitchen staff. Nice to meet you." *Keep on moving. No fraternizing with the guests.*

"I'm Jeremy. Jeremy Bradway. I'm here for a few days. Maybe we could get together."

"That's not permitted, sir. No socializing with the guests. It's a rule." She tried to make her voice sound stern, but he wouldn't take the hint.

That proved to be the way it was with Jeremy. He never took no for an answer. It seemed that if he wanted something, he just figured he could have it. He decided he wanted Amanda. It took several months of pestering, turning up at the lodge unannounced, staying for days on end, until finally she agreed to go to his home and meet his family.

Amanda was overwhelmed. The Bradway family was much richer than she could ever have imagined. Jeremy's father owned vegetable processing companies. They had more money than God! Their house resembled a mansion you'd see in the movies. The front foyer, with its pink marble floor, was bigger than the whole lounge at the staff residence. She tried desperately not to gawk.

"So, you're the chef at the Long Point Lodge, my dear?" Mrs. Bradway held an exact inch of Scotch in a crystal tumbler probably worth more than what Amanda had paid for her 1965 Ford Bronco the previous year. The woman was dressed in a navy blue silk wrap dress that hugged her perfect figure. The pearls around her long and aristocratic neck were outrageously beautiful. Her soft blond tinted hair was coiffed to perfection. Amanda assumed it probably never moved, even in a stiff breeze. Mr. Bradway was in his office out of sight. Jeremy said that was normal.

As she stood in the living room of this modern-day castle, on a carpet that felt like it came up to her ankles, Amanda was forced to reveal that she worked *for* the chef. She felt wilted inside the flowered shirt dress she had scrounged from one of the waitresses. A dress was important but she didn't own one. Mrs. Bradway's sniff of disapproval was unmistakable.

"You are from around here are you not?" The grilling continued. Amanda explained, carefully, that she was born in a town nearby where she was raised by *friends of the family* after her parents tragically died in a car crash. This small white lie sounded better to her than revealing foster care. It made her sound like she had a decent, if not privileged, upbringing. "I have wanted to cook since I was a little girl so grabbed the opportunity to study when I had the chance. I apprenticed at the lodge and they were kind enough to ask me to stay on. I've been with them more than a year now." She finished with a flourish.

"So you studied here? Not abroad at a culinary institute?" Mrs Bradway looked aghast and turned to Jeremy. "You told your father she was a chef!" Her accusations dripped with disdain. Amanda felt flushed and shaky. She wanted to go home.

Jeremy started to stutter and then collected himself. "Amanda and I are engaged, Mother. It doesn't matter whether she's a chef or whether she's a short order cook. We will be married and she will be Amanda Bradway. That's all."

And that's exactly what happened. Much to Amanda's complete and utter amazement, they were married a couple of months later. She simply permitted the tornado that was the Bradway family to scoop her up and move her life along. The wedding was small. She didn't tell the Tallards. It was in the Bradway garden, with maybe fifty people Amanda didn't know. His family planned the whole affair. They bought her dress. It was short and lacy with an empire waist. Amanda liked it in the end, even though it seemed Jeremy's mother was convinced she was pregnant and needed the style to have a high waist—just in case. She walked across the grassy lawn toward her future husband. How had she managed to let this happen? Even the grass felt like carpet up to her ankles. She walked alone. Her bridesmaid was a cousin of Jeremy's. She was nice, although indifferent to Amanda. People obviously thought she was a gold digger. She was expected to quit her job. They moved into the guest house on the family property. His parents never really warmed up to her, no matter how hard she tried. She even attempted to cook for them and help with a party one weekend. Mrs. Bradway was never satisfied and exceedingly skilled at making her opinions known.

Jeremy got his way with his parents—Amanda and marriage. After that, he paid little or no attention. She didn't want to forfeit employment and argued with as much patience as she could muster. She really needed a focus, because he was always off somewhere with his friends and she could not bear the idea of sitting alone in the guest house all day. No one seemed happy with any of these arrangements but she stood her ground and continued to drive her old Bronco back and forth to the lodge.

After four months of marriage, Amanda came home one night to find Jeremy, and some girl she only knew as Molly, tangled up in her bed linen. He was apologetic and contrite. Mr. and Mrs. Bradway seemed to think their son's behaviour was Amanda's fault because she refused to give up her old life. She went to work the following day to tell them she was leaving. She picked up her last cheque, went back to the guest house, and packed up her few possessions. She loaded her Bronco, drove down the elegant tree-lined driveway, and pointed her vehicle west. She never contacted them again and, to her knowledge, they never tried to find her.

Once she made it to Alberta in late 1974, her circumstances became easier. Oil and gas exploration camps were crying for qualified cooks and she got a job near Crete River with no problem. Amanda was a good organizer and planner. She could run a kitchen and turn out wholesome and tasty grub. She cooked three meals a day and an evening snack for thirty men. She had two helpers in her kitchen—both women and both considerably older. They did their jobs well. The dining hall ran like clockwork. She kept to herself. Relationships were always arm's length. Life was safer without involvements.

By 1977, oil companies started to slow down. Her employers decided they didn't need this particular camp any longer and Amanda got laid off. Someone mentioned a diner in a town called Hayworth a couple of hours south. Maybe she could get on there. She packed up her Bronco and went to Hayworth.

She got the job as the short order cook on the back shift, working from three until eleven five days a week. It wasn't fancy but the owner relented and permitted her to do a dinner special every night. The place started to get busy. People were nice. The boarding house where she stayed was adequate—clean and well managed. The old lady who owned it didn't put up with drinking, big dirty boots, or loud parties. Amanda felt safe but without a future once again. Then she met Chester, thanks in no small measure to her old Bronco. And the rest, as they say, is history.

****

She bends over the playpen and picks up Mason. What a sweet baby—never any trouble. After giving him a bath and playing for a little while, they'll go for a walk and maybe stop in to see how Ben is doing. Since Rose will be away for almost two weeks, Amanda will make it a point to keep closer track of the old gal.

Chapter 10

Rose

Rose sits at the tire shop after work on Tuesday. New tires are an absolute necessity if she intends to drive to Penny Falls, Ontario in the standard three days. Penny Falls is about one hundred kilometres past the Manitoba border, and the location of Forest Hills Institute, the current home of her younger sister, Margaret. Rose has always called her Maggie.

Throughout what perhaps best can be described as a tumultuous childhood, Rose and Maggie lived with their parents at the Abide A While RV Park and Campground just outside Penny Falls. The whole place was owned by a German couple who lived in a Swiss chalet style home on the property in the summer and then went back to Germany every fall. The Woodwards lived in a winterized house trailer and managed the place. They worked the office, cleaned the public washrooms and laundry room, mowed the lawns, raked the beach by the lake below the falls, maintained a modicum of security, and did any minor maintenance that might be required.

One might think this an idyllic life for two little girls and their mother but circumstances are not always as they seem. Rose's father, Abner Woodward, was a mean drunk. He presented as pleasant to the park guests, always willing to go above and beyond, but behind closed doors he was a violent and hateful man. Abner was short by most standards, with dark mottled skin and a heavy belly brought to him courtesy of too much whiskey and too many beers. He could be brutish but in a stealthy, catlike way. No one in the park would ever know when he grabbed you and held you down. The girls' mother, Ruth, seemed vacant of personality most of the time. She was probably starving herself in a vague attempt to fade away while no one noticed. As a child, Rose just considered her mother thin—a light eater. Over the years, she came to understand that Ruth had her own ways of courting invisibility. It was as if her eyes were open but there was emptiness behind them—no softness, no empathy. It scared Rose a lot more than her father did if the truth be known. She remembers the day, very clearly, when she came to understand her mother would never be there for her.

Winters were the worst. There wasn't that much for Abner to do. He made sure the road to their trailer was plowed and that the place was secure, but mostly he collected pogey and drank. He could be as mean as he wanted in the winter since there was nobody within a couple of miles to hear their screams. How could somebody plan to be a different kind of mean depending on the season? Rose fantasized, often, about killing her father.

It used to be hard to go back to the area and for many years she didn't, but the Woodwards eventually stopped running the RV park when the Germans sold the place off and the new owners developed a golf course. Abner and Ruth moved into cheap seniors' housing in a neighbouring community, and Rose no longer worried about a chance encounter at Forest Hills Institute. She learned, from the staff, that they absolutely never visited their daughter.

****

As she sits and waits for her car, Rose goes through the pattern of her trip in her mind. She has done this many times now and considers her choices to be safe and secure. On her first day she drives to Lloydminster, a lovely town situated precisely on the Alberta and Saskatchewan border. She stays at a motel right on the main drag. They permit pets. She goes nowhere overnight without her cat if she can help it. She travels in May and early June so the car won't get too hot for him, no matter what. She can take him in to see Maggie, so there's never a problem. On the second night she goes as far as Russell, Manitoba, where she reserves a little cottage from the Riley family who have a complete village of cottages just off the highway and down around a man-made lake. She sometimes stays two nights here on the way back. It's so tranquil. While in Penny Falls, she stays at the Aurora Inn. It's not fancy and probably isn't the cleanest place in the world, but the price is right and they have an old-fashioned diner-style restaurant with great meals. She stays three nights and has two full days with her sister before she makes the return trip. Most of the time, she's gone nine days of her two-week vacation.

Sun streams through the big front window of the tire shop. Rose sits on a worn stacking chair and thumbs through a three-year-old magazine about business in the United States. She rarely glances up to make contact with the reception guy behind the high wicket. Rose's mind wanders back to the barbecue last week and how Ben hinted about making the trip with her to keep her company. At the time, Rose was pretty sure Ben would not get good news from her tests and so carefully avoided the topic. Today was the appointment with Alex. There would be no road trip for Ben. Although Rose protects her privacy when it comes to both her sister and her atonement, she is deeply sorry for the reason Ben cannot accompany her.

When the boy calls her name she glances up at him, drops the magazine, and approaches the service desk to pay the bill. "If you ever want to sell your Nova, let me know," the kid spits at her out of nowhere. "It would be great to refinish the paint and soup it up."

Rose is a bit taken aback. She didn't think her car would be of interest to anyone. "It's gonna' be a classic," the kid continues. "You take good care of it. Let me know before you trade."

Rose responds with indulgence as she digs in her purse for her cheque book. "I'll keep that in mind. I want to trade in the fall. Maybe you can watch for a newer model for me—a sedan in good shape and not expensive." Give him a challenge. Nothing ventured, nothing gained.

"I'm on it." The kid grins broadly as he turns his perfect, white T-shirted torso toward the back shop and hollers that Rose is on her way to meet the car. She watches as it is slowly manoeuvred out of the garage.

It doesn't take long to pack for the trip. Rose's routines are a comfort. She packs a small suitcase with soft cotton pants and a gathered skirt. She has sweater sets and baggy blouses. She has a warm velour track suit in case she runs into colder weather during the drive. Her spare room is controlled chaos as she organizes her travel clothes. Caesar wanders in and out of his crate and practises for the trip as he does every year. First, he stands focused on the thing like it's the enemy; then he creeps inside as if he expects to find his foe lying in wait; finally, he sits down and surveys his surroundings. Without preamble, he jumps through the opening like his tail's on fire, and proceeds to repeat the process again and again. Rose knows the drill. He'll sleep in the crate tonight with the door open and his furry little face hanging out. By the time they leave on Thursday he'll be ready to go. She rolls up a blue cardigan. It's one of her favourites.

One more day at work. The current program on TV reminds her it's only seven-thirty. Still time to go across the hall and have a visit with Ben. She leaves Caesar to his crate war and crosses to her neighbour's apartment, carefully closing her own apartment door behind her. It takes some time for her knock to get a response.

Ben opens the door just a crack. When she sees Rose, she widens the gap. "I suppose you're here to see how I'm doing. I haven't slit my wrists if you're worried." Her white hair hangs in disarray around her face. She is clad in baggy pyjamas and a housecoat that's seen better days. "Come on in."

"I won't stay, Ben. I leave for Ontario day after tomorrow and I wanted to check on you since you met with Alex today. When's your ultrasound?"

"They haven't called yet; probably by the end of the week. It doesn't matter. Alex says he's sure he's right. He may be an asshole but he's usually right." She sighs with conviction and tosses herself down on her big blue sofa. "Have a seat. Have seat." Her voice reveals the strain and the irritation. "You know what pisses me off the most? Right now I feel pretty good. I felt like crap for almost all of the last year. Now he tells me I'm about to die and I'm actually not sick at all." Her laugh is more like an ironic snarl.

Rose is careful about what she contributes. Ben is in shock and easily influenced. "Just wait until after the ultrasound, Ben. Enjoy feeling good. Take it one day at a time." Her face dribbles platitudes. She sticks her knuckle between her teeth to shut herself up.

Ben smiles the way you'd smile at a puppy that just tripped over its own feet. "I have to find a way to get organized to die. I suppose I'll have to go into the hospital. It's not like I have any family."

Rose watches the older woman talking, almost to herself, as if she's alone and exploring her limited options out loud. "Everyone needs to get their affairs in order at some point, Ben. As long as you're okay right now, it's probably a good time to start." She attempts to be practical and offer more than empty platitudes. "We'll all help. I'm sure everybody here at The Station will do whatever they can." There, she's just committed the whole building. That was smart!

Ben's voice is softer. She looks across at her neighbour with tears in her eyes, but refuses to cry. "I don't know what to do. I guess I've always just hoped I'd have a heart attack and die in my sleep. It would be a chore for the cleanup crew but not for me. I don't know how sick I'll be or how long I have. My life has just become a black hole." She stares at a corner of the couch and avoids Rose's eyes.

Rose is at a loss. She sits up straight and puts on her in-control voice. "Now listen! I'll be back in ten days. By that time you'll have some more information and we'll make a plan. Everybody will help. I know they will. Give yourself a break right now. Eat what you like. Put a few pounds back on while you can eat. Start to get organized—you know—legal stuff." She doesn't want to itemize the details about power of attorney, wills, or executors just yet. If Ben hasn't gotten to this point by the time she gets back from Penny Falls, they can talk about it then.

"I guess I need to write a will."

"That's a good start, kiddo. You could see a lawyer and start the ball rolling. If you want me to help, I could review a draft with you when I get back." Thinking quickly that Ben may have someone else in mind to help her, even a long-lost family member, she quickly adds, "Of course you can get a second opinion from anybody. It doesn't have to be me."

"I know. I know." Ben waves a limp-wristed hand through the space between them. "I'll call the lawyer I used for the business. Maybe he can recommend somebody. You have a good trip now, visiting down east. Don't worry about me."

Her tone is dismissive. It's time for Rose to return to her apartment and get ready for her last day at the office before vacation.

****

The three-day trip across the Prairies and into Ontario is uneventful. Her room at the Aurora Inn is serviceable. Rose thinks that if she makes this sojourn too many more times, she might find a classier place to stay. On her first full day in Penny Falls she loads Caesar into her Nova and traverses the few kilometres to Forest Hills Institute. Every year the driveway appears more spectacular than the last. It must have been ten years ago now, that they planted Lombardy poplar trees on either side of the nearly one kilometre paved drive leading to the building. The grounds are perfectly flat and mowed until they resemble Astroturf, or a golf course, instead of a regular lawn. The poplars are about ten feet apart and their spectacular vertical growth of more than fifty feet in ten years has created a corridor along the slightly curved approach to the five-story brick building. Long ago this place was known in the neighbourhood as the Crowbar Hotel, home to misfits and the insane. It is significantly more upscale now but the residents tend to remain classed the same way.

Rose engages her supportive smile, parks her car, and grabs Caesar's crate before she goes inside. There's no need for introductions at the big oak desk with the marble trim. Ben would absolutely love that desk! The staff knows about her arrival so she just waves and trundles down the hall and up one flight to Maggie's room.

Maggie sits in a leatherette hospital lounge chair and gazes out at the wide expanse of lawn below her second-story window. Her straight hair is long, tied back in a pony tail at the nape of her neck. She is dressed in sweatpants and a pullover sweater. The room is bright—painted a soft lemon shade. The windows, although the sashes need the attention of a paint brush, reach almost to the ceiling which is twelve feet high at least. The bed is made and the quilt, which Rose toiled over for two years and delivered a couple of summers ago, rests in pride of place at the foot. There is a faded black and white picture of the two girls, arms around each other's shoulders and taken when they were fifteen and eleven, on the metal bedside table. Maggie does not immediately turn when Rose enters the room.

Today will be a quiet day. The first day always is. Rose will close the door so she can let Caesar out of his crate. He will do his duty by jumping up to sit majestically on Maggie's knee for the morning. Maggie will start to pet him after about half an hour, during which time Rose will prattle on about her job and the drive out. Maggie will not make direct contact with Rose. Just before lunch Rose will scoop up Caesar and put him back in his crate. She will accompany her sister to the dining hall where they will eat white bread sandwiches, drink lemonade, and have a cookie for dessert. After lunch they will spend another couple of hours together before Rose returns to her shabby hotel room for the evening. The second day is always better. Maggie will talk on the second day.

Maggie has been in Forest Hills Institute since she was eighteen years old—a total of thirteen years. Rose left home when Maggie was twelve and by the time her younger sister was sixteen, she had run away from home many, many times. Rose was estranged from her family. She never contacted them or provided information on her whereabouts. Would Maggie have come to her if she had known her sister's location? Rose will never know. Abner and Ruth finally dumped her into a mental health clinic. At that time they were told their daughter had a depressive psychosis that required medication. The medications never seemed to work. She would stop taking them. She would run away. Finally they had her moved to an institution. Rose only found all this out after contact with her Aunt Betty. Rose always felt it was her fault Maggie ended up mentally ill. After all, it was she who had abandoned her sister to the whims and cruelties of their father as well as the passive neglect of their mother. She would never be able to right that wrong.

On the second day of the visit, Maggie turns when Rose taps softly on her door and lets herself in. She beams as she bends to peer into the crate. Caesar is the great equalizer.

"How are you, today?" Rose starts off slowly. It is an unbelievable disappointment on the occasions when Maggie refuses to talk on the second day. Caesar has been a big help over the years. Her short meeting with the staff has yielded very little. Their parents are still her guardians although they haven't darkened the door of Forest Hills in more than four years. This year was no exception. Maggie manages on her medications, has no close relationships with other residents, takes an interest on pet day, and follows her routine. The good news is that there continue to be no more hallucinations and no delusions, at least that she has voiced to staff or her psychiatrist. That's all Rose knows.

Caesar jumps up on Maggie's knee, settles in, and purrs rhythmically. The girl strokes his soft tortoiseshell coat and stares out the window. It's misty today. There's a fog that wraps itself around the poplars farthest down the driveway. It's eerie and beautiful at the same time.

They sit. Rose isn't sure what to talk about. The chair gets harder under her bum. The view does not mesmerize her as it does Maggie. "Can I live with you instead of here?" Maggie's hesitant words clatter off the lemony walls and crash to the floor. Each one stabs Rose on its way down.

"You want to come out west and live with me?" She's flummoxed. She doesn't know what else to say.

"Yes." Maggie turns her round face and focuses her big brown eyes directly at her sister. "I want a life, Rose. I don't need to be here. I just can't go home to them. I could work. I took a bookkeeping course. I could contribute. I'm not stupid." She turns back to the window as if she already knows the answer; as if she has already dismissed Rose's response.

"You took a course? Really? Can you leave? Don't Mom and Dad have a say?"

She focuses on the fog. "The psychiatrist told me that if I can show them that I'm capable of living on my own, they can't keep me here. No one can keep me here. She doesn't even think I need supervision for my medications anymore. She doesn't think I am any more depressed than most people. She says I have a dissociative disorder as a result of the abuse. She says that, with therapy and separation from him, I will be fine." Rose has never heard her sister talk so much.

"I've been waiting for you to get here before I talk to the doctor. I need to be able to tell her I have somewhere to go; someone who loves me and will help me. I don't want to go to some halfway house. Will you help me?" She turns from the window. Her eyes are big and bright, not glazed and distant.

On the ride home from Forest Hills Rose thinks about her sister and the plan. She will have to speak with the psychiatrist first. Maggie will take over her own responsibilities and ask that Rose be her contact person. They don't know how long it will take but her sister is bound and determined to leave Forest Hills and Penny Falls. She wants to come to Hayworth and Rose can sense the ground shift beneath her feet. Life is about to change.

Chapter 11

Joe

After reading the letter he received from his sister this morning, Joe finds it difficult to concentrate on the marble fireplace he's in the process of installing. Yesterday, with the skill and attention for which he has become known, he carefully constructed the plywood base and the box used to frame the airtight insert. The antique oak mantle lies sedately on the hardwood floor across from him, wrapped loosely in a cotton sheet and ready for its big reveal after the Carrara marble is set and grouted.

The house is quiet. Family members are at work or school. CBC plays quietly in the background. Information about Mount St. Helens and the pending Quebec referendum float through the dusty air, unabsorbed by Joe as he focuses on the letter as well as the task at hand.

Christine wrote to tell him his mother is getting sicker all the time. Her health has been deteriorating pretty steadily since spring. She's had two heart attacks now and is short of breath, so requires oxygen. Chrissie thinks he should come home. He assembles his wet saw and then measures the marble. Measure twice and cut once. This stuff's expensive. He flips on the switch and the motor roars to life. Water flies off the blade, caught by the heavy fibreglass pan and the yards of plastic Joe has already employed to protect the floor. He will need six pieces cut this exact size. Chrissie's letter caught him off guard, since she usually just writes at Christmas. She also included news about his nieces. One's in college while the other will graduate from high school next month. Hard to believe. Maybe a visit back to the little Nova

Scotia community where it all happened wouldn't be as bad as he fears. What would Anita say? He's had no contact with her since he left back in 1966 and came to Hayworth. Married to a cement contractor, Anita manages her husband's business. They never had any kids.

****

It was Anita's fifteenth birthday on March 11, 1945. The old farmhouse was full of people—aunts, uncles, cousins, friends, and neighbours. The dining room table was covered in food—whatever you could imagine. The sideboard was stripped of the silver tea set and instead supported a heap of presents like he had never seen before. As a ten-year-old, Joe guessed you must clean up when you get to be a teenager.

Joe's assignment for the afternoon was to take care of his five-year-old brother, but Adam wasn't in the mood to cooperate. A fitful child at the best of times, Adam was cranky and weepy. He needed a nap but wouldn't go near their room as long as the house bulged with people. That situation was not about to change. There would be food, presents, and cake before everyone cleared out. He located his mother and pleaded to be relieved of his responsibilities.

"All I asked you to do was mind Adam. You are ten and he's five. Play with him. Take him for a walk. He idolizes you, Joe," Alice lectured with impatience in her hurried voice as she returned to the kitchen to refill the teapot.

Joe did his best. He grabbed Adam's pudgy and sticky hand in his own, and they took off into the backyard. The mid-afternoon sunshine was warm on his face and Joe felt the freedom of actually moving outside without the heavy coat, mitts, and hat of winter. "Come on, Adam. Let's go for a walk. What a great day! You don't even have to wear a coat!" He tried to exhibit enthusiasm he didn't feel.

Adam was having none of it. "Not going!" His words seemed ferocious, spit from such a young mouth. He dug the heels of his new brown Oxfords into the soft dirt of the driveway while he tried with his free hand to escape from Joe's grip. "Not going!"

Joe tried again. "Let's follow the creek, Adam. We can see if that old beaver dam is still there. I bet you've never seen a beaver."

The little boy relaxed, stopped pulling all together. "Okay."

Joe couldn't believe his ears but wasn't about to waste the moment. Off they went. Joe tried to hold his brother's hand as they followed the gurgling stream, anxious with spring runoff and noisy in its trek across the Dodd property and down to the lake. The farther into the woods they got, the more excited Adam became. He skipped ahead and ran off the path. Joe traipsed after him, but it wasn't long before the little guy started to get cranky once more.

Joe was exasperated. "Adam, you have to stay beside me. Come back here!"

Adam took off. "Going home. No beavers. Going home." He was travelling in the right direction although not exactly on the path, so Joe gave up his charge and let him go. After another ten minutes of continuing his trek in the opposite direction, he decided the dam must be gone and started back. It would be best if he caught up with Adam before the little bugger turned up at the back door.

As he reached the yard, Joe became aware of the icy nip that had developed in the wind. It was late afternoon by this time and the warmth of the sun had dissipated. Glad to be home before he needed a coat, he wandered through the house in search of Adam. He avoided eye contact with either of his parents and simply nodded to relatives, as his heart started to beat faster and his palms began to sweat. He took the stairs two at a time, but the little monster hadn't been near their bedroom. Joe would know because Adam was incapable of entering their room without getting into something that didn't belong to him.

He grabbed his winter jacket off the hook at the back door and went out, snatching his father's flashlight in the process. Back down the path and out of earshot of the house, he started to holler Adam's name. He startled himself, suddenly aware of the panic in his voice. He followed the same path as far as he had gone before. He yelled and yelled. All he could hear were barren branches as they rattled in the wind, and the purr of spruce bows brushing softly against each other. Now it was dark. Now it was cold.

He ran back to the house. Alice was just starting to set out more dishes for the supper buffet. She caught Joe's eye. "Get your brother washed up, Joe. Supper's almost ready. You two can sit on the floor in the living room but keep an eye on him. I don't want his supper on my clean carpet." She obviously missed the look of sheer terror bleeding out of her elder son's eyes.

"Ma," he whispered. "Ma!" She glanced down with one hand gripping a bowl of salad and the other a plate of ham. "I can't find Adam!"

She turned and yelled into the main part of the house. "Adam, come into the kitchen so your brother can help you wash up for supper." She nodded to Joe, seemingly satisfied to have helped him.

"No, Ma! Listen. We went down the path. He wouldn't stay. He wanted to come back and I can't find him!"

For a split second, Alice glanced out the window into the now indigo blackness of the spring evening. Reality registered. Joe saw it in her eyes. She set the plates back down on the counter and went into the living room. "Everyone! Everyone!" Her voice was a little shaky as people started to mill around. They all expected to begin eating; to get well on their way toward a good old-fashioned birthday party. "Adam's disappeared. We need to find him. I don't think he had his coat and it's starting to get chilly."

"It was sunny and warm two hours ago." Joe's voice sounded whiny even to himself. His mother ignored his fear-wrapped words. The door opened and closed a dozen times as people rushed to their vehicles for coats and flashlights. The woods started to look like Christmas with all the twinkling lights, as everyone took off out into the night. No one spoke to him. He sat down on the back step.

Eventually, Anita approached him after she had changed from her party dress into her coveralls. "You managed to ruin my party," was all she said as she clomped down the steps and followed her mother across the yard.

After an hour of fruitless calling and wandering in the woods, the police were summoned. The yard was full of people. There were lights flashing and the volunteer search and rescue folks came. They wanted the family to stay put. A policeman sat with him in the kitchen and asked him what happened. Joe cried a lot during this time. He tried to tell the man his story, but the questions hurt and he cried some more. "When your brother left to come back to the house, why didn't you follow him? Did he know his way back on his own? Was he upset? Did you hurt your brother, Joe?"

After the policeman left the kitchen to go talk to Alice, Joe quietly went up to the room he reluctantly shared with Adam. He sat on his bed, legs pulled up to his chin, and stared at the blue and white quilt his grandmother made for Adam when he moved from the crib to a real bed. It had dog and cat pictures sewn on it. His room faced out toward the backyard and, despite the closed curtains, the flashing orange light of the search and rescue truck danced with the red and blue lights of the police cars. They reflected off the walls and made his room seem happy and sad at the same time. No one came to see if he was okay. He sat in the same spot until dawn fought for a place on the walls with the orange, red, and blue.

Joe crept downstairs when he heard the commotion outside. His mother screamed. He held the railing, crouched, and turned backwards so he could see through to the kitchen and toward the door. A big man, in dark blue coveralls with an orange vest, carried Adam into the house. It seemed like he was asleep in the man's arms with one grubby hand flopping in the air. For a second or two, Joe felt that his little brother would be fine but he knew the truth. Somewhere deep inside, the horror of his mother's screams started to make sense. Adam was wet. His hair was matted with ice and blood. His shoes were gone. Joe ran upstairs and into their room.

The time between when they found Adam's body in the stream beside the beaver dam and the funeral was terrible for Joe. No one said he was bad; no one told him he committed a terrible act; no one accused him of abandoning his baby brother in the woods so he could fall in a stream, hit his head, and drown. No one yelled at him. No one ever asked him again what happened. His parents stated facts and issued instructions: "Come to the table for dinner." "Put your boots in the porch." His sisters didn't talk to him at all. Chrissie looked at him with sympathy akin to pity in her big brown eyes. Anita glared with a hate that burned black in hers. They didn't go back to school until after the funeral, so he spent a lot of time in what had been their bedroom or on the back porch. One day he came in and found Adam's bed gone. There was no furniture to replace it, and the dust bunnies still floated in the corners. He got the broom and swept the floor but it didn't help. Every time his eyes rested on that side of the room he saw the blue quilt.

He was scared to go to the funeral. He worried people might try to hurt him and his family wouldn't care enough to protect him. He wanted his mother to hold his hand. He wanted his father to put a big, tobacco scented arm around him. They walked into the church behind the little blue coffin carried by uncles and family friends. It had small white handles. Joe's parents walked first, with Anita and Christine right behind them, heads bowed. His mother and sisters sobbed softly all the way down the center aisle to the front pews. He walked behind them all. He could feel the eyes of everyone near the aisle and close enough to observe, burning holes into his brain. It took every bit of courage and control contained in his ten-year-old body not to run from the church.

When they got to their seats behind the pallbearers, they stood and waited for him to go in first so he would sit the farthest away from the minister and the coffin. He sat on the hard oak bench in the second row behind one of his uncles and focused his eyes intently on the floor. As much as he loved to gaze up at the wooden ceiling and the plaster angels mounted on the support beams, as much as he always loved to examine the stained glass pictures of the stories from the Bible, he refused to allow himself those pleasures and kept his head down.

Back at the house after hymns and tears, after the minister talked about forgiveness, after Adam was pronounced heaven bound, Joe disappeared into his room. He carefully removed his Sunday pants and jacket, hung them in the now half empty closet, wiggled into jeans and a blue shirt, and settled on his bed. He pulled his knees up to his chin and rested his forehead on the rough denim. He barely heard the latch move as the door opened and Chrissie came in. He knew it was Chrissie. It just couldn't have been anyone else. She soundlessly offered him a pink glass plate burdened with funeral sandwiches—egg salad, cheese and cherry, ham and cheese—all with the crusts cut off. There were two squares, both chocolate. When he lifted his face, the tears in his eyes fell down his flushed cheeks. He was afraid to say thank you. He appreciated the effort from his sister but his mouth felt full of saw dust and his throat burned as he tried not to cry. She placed them carefully on the tiny table beside his bed.

She turned to leave. With her back to him, he heard her whisper, "I still love you, Joe. I know it wasn't your fault." As the door quietly closed, he returned his cheeks to his knees and could no longer prevent the torrent of unshed grief from pouring down his young boy face.

****

He hears the front door open just as he returns his attention to the task at hand, startled to realize he was about to cut a piece of marble that did not require the attention of the saw. Momentarily confused, he raises his eyes to see his client, Mrs. Rakowski, walk in. All aflutter in her designer coat and leather gloves, she appears as surprised as Joe.

"I expected you to be gone by now. It's after five." Her attitude is no nonsense. Joe has worked for her before. Although meticulous, she's a good customer and they have always gotten along.

"Not quite done, yet, Mrs. R. I wanted to finish the hearth today so I can do the surround tomorrow." The attempt to cover his serious lapse into reverie seems to work.

"It will be fabulous. The marble is exactly what I wanted. The fireplace will be a focal point, Joe. I'm very happy." Without another glance in his direction she retreats to the kitchen, with her green leather clutch purse jammed tightly into her armpit and her gloves dangling unceremoniously in her hand.

"I'll be out of your hair in a half hour." He tosses the words carefully at her back. His hope is to provide the information without annoying her. His original goal was to be gone before she got home from her bridge club. He shakes his head in a futile attempt to shatter the images that still linger behind his eyes. The wind rustles the cedars, planted as columns on either side of the living room picture window. The sound wraps him up in a cold loneliness.

He finishes the hearth, packs up his tools, and loads his truck. Time to get home to Blanche, who is no doubt anxiously awaiting the arrival of her meal ticket. He'll write to Christine. His biggest fears could be realized if he finally gives in and goes home. He doesn't know if he could bear the rejection all over again.

Chapter 12

Patrick

Patrick arrives at the diner just after the lunch crowd starts to disperse. Nancy's obviously frazzled working alone. She nods when he walks in but continues to wait on customers. She delivers lunches on a big tray. The booths along the window are cluttered with dishes. Dirty and crumpled paper napkins are the only garnish on empty plates while plastic soda glasses sit bereft, except for bent straws and melting ice. He wants to relax at the counter and have a quiet lunch before he fires up the big old dishwasher. Instead, he nods to Nancy, grabs a tray, and starts to bus tables. He knows he's supposed to be in the kitchen except when he eats, but Nancy is so nice to him and seems to need his help. She glances up again from the soda fountain where she's refilling glasses with ice and coke, wipes a strand of dark hair off her forehead with the back of her hand, and simply nods.

She's wearing the standard black trousers and black shirt with a white bar apron. It's stained and needs replacing. Patrick thinks that if the boss came in and saw her in that apron, she'd have a fit. The owner is a local accountant who bought the business as an investment. She's a big woman with hair too long and straight to suit her heavy and drooping features. She dresses to the nines in business suits and high heels. She wears lots of colourful scarves and sometimes ties her hair up in a knot. She's prettier when she does that. The Hayworth Diner seems to run itself after all its years of operation, but Margo Johnson keeps pretty close track despite her full-time job. Everybody out front must be neat and tidy. She would hate to see that dirty apron as much as she would hate to see Patrick expose his less than desirable hygiene habits to the customers. Patrick knows he only keeps his job because he's reliable and will take extra shifts at a moment's notice. Still, Margo wouldn't be happy today.

He picks up all the clutter from the first two booths and shoulders his way through the swinging doors into the kitchen. Danny, the cook, is jumping from one plate to another in a valiant attempt to get meals out for the latecomers. Dishes are piled high and cutlery is scattered. Patrick keeps his eyes down. Danny, a big and burly character with a pot belly and handlebar moustache, can be mean if he's busy. Oftentimes, he takes his bad moods out on the weird guy who does the dishes. Patrick knows this is how Danny sees him. It's hard to believe he has such a cute wife and two little girls. He's a different person when they're around.

After he empties his tray and scrapes the garbage, he returns. This time he grabs the cleaning rag and spray bottle from behind the counter. He wipes the first two tables before he loads up the next two—almost half done. After twenty minutes, the eight booths that stretch along the front windows are clean as a whistle. Patrick smiles as he gazes out over the handmade pine creations, urethaned to a high gloss and trimmed in red leatherette. The actual tables are pine, too, with glass tops that protect the wood. He admires that 1950s style and imagines his toy collection displayed in one of the booths. Perfect! He returns to the kitchen and loads Old Bertha, as they so fondly refer to the vintage Hobart counter dishwasher with the rack conveyor belt. He loves this machine. They have a bond of sorts. He's actually managed to fix her twice all by himself.

Once the old girl starts to purr, he ducks through the doors to see if Nancy needs more help. Nancy rushes past him with a second tray of food. "Patrick, can you bus that table in the back, the one with the woman by herself? Tell her I'll be over in a minute with a dessert menu and see if she wants tea or coffee. Will you do that?"

He nods but keeps his eyes on her shoes, secretly pleased Nancy seems to need him. As he scoops up the woman's dishes and starts to repeat Nancy's request, he notices the long red nails wrapped around the tall glass of orange pop. Before he is fully aware of what has happened, he runs to the kitchen with her plate and leans against the counter, soothed by Bertha's quiet vibrations. His eyes are closed and he sees the image of her; the orange extension cord that was always rolled in a box beside the outdoor Christmas tree lights tucked away behind the furnace; the orange chair from the girls' tea party table and chair set, tipped and guilty looking, lying on the floor; hands hanging straight down by her sides with one scraped clean of the hateful red polish, while the other glistened under the glow of the sailboat light in the corner.

"Patrick! Are you okay?"

Nancy leads with her hip and pushes in through the doors. He can hear them flap, signalling her entrance. He takes a deep breath and opens his eyes. "Sorry, Nancy, I'm okay. Don't know what came over me." He tries to shake off the anxiety and forces himself to meet her eyes and ignore the images in his head.

"You look awful. I bet you haven't eaten—out there helping me because Tammy didn't show. Listen. We're under control. What do you want for lunch?"

Patrick quickly glances over at Danny, who just stands there, arms crossed, as he watches them. Afraid to reply, his eyes focus on the linoleum.

"Make him a club, Danny, and add lots of fries. Wash your hands and go out to the counter, Patrick. We're under control now," she repeats for emphasis. "Couldn't have done it without you." She tilts her head in order to better see his eyes and nods her thanks.

The rest of the day is calm compared to that first hour. He starts to unload Bertha for the third time. Danny is busy with supper prep, and Nancy's in the restaurant filling coffee cups and cutting pie for the mid-afternoon regulars. Patrick starts to think about the day he found his mother.

****

By fourteen, his routine was entrenched. He attended school by rote and trudged home along the tree-lined suburban streets of Alystair, a small factory town in central Ontario. He hated school—not so much school, exactly, but the kids who were mostly mean to him or ignored him altogether. They could sense he had issues and their sensitivity was manifested in name-calling, tripping, poking fun, or outright cruelty. Breaks from this daily grind occurred only in class but Patrick was unable to concentrate the majority of the time. His voices argued with the teachers, preoccupied his thoughts, and caused him to avoid the eyes of others often by simply keeping his closed. This caused problems. Teachers said he was asleep.

Classmates called him stupid. No one ever seemed curious about the truth. Patrick kept his secret safe.

His trip home each day was filled with anxiety and fear of what awaited him. His mother could be fine; she could be in a blind rage; she could be holed up in her bedroom while his sisters aged eleven and ten at the time, sat at the kitchen table frozen with eyes locked on each other. Most days, he would open the back door and listen for a few seconds. If he could hear the girls talking, he knew the situation would be fine. If the house was uncommonly silent, or if he heard his mother screaming, then he would be forced to call his father to come home.

On this day, it was quiet. He loped up the stairs from the back entry and saw both girls sitting at the kitchen table, still in their school clothes. The table was set for supper. There was a stew in a pot at the back of the stove, with a note taped to the lid—instructions for heating. *Maybe she went shopping.* He realized how unreasonable that seemed even as he considered it.

When his sisters saw it was him they jumped down and ran over. Natalie, the older one, grabbed Patrick's hand and stretched up on tip toes to whisper in his ear. "She's not here. We tried her bedroom, but she's gone."

Sarah, never one to be left out, added, "We looked upstairs, too, Patrick. She isn't here."

"Did you check the basement?" His eyes darted from one of his sisters to the other. They were beautiful girls with long and thick straight ebony hair that shimmered in the afternoon light. They inherited their mother's slightly olive complexion. Born a year apart, they were often mistaken for twins. They would be tall in the end but right now he towered over them both. He, on the other hand, inherited his father's pasty complexion now peppered with adolescent acne, and scraggly brown hair that could best be described as shitty looking.

The younger girl quickly defended their inaction. "We aren't allowed to go down there if you're not home, Patrick! We would never do that!"

Sarah was right, of course. He had insisted, when they were much younger, that the space was his and their presence would be by invitation. Neither was a nuisance. They both abided by the rules and even appreciated the modicum of structure rules provided, considering the circumstances. "You two go change your clothes. I'll just run downstairs and then I'll call Dad. Don't worry. We'll find her. I'm sure she hasn't gone far." *When are the nurses due? Not for a day or two. She was funny this morning, talking to him and doing dishes. She acted more like she would right after the nurses' visit, not before. It was nice. Maybe she's getting better.*

As he switched on the cellar light and navigated the stairs to the basement, his stomach was doing flips. The sweat poured down his spotted face. The voices were mercifully quiet. His physical self knew it would be bad even as his mind attempted argument.

There she was, framed by the light of a tiny table lamp shaped like a boat with a yellow sail shade. All he saw at first was the orange extension cord and the orange chair from the girls' table and chair set. All he could think about was Christmas lights and tea parties with little sisters. That cord was always kept behind the furnace with the strings of lights he would help his father put up and take down every year. The cord matched the chair, upended in the middle of the floor. Somehow, in his mind crowded with bits and pieces of television characters, news stories, fears, hallucinations, and logical fallacies, Patrick realized his life would never be the same again. Calmly, he approached his mother and lifted the long strands of unwashed hair, revealing a face swollen, blotchy, and contorted. Her big green eyes were mercifully closed. She wore a blue floral flannelette nightgown with long sleeves. They were trimmed in bits of lace. It seemed she had made an attempt to take off her nail polish. One hand was scraped and raw around the cuticles. The other flamed red.

He heard the girls at the top of the stairs. "Don't come down." All business. "I'll come up. We need to call Dad." He trudged up the stairs and turned out the light so just the sailboat remained to shadow her spot. He dialled the number for his father.

"Alystair Pontiac Buick. We deal in only the best. How can I help you?"

"Raymond Hollinger, please."

"One moment," came the singsong reply.

After a click that seemed to last for minutes, Patrick heard his father's voice. "Raymond Hollinger, Assistant Sales Manager. Good afternoon."

"Dad, you have to come home now. It's bad." His voice started to shake. He needed to calm down.

"Are the girls okay? What's the matter?"

"The girls are fine. Just come, Dad. Now!"

He sat down at the kitchen table after getting his sisters each a drink of juice and rummaging in the cupboard for a box of cookies. They were suspicious but didn't ask questions. The Hollinger kids had learned at a very young age how to keep their mouths shut and stay out of the way. It wasn't long before a Buick demonstrator with dealer plates pulled into the driveway and Ray bounded up the back steps. Patrick met him at the door.

"Downstairs, Dad. Natalie and Sarah—stay put," he demanded over his shoulder. Patrick led the way and returned to his mother. He could hear his father's footsteps behind him.

****

After the police were gone; after the ambulance took his mother's body on a stretcher covered in a sheet; after he fixed his sisters a sandwich and their father had tucked them into their beds; he returned to the basement—his beloved basement where he always felt safe and where he could be himself. He had many questions: *Why did she choose to hang herself in my space? Why did she choose today? Why didn't she leave a note? Was there a message for me that I don't understand? Why was she trying to take off the polish before the nurses came?* He sat for a long time in the big leatherette recliner across from the television and across from the spot where his mother died. He didn't watch TV. The voices were coming alive now. He waited for her to talk to him.

It didn't happen that night or for almost a year after that. Then she started to appear as Patrick sat in his recliner watching television and listening to the cacophony of voices rollicking through his mind. She stood on the spot below where she hanged herself, dressed in her flannelette nightie with the lacy cuffs, her face smooth and beautiful once more. She most often stared at him without speaking, but he could sense her words somehow. She always had that orange extension cord draped around her neck and tossed over one shoulder like a scarf.

As time went by, his father focused almost exclusively on the girls. Patrick knew his dad was frantic that Natalie or Sarah might end up with schizophrenia like their mother. Everybody knew it ran in families. They thrived on all the attention and especially enjoyed visits to their counsellor. The death of their mother freed them from the burden of her disruptive episodes and bouts of depression, anxiety, or frenzy. Patrick knew that most of the girls' friends, who now came over on a regular basis, considered the brother in the basement to be weird. It was okay. He kept to himself. He helped around the house and tried to ease his father's burdens as much as he could.

By the time Patrick turned sixteen, he had started to change and he couldn't seem to help himself. He skipped school, stayed in the basement, mumbled under his breath, and fought with his father. Natalie and Sarah, who used to go to him for help and advice even before their mother died, started to avoid him. He lost interest in his appearance. He wanted to try and outrun the voices. He didn't want to end up like his mother although he was smart enough to realize he was embarking down the same path. His worst fear was that his sisters would find him the way he found his mother, so he left.

He was sure they would find the note taped to his television, after he had been gone a couple of days. Eventually, one of them would go down to the basement even though he knew they all avoided the rec room as much as possible. He was eighteen. He told them not to come after him; that he had to get away; that he was sorry.

****

As he starts his walk home to The Station after a full day at the Hayworth Diner, Patrick thinks again about the woman with the long hair and the red nails. She wasn't as pretty as his mother had been. His family never came after him and never attempted to find him, as far as he knows. What about Sarah and Natalie? They would both be around twenty now. He bets they're tall.

Chapter 13

Cheryl

She closes her daily planner and places it precisely in the upper right-hand corner of her spotless blotter, so it sits exactly in the centre of the working side of her desk. She stands up, puts on her dark blue sweater-jacket over the pale blue and patternless shift dress she carefully chose that morning, and walks on clicking heels down the hall to greet her last client of the afternoon.

All she has for reference is the referral. Lorna is a seventeen-year-old who made the appointment to talk about her options. She's currently about six months pregnant and on the verge of graduating from high school. Her parents haven't disowned her exactly. They just choose not to be involved in her decision-making process. The referral said she doesn't want to keep the baby, so Cheryl's role is to assess current conditions and present her client with options.

As she turns the corner into the waiting room she sees her new client right away, sitting in the corner, focused on her lap, and fidgeting with her fingers. She has delicate hands although the dark pink nail polish is chipped and chewed. She's wearing black sweatpants, a huge grey sweatshirt, and sneakers. Her long, and terribly thin, brown hair hangs curtain-like and obscures half of her downturned face. One ear protrudes through the strands.

"Lorna?" Cheryl announces the first name only, with a slight question and a small smile focused on the girl. She responds to her name although startled like a rabbit one would meet on a hiking trail, and nods.

Cheryl extends her hand. "I'm Cheryl Nadler. It's nice to meet you." They shake hands. Cheryl can tell the girl has probably never been on the receiving end of a formal introduction like this before. Most kids her age don't shake hands voluntarily. Cheryl is well aware but she tries to treat her young charges as adults. After all, they come to her with very adult issues. "You can follow me." The girl stands and obediently falls in line.

Back in the office, secure in their privacy behind a closed door, Cheryl encourages her client to be comfortable while she attempts to elicit basic information. Some aren't anxious to talk. Lorna is not like this.

"So, will you tell me a little bit about your situation, Lorna? All I know is that you are currently exploring your options. You didn't bring one of your parents with you today." Cheryl is careful that her tone does not hold a judgment or a question. It will be entirely up to the girl as to what she chooses to reveal. The story, not unlike the many, many Cheryl has heard before, comes out in a rush.

"I made a mistake and now I'm paying the price." Her voice is harsh. "My parents aren't here because they said I'm old enough to get into this mess and now I have to get out of it. No boyfriend." She is blunt and answers questions before Cheryl can ask them. "He's at college; home for Christmas; you get the picture." She pushes her hair back behind her ears and gives Cheryl a grimace. "He's not interested in me anymore. I applied to go to the same school as him but don't think I'll go there now."

Cheryl waits patiently for her to get the history off her chest. She's found that it's easier to let a client dump out all that's on their mind before she attempts to organize the situation. As the girl meets her eyes and pushes her hair behind her ears yet again, Cheryl knows she's ready for a discussion. A head turned down with a curtain of hair protecting a face is a bad sign, but Lorna appears open to the process. Cheryl leans over in her chair, making the gap between them slightly smaller.

"How about you start from the beginning. Tell me your plans and how you think I might be able to help."

Cheryl watches closely as Lorna visibly relaxes. She stops picking at her fingers. She leans back in her chair so she is no longer hiding her belly with poor posture. "I think my due date will be September, probably the middle. I'm accepted at two different schools, like I said. I won't go to the same school as Doug so that leaves U of C. They have already told me I can start late. My marks are really good." Her face is flushed as she adds this bit of information.

Cheryl counters. "So, you're such a good student they are telling you starting late won't be a problem? You must be one pretty smart cookie!"

Lorna beams with pleasure. "I want to put my baby up for adoption. My parents and I have talked. They tell me not to ruin my life, or theirs, by trying to raise a child while going to university. I don't think I could do it anyway. Besides, there are lots of people out there who want babies, right?"

Is Lorna trying to convince herself or Cheryl? "You've made up your mind?"

"Yes." She focuses on a spot on the wall behind Cheryl's right shoulder while she speaks. "I wish I knew how it'll feel when I'm thirty and I know there's a kid out there that's mine. I wish I knew if it will always feel as awful as it does now even though I'm sure it's the right choice. I want to be a scientist, a chemist, actually. This is hard." She returns her attention to Cheryl and repositions her hair away from her face. Her blue eyes are bright but damp around the edges.

"Let's talk about options, Lorna." Cheryl is all business. She explains to her client about traditional adoption, where the baby is given up almost immediately to a family chosen by the department. Lorna's privacy, as well as that of the adoptive parents, will be protected. There are also a couple of New Age options just now becoming more popular. Prospective adoptive parents can sign on for an open adoption. After the normal screening process, the birth mother is able to choose from a list of qualified parents and can also choose how involved she would like to be. Sometimes birth mothers stay involved. Other times they get a couple of pictures from the adoptive parents and then prefer to be in the background. It can be tricky. "Did you know about these options, Lorna? Did you think about it before our appointment today?" Most often, girls who plan to surrender their baby have weighed all the options but the responses sometimes surprise Cheryl.

"Right now, I think I want to know who the parents will be but not be involved. Can I do that?"

"You most certainly can. You can even help choose them and meet them beforehand if you want."

The shake of her head is barely discernible. Her hair has drifted down over her face again, curtaining her eyes. "No. If I get too involved it won't work. I know me. I'll change my mind. You choose and tell me a little about them; just enough so I know my baby will get a good home. I'm sorry."

"Oh, Lorna, don't be sorry. You've just made a huge decision. We'll work together for the next couple of months. You can ask me any question you want. I'm here to help and we'll make sure your baby has a good home. Now, when you come in next week, how about you ask your parents to tag along? I would very much like to meet them and we can explain the process. Will that work?" Cheryl leans over and pats Lorna's hand.

The girl lifts her face and presents a sad and resigned sort of smile that Cheryl has seen a hundred times—one that Cheryl understands only too well.

****

After she turned fourteen, Cheryl spent very little time at home with her mother. She attended school when she felt like it and hung out with her boyfriend, Jason. He was a small-boned and wiry boy, a number of years older than Cheryl. He had his own apartment—a room, really—with a hot plate. The bathroom was down the hall. He sold drugs and was high, himself, most of the time. Cheryl drifted into spending most days and nights with Jason where she could forget about her mother, her mother's boyfriends, and lying in bed awake at night waiting for one of those guys to try and get into her room. Her mother didn't care where she was or what she did so she started to stay at Jason's, mainly so she could sleep. She felt safe there. They began to have sex just after she turned fifteen. He was probably nineteen; she wasn't sure. He didn't seem all that old but Cheryl knew he was.

She didn't know she was pregnant when he died. She turned up and crawled into his grubby bed one night when he wasn't there. She could sleep in his room with the door locked and know that if the key turned it would be Jason. She had been asleep for a couple of hours when she woke to that familiar sound. He was high, really high, and seemed surprised to find her there. She wasn't totally convinced he knew who she was. He flopped on the bed and was out cold. She got up and locked the door before she crept back in beside him.

She woke up in the morning because of a horrible smell. In her dream, someone was throwing up all over her. Her mind tried to sort the dream from the real when she saw Jason with his face in a puddle of vomit. He was grey—and cold. She knew he was dead.

Cheryl called the police and an ambulance from the pay phone in the hall.

She answered all the questions the cops put to her. She felt sick to her stomach as she sat in the tiny, dirty room that smelled like vomit. It got worse as more people turned up and she finally asked a policeman if she could sit in the hall. After about three hours, they told her she could go home. When she arrived at her mother's apartment it was almost noon. Her mother was drinking and some guy who didn't look familiar was still asleep in her mother's bed. She went into the bathroom and threw up. She escaped to her room, wedged a chair under the doorknob, and stretched out on her bed. There were no linens—just the mattress. Her mother must have wanted clean sheets so used hers. She stared at the ceiling as waves of nausea and sensations of loss she couldn't explain rolled over her. Her mother hollered through the door. She wanted to know if Cheryl had any money.

It wasn't long before her mother asked if she was pregnant. Cheryl didn't know. She went to a clinic for people who didn't have a doctor. They gave her some vitamins and sent her to a home for unwed mothers. In 1966 in Cape Breton there were no options such as open adoption and abortion wasn't even legal. She would never have had an abortion anyway. So, basically, the home paid for her food and kept a roof over her head until she went to the hospital to have the baby. They took it. She was never told if it was a boy or girl. She heard it cry so she knew it wasn't dead. After she returned home from the hospital, her mother kicked her out; said she was moving to Halifax with some man and Cheryl couldn't come.

She worked at the bus terminal diner and slept in the back room until she earned enough money to buy a discounted ticket to Alberta. She never saw her mother again. Life was not easy and she mostly remembered Jason and the cry of a newborn she would never know.

****

She writes up her case files before going home. She hopes Lorna will be able to persuade her parents to come in for the appointment next week. Deep down, she wishes Lorna could find a way to keep her baby and still become the person she wants to be but there are no guarantees. She carefully files the chart when she's finished. She removes her heels and puts on her sneakers. She closes her office door and walks down the hall being sure to take a moment to nod "good night" into any office with an open door. Cheryl is aloof at work. She doesn't fraternize with the other staff. She has always had trouble bonding. She knows she judges. Awareness of all this doesn't help that much. She is definitely safer when she follows her routines. Some of her co-workers are buried in paper. You can't see the tops of their desks. Cheryl shudders, thankful she's orderly. She anxiously anticipates her arrival at home and going for her run.

As she approaches The Station her eyes fall on Ben and Rose standing outside in the glare of the late afternoon sun. It won't be dark until after ten at night so it almost seems like noon, even now. Rose looks concerned and Ben is flapping her arms, appearing to argue. There must be an issue. Rose is just back from a trip east and Ben has been lying pretty low the past few weeks. No harm in saying hello.

Rose turns toward Cheryl, first. "Hi. Just getting home? Too nice to be inside all day, don't you think?" Ben continues to study the gravel in the parking lot. She does not appear well at all.

"Going to go for my run in a few minutes; just want to shower first. How's everybody doing?" Cheryl knows it's probably a mistake to ask this question. She will more than likely get a protracted answer that will undoubtedly put her schedule out of whack, but her concern for Ben takes priority.

"I'm fine. Just got back from my trip east and have some organizing to do before I hit the salt mines again." She grins at her comparison of Dr. Gunton's office to a salt mine. "Ben, here, isn't up to snuff and I'm trying to convince her to go back to the doctor."

The expression on the older woman's face is black with barely concealed anger. "I'm sure Cheryl has better ways to pass the time than hearing about my problems. She listens to people's problems for a living, for God's sake! Give the girl a break." She points a vacuous smile at Cheryl. "I'm fine, really. Just a little under the weather."

Cheryl assesses the situation right away. "If you need to see the doctor, Ben, I'm sure you'll go. You are a very smart lady who knows her own mind." Cheryl glances at Rose but never changes expression.

Ben nods. "I thought I might make an appointment anyway. No big deal." She shrugs her shoulders and turns to go into the building.

Cheryl refers back to Rose. "Well. Off I go. I hear a salad calling my name but I have to have my run first." She trots toward the door right behind Ben and enters the foyer at almost the same time. "Never hurts to see the doctor," she whispers over Ben's shoulder as she starts up the stairs. "If I can help, just let me know."

As Cheryl unlocks her apartment door, she is certain Ben will make an effort to contact Dr. Gunton. Now that she doesn't think Rose is telling her what to do and trying to take charge, Ben will do what needs to be done. Instil in someone the idea they are perfectly capable—the old "you can do this" approach—and they will likely follow through. It works with all ages. Sometimes it would be nice if she could make it work for herself.

Chapter 14

Ben

"The Tylenol doesn't work anymore. I take three at a time but the cramps are worse than ever." Ben sits across from Dr. Gunton. Her once shockingly white hair, now strangely grey and drab, hangs across one eye and doesn't seem to suit her at all anymore. She drags it out of the way with hands she once considered her best feature but now knows must look like claws as they scratch through her mane.

Alex Gunton finally observes her from across his desk. "How bad is it?"

"It makes me scream. I hold a pillow over my face. It's like my insides are going to explode."

"Are you eating at all?"

"Cream of Wheat, Arrowroot cookies, and applesauce. Mostly weak tea." Her voice is raspy and sounds like dry leaves being crunched by a fist. She no longer even attempts to put her best foot forward. Ben needs more time. She still has unfinished business—issues she's put off addressing for years. "Can you give me stronger pills for the pain?" She doesn't want to beg but her voice has a ring of desperation she can't prevent.

"I can give you hydromorphone, Ben, but it's highly addictive. It will work but only for a couple of hours at a time. If you take too much, you'll just sleep and get confused. Do you have anybody taking care of you?"

Ben starts to say no but realizes that isn't the complete truth. Her circumstances started to change earlier this month. She hasn't driven in weeks. Her little blue truck sits idle in the parking lot at The Station. Joe took her to the hospital one night and has acted in the capacity of chauffeur ever since. He's waiting outside now. Rose does any grocery shopping she needs and picks up her mail. Cheryl has come down half a dozen times to get her laundry. The girl has her own machines upstairs. She's obsessed with clean linen. "Some of the people at my building help out. I don't drive anymore either."

"Well, no more driving under any circumstances and you will probably need someone with you all night if you want to take this stuff. It's powerful, Ben." He glares at her over the top of his wire-framed reading glasses. He's paying more attention to her than ever before. It must be serious. "Ben, you need to get your affairs in order." His tone is forceful. It's not a suggestion.

"I'm not sure where to start. I have a little bit of money saved but not much else"

"You need to see a lawyer. Have you got a will? You need a will. Do you have family? Your chart says to contact Rose Woodward if there's a problem. Don't you have family? You need a power of attorney, an enduring power of attorney, and an executor. You need to do this, Ben." He stands up and hands her prescription down to her.

She reaches out but isn't prepared to stand just yet. "So how long do I have, Dr. Gunton?"

"Can't say. Won't say. This pain medication is highly addictive. I give it to patients when addiction is no longer an issue. Ben, get your affairs in order." She stands. "I want to see you again in two weeks. Tell Rose to put H.C. beside the appointment." She is dismissed.

Back in the waiting room, she repeats Dr. Gunton's instructions. "What does H.C. mean, Rose?"

Her friend and neighbour peers up from the doctor's schedule. "It means if you're too sick to get here, he'll make a house call. I allow extra time just in case."

Ben gets sweaty. Her face flushes before she can gain control. "I guess I'd better get busy." She attempts to cover her shock as she points out the obvious. All of a sudden her circumstances seem so real.

Back in the truck, she asks Joe if they can stop to get her pain medication on the way home. "If I set up a time to see a lawyer, will you drive me?"

Joe, always patient and kind—never prying, never gossiping, never asking too many questions—glances over at her for just a second before he returns his eyes to the road. "I'll take you wherever you want to go, whenever you need to be there, Ben. Just let me know." She thinks his eyes look sad.

That evening Cheryl stops by to pick up laundry. The girl certainly is reliable. She offered to help one Sunday when she saw Ben struggling up the stairs from the laundry room and since that encounter, every Sunday and Wednesday, like clockwork, the little social worker is there. She comes down after she has her supper, always crisp and fresh like it's the beginning of the day instead of the end. The fresh laundry will be outside Ben's door all folded in the basket tomorrow morning. She leaves it there on her way to work.

Before Cheryl has time to turn around, Rose opens her door. "I thought I heard you two. Can I come over for a minute, Ben, just for a wee talk?" The expression on Rose's face clearly describes the concern Ben knows is there. The doctor said she shouldn't be alone overnight if she takes this new medication. Well, she doesn't want strangers to sit in her apartment and watch her sleep. That would be creepy.

"Sure." Ben opens her door wider so Cheryl can leave with the laundry basket, and Rose jumps across the foyer. Caesar trots along behind her.

Rose enters Ben's apartment with a measure of hesitation that doesn't go unnoticed. Without ceremony or pleasantries she begins. "I have an idea. I think we need to have a building meeting to see if people will rally around to help you while you're sick."

"What? I can't ask people to stay overnight with me. You aren't family."

"Well, what do you think will happen when you need more help? I just want to explore your options with you." She sounds exasperated. "I think I know you well enough to know you don't want to go into hospital for months on end. That's no way to spend what time you have. Let's be honest. Joe is already driving. Cheryl does your wash. I do your shopping and mail. Let's have a meeting and see what else people can do so you don't have to worry, and so you can stay here as long as you want. If Amanda and Patrick don't want to pitch in, that's okay; but let's see."

Ben suddenly has a clear appreciation for the fox cornered by a bunch of yapping hounds. She sees her life, or what's left of it, begin to spiral out of control. This wasn't how it was supposed to be. "I'll make an appointment with a lawyer tomorrow—probably the same guy that handled the business stuff for me. At least I know him. Joe said he'd take me. Let me do that and then we can have a building meeting. You're right, I'd prefer to avoid the hospital as long as I can but I don't want people to do chores they don't want to do. I'm worried certain people might feel obligated to help. I don't want to be a burden, Rose. I don't want to be a project." Her voice is vehement. She's out of breath and starts to cough.

Rose nods and the matter is closed. "Let's have tea. You sit down. I'll make it."

****

Joe takes her to see her lawyer. Ben has had little need for a lawyer during the past years. There was her lease and a couple of business documents but nothing too compelling or even interesting, for that matter. She called and asked if Murdock Blackney does documents like wills and was told by his senior-citizen secretary that Mr. Blackney does general law and that certainly includes wills.

It's a sunny Friday afternoon in mid-August. Joe said he was happy to quit early and take her. She chokes down a pain pill and is ready when he rumbles into the yard right on schedule. Her appointment isn't for forty-five minutes, but she wants to talk to her friend and figures she'll need the extra time. She climbs into the cab after he opens the door. She's cold constantly and has on heavy slacks, a pullover, and a coat sweater. Joe is dressed in a cotton T-shirt and blue jeans. "Hi, Joe. We've got a few minutes. I need to talk to you first."

"Sure, Ben, what's up?" He's hoisted himself back up into the truck cab after carefully closing her door.

"I need to see Murdock Blackney today so he can draw up a will for me and put the papers together for the power of attorney and other stuff. I need to ask you if you'll be my power of attorney and my executor when I die."

She sees a look which could easily be interpreted as horror wash across the carpenter's face, so she thrusts forward. "You're in business, so you probably have as good an aptitude for this kind of stuff as anybody. I don't have much and I'll leave most of it to my grandson if I can find him." Joe's eyes have questions but he remains quiet. "It's a long story. Anyway, I've got to take really strong pills now. It helps with the pain but if I take too many I get stupid. Eventually, stupid will be better than pain and I'll need someone to pay my bills. I trust you."

She knows her expression is sheepish. "And I don't want to be kept alive with tubes and machines. Just keep me out of pain so I can go when the time comes." Her body slumps. She's empty of words.

Joe's voice is soft. He puts a big hand on her shoulder. "You tell me what to do and I'll do it, Ben. I wish things were different."

Relief spreads through her like warm tea. She practised this speech for two days. "Okay, you come in with me so you know all the details about what's going on and then old Murdock will have no issues talking with you later. Let's go." She buckles up and focuses on the windshield in the hopes that her friend isn't as nervous about all this as she is.

In the end, there isn't much to it. Ben and Joe sit across from Murdock Blackney. He's a little and bulbous man with a bald dome perched on top of unruly grey sprigs of hair that sprout from in and around his ears. His suit is brown. The office panelling is brown. The desk is brown. Ben absently thinks that the décor looks like shit, which is fitting considering her circumstances.

She has to find out the location of her grandson. She determines that her neighbours may choose whatever they like from her apartment after she dies and before the remainder goes to charity. Choice will be by rotation and in alphabetical order including Joe. Patrick will be given enough money to fix his tooth, and Joe will get a stipend for all his work. Money left after the bills are paid will go to Charlie Collins, now twenty-eight, the son of Butler (Butch) Collins and Ben's deceased daughter, Grace. There is no one else. Ben's husband died shortly after her move out west in 1955. She never saw him again after she fled the east coast. Grace died in 1953.

Joe doesn't ask her any questions. She assures him she will find Charlie. It won't be that hard. She has a little savings she wants him to have. It would be enough to possibly buy a small house but that would depend on where he is. There are people she can ask; people who are no doubt still where they used to be.

****

After a couple of long distance phone calls, Butch Collins actually answers the phone on the first ring. "Hello."

She recognizes his voice but asks anyway. The pain pill has kicked in and she wants to get this over with while she can or before she has a heart attack, whichever comes first. "Hi. Can I speak to Butch, please?"

"Speaking. Who's calling?" *Does he sound gruff, suspicious?*

"It's Benjamine, Butch. Don't hang up. This will only take a second."

"Ben? Benjamine Tullis? What the hell are you doing calling me? What do you want?"

"Charlie's address for my will." She tries to be blunt, hoping he'll just give her the address and not ask any questions.

"He wouldn't even know who you are, Ben. He thinks you and his mother were killed at the same time."

The shock of this information staggers her. For a second she almost physically loses her balance. Her grandson has been kept in the dark all these years. "Listen, Butch. I've got some money saved and I'm sick. Only have a few months I think. I need contact information for the will. It doesn't matter what he knows or doesn't know. I just want him to have it."

Surprisingly he gives her the address. "A lot of water under the bridge, Benjamine. Are you going to contact him? What are you going to do?" His voice is not unkind.

"I'm just going to give the address to my lawyer, Butch. You can tell him whatever you want after I'm dead. You're right. A lot of water under the bridge. Thanks for this." Her voice is flat, without inflection. She is mildly curious about how his life has gone over the past twenty-seven years and how her grandson has turned out, but she doesn't want to hear him blame a possibly miserable existence on her. She got what she wanted. She's done. "Take care, Butch. Bye now." She hangs up the receiver and is unsettled by how violently her heart pounds.

After she provides Blackney's office with the information, she stretches out on the couch to relax. She has a couple of hours before the pain comes back. She can't take any more pills until shortly before everyone turns up for what Rose has called their "organization" meeting tonight.

Ben's couch has four feather pillows piled in one corner. They smell good today—Cheryl and her fabric softener. When the pain starts to move across her in waves of cramps that feel like her bowels will explode and fly out through her abdomen, she braces with the pillows. Two are placed behind her back, one is held on her lap, and one is to cover her face as she folds into a ball and screams. It's her way to cope without alarming the whole building. Ben knows the waves will flow past and subside once she takes the hydromorphone again, but she can't take the pills every three hours or she'll just get dopey and sleep all the time. She has too much to do. Everyone will find out about this soon enough, but for now she tries to keep her secret.

****

Joe arrives first. He's armed with a platter of cheeses and crackers. He's no longer in his work clothes but dressed in khakis and a blue cotton shirt. Ben still thinks he'd make a good catch. "How are you doing? Did you get that address you needed? How about I make a pot of tea?"

Ben still sits on the couch, surrounded by pillows and dressed in loose cotton pants with a drawstring waist, an over-sized blouse, and a heavy cardigan. She has sheepskin slippers on socked feet. She can't keep warm and wants no tight clothes around her middle. Her medication has begun to kick in so she's relaxed and ready to handle whatever her well-intentioned neighbours have in store for her. "Sure. Make yourself at home. The teapot's in the cupboard by the window. Teabags are right beside it. Most people prefer the regular tea so grab the Red Rose. Aren't you the man about the manor with your tray of nibbles?" She grins as she teases her friend. They've developed a bond of sorts. It's odd to experience the emotion of dependence on others. She's not used to it.

"I got hold of the people I needed to. Gave the address to Murdock's secretary." Joe's eyes look puzzled. "I'll tell you the whole story some evening when you decide to pop down and keep me company," she adds as she responds to his unasked questions. "You'll need to know what you're dealing with in a couple of months."

His facial expression morphs from puzzlement to surprise. "A couple of months! God, Ben, is that what Gunton told you?"

"Not exactly. He just told me to get my affairs in order, but the way I feel I don't imagine I'll see Christmas." She raises her hand for effect. "Now don't worry. The paperwork's all done but the signatures, and Blackney said we could come back early next week. I should last until then." She hopes her sarcasm will cover the fear that inserts itself between her words.

She hears a knock on the door, which opens at the same time, and the rest of her neighbours pile in. Amanda is first, with Chester holding Mason. Cheryl and Rose appear behind and just as they're about to close the door, Patrick pokes his head around the door frame. "Come on in, Patrick. Don't be a stranger. You know everyone. Come sit by me." Ben wants him to be comfortable and feel part of the group. Who will tell him to take a bath once she's gone?

With his face focused on the floor and stringy hair covering one eye, he virtually slinks over to the couch by Ben and barely acknowledges his neighbours. There's lots of jostling for seats, but Joe takes charge and ensures everyone is comfortable. Those that want tea are served. Mason has a couple of Arrowroots, and the platter is passed around.

Rose starts. "Ben, the reason I wanted us to get together is that we all agree you need help and everyone wants to pitch in. Is that fair?" She surveys the little group and there are mutual nods of assent.

Ben interrupts. "Listen, you guys. Cheryl is already doing my laundry." She acknowledges the social worker in her matching beige linen pants and pullover top, with a nod. "Rose, you do my shopping and get my mail." Another nod. "Joe is my chauffeur and has just taken on the task of power of attorney when I need it and executor of my will." She observes the glances of surprise at this last statement. "What else is there?"

"Well," starts Rose again, with a little less authority, "we don't want you to be offended but we think you probably need someone here overnight."

"Did Dr. Gunton tell you that? That's breaking confidentiality." Ben's eyes burn straight into Rose's.

"No." The woman's voice is strong again. "You told me you take hydromorphone now and I know it makes patients really drowsy. I just think you might fall in the night." Her voice is softer as she continues to hold Ben in her gaze. "It's hard if you only take the pills after long intervals. The pain comes back and it can be bad."

Ben doesn't want people in her apartment with her all night. She's certain it hasn't come to that just yet. Patrick starts to squirm beside her. He must be upset. Maybe this is too much for the kid. He stands up quickly and bolts for the door. They all hear him tear up the two flights of stairs. Before much else is said, he's rushes back in with a plastic encased package in his hand. He slows down and walks over to the couch. With a reverence only Ben understands, he places his offering on her lap.

Everyone stares at James Bond walkie-talkies in their original box. Ben knows they are circa 1965. "What's this for, Patrick?"

He runs a hand, rubbery and pale from doing dishes at the diner, over the box. "You can keep one and one of us can have the other. Then, if you need someone we can come running." He smiles with satisfaction and the gaping hole from the missing tooth is exposed for everyone to see.

"Do they work?" Joe, ever the practical one, asks the obvious.

"They need batteries but then they'll work." He quickly glances around the room. "I'll make sure they work." Ben pats his hand.

In the end, Rose says she'll draw up a schedule and each night someone will have the second walkie-talkie. If Ben needs help she can call. Amanda is quiet throughout most of the evening, sitting on the floor, playing with Mason, and leaning against her husband's leg. Ben feels sorry that she seems so sad. Before they get ready to leave, the young mother looks up.

"I would like to be your housekeeper, Ben. I can come in every morning after I do the stairs. I'll do what needs to be done—clean up any dishes, help with the grocery list—you know that kind of stuff. May I do that to help you?"

Ben turns to Amanda. "My dear, you are welcome in my home every morning you want to be here. I will always appreciate your company." Ben knows in her heart this will be hard. For a person who prides herself on her independence and has always protected her privacy to a fault, she expects challenges ahead.

Chapter 15

Amanda

"I thought I might make you a more interesting lunch." Amanda wipes out Ben's refrigerator, while the older woman is stretched out on the couch watching. "I brought some banana bread with me, and you have applesauce. That's all I need." She turns just as a wince of pain flashes across Ben's pallid face. It's like you could look through her skin and see the veins working. Her face has a tint of bluish-green against her white hair. The medication should kick in soon. Amanda knows that the hydromorphone makes her friend sleepy. She slurs her words like someone who's had one too many but she somehow remains alert and oriented. It must take an incredible effort.

Their morning ritual has been going on for a number of weeks now. Amanda will tidy her own apartment, give Mason his bath, and then go about sweeping the apartment foyer and staircases. Once she's finished, she pops in to Ben's. There are times she has to help her out of bed, but most often it's like today. Ben sits on the big blue leather sofa, cocooned by pillows. Amanda makes her tea, gets her what she wants for breakfast—which is usually not more than a couple of Arrowroots or a small bowl of Cream of Wheat— washes any dishes, sweeps, tidies the bathroom, and then they visit together. Sometimes they complete a grocery list for Rose, or put the laundry in the big plastic basket for Cheryl. Amanda usually makes an attempt to create a lunch that might inspire Ben to eat more than applesauce, hence the banana bread.

"Talk to me about how you came to Hayworth, Amanda. If my memory serves me, you just kind of appeared out of nowhere." Ben always shows an interest, no matter her condition on any given day. It's easy to let your guard down.

"I was a camp cook up north, Ben. I got qualifications when I lived back east. I did pretty well until they started to lay people off during a slowdown." She starts to cut up the banana bread into bite-sized chunks. Her goal is to make a bread pudding with a twist. "Somebody said the Hayworth Diner needed a cook on the back shift, so I took a stab at it and got lucky."

"But why did you want to go up north? Couldn't you get a job back home? You had qualifications, right?"

For a heavily medicated woman, she can certainly stay focused. Amanda continues to work with her back to Ben. She's never sure what to reveal. Mason gurgles, asleep in his little stroller in the middle of the floor between the peninsula and the couch. She glances over, satisfies herself he's okay, and takes a breath. "The truth is, Ben, I needed to get away. Sometimes money isn't the solution to your problems."

"You're rich? Really?"

"No, no. Don't misunderstand!" *God, I'm making this more complicated than it really is!* "I grew up in foster care. My parents were killed when I was just a kid. I was penniless but I married a rich guy. Wealth isn't all it's cracked up to be."

Ben, fully supported by pain medication that's finally kicked in, observes Amanda with an expression of surprise blended with curiosity. "So you've been married before. I didn't know that." Amanda detects no sign of judgment in her voice. "Will you tell me what happened?"

"Nobody knows about this, Ben—not even Chester."

"There's an old expression, Amanda. It goes: 'Dead men tell no tales'. I assure you, I'll take whatever you intend to tell me to my grave. I really mean it—and it won't be that long." She laughs quietly and seems to study Amanda with slightly hooded blue eyes that, just now, appear faded.

Amanda tells her story but abbreviates the part about her parents. She says that she landed in foster care after her parents died. She talks about how she learned to be a chef and worked at Long Point Lodge. She tells Ben about the Bradway family and about the day she met Jeremy. She describes how rich they were and probably still are; how out of her depth she was; how inadequate she felt around Mrs. Bradway; and how she seemed to have no control over the succession of events that led to her eventual marriage to this young man who wouldn't take no for an answer. She tells Ben all about the day she caught him at home in bed with somebody else, and about her subsequent departure. "So that's how I ended up in an oil field camp in northern Alberta, Ben." Just to finish, she quickly adds, "And when I came down here and experienced trouble with my old Bronco, it was Chester who came to my rescue. I guess he saw me as a damsel in distress!" She winks at her friend as she gets up from her seat on the couch to pull the pudding out of the oven.

"Can I ask you a question?"

Amanda's heart beats just a little faster as she carefully sets the bubbling banana and applesauce bread pudding on the cooling rack. "Sure, Ben, you can ask me whatever you want."

"Did you ever divorce the guy?"

Amanda can't prevent a huge sigh from rolling out of her. She turns around as she tucks unruly red locks that have wiggled out from her knotted bun, back behind her ears. "You said you could keep a secret, Ben. No."

"So you married Chester while you were still married to, Jeremy, was it?"

"Yeah, that about sums it up. I guess I could go to jail for bigamy? And Mason is illegitimate?" Her voice sounds questioning but she can guess the answers. "Who knows? Maybe he's divorced me and I don't know it. The family never tried to find me. With all their money, they probably just got the divorce."

Ben surprises her. She doesn't gasp. She doesn't lecture. "You know that after three years, you can just file and get a divorce. Maybe he did that. Maybe you could do that if he hasn't. Murdock Blackney is coming by this week. I want to formally give my power of attorney to Joe. How about I ask him to look into it for you—in total confidence of course? Might as well put the mystery to bed, eh?" Amanda sees reflections of a mother in the woman's eyes.

Amanda nods. "That's probably a good idea. It's been almost ten years. What's this about turning over your P.O.A., Ben?"

"Changing the subject, are we? No big deal. I just don't want Joe to have to manhandle me down to the bank every time I need to cash a cheque. This way, he can have signing authority. It's time." She nods to herself.

Amanda knows the inevitable steadily approaches. She's awash in the sadness that realization brings.

"Amanda," Ben continues. "What do you remember about your parents?" Her voice is soft and Amanda, as she sits across from her dying friend and bounces her beautiful baby boy in her lap, begins a story she can't remember having ever told anyone before.

"My parents were young and happy. I know they loved me. I can still feel it. I can't explain why. They were both killed in a car crash. I was in the back seat, Ben. I held my mother's hand while she died." Despite her best efforts, Amanda's face crumbles. She hugs Mason a bit tighter and buries her face in the sweet smell of his little neck.

"You poor dear. That guilt about surviving when others don't—it can eat you up."

Amanda lifts her face and studies her friend. "I wished for a long time that I had died, too. I needed to repay the universe by being perfect in school. I was afraid that if I wasn't perfect, my foster family would throw me out. Now, after all this time, I'm still a mess. I think I need to be a perfect mother and wife but, instead, I've broken the law. It's like I want to ruin my lovely life!"

Ben's voice is quiet. "You can fix it, Amanda. We'll start by talking with Murdock. It's okay. This'll be between us. Let me help. It's almost lunchtime. Can I try some of your pudding? Is it cool now? Maybe we can all have some."

Amanda places Mason carefully back in his stroller. She gets him a cookie and dishes out some of her creation for both of them. Amanda's not optimistic that Ben will eat all that much. It's amazing she can stay alive on what little she consumes. Amanda watches her try the banana bread pudding and, much to her delight, her friend actually eats it with enthusiasm.

"This is so good! I can't remember eating a bite in the last couple of months that tasted this good. Will you get me some more? I want to tell you a little about my daughter. You remind me a bit of her.

"Her name was Grace. That's my middle name—Benjamine Grace Tullis, I am." Ben smiles over at Amanda, who knows they don't have much longer before the medication starts to wane. Ben will want to be alone then. She tries not to take more pills until mid-afternoon and then a third dose before bed.

"Grace wasn't a bad girl, but we argued a lot. From the time she was a teenager, we always managed to find topics to fight about. She was twenty-two when she married Butler Collins. Everyone called him Butch. A nice enough guy, but wild and crazy; liked to spend time at the pool hall and the bar. He and Grace always seemed to be partying. I didn't think she should marry him. I wanted her to finish college, but she wanted to be a mother. She always reminded me that I was exactly the same age when I married her father. All she seemed to want was to be a mother, although Butch didn't strike me as a family man at all. He drove a delivery truck for the grocery store. I expected he'd never be able to take care of her. Richard, my husband, was sick a lot by the time Grace was in high school. He had back problems and what he called bad nerves. He couldn't spend any time at the store. He worked at the local hardware store and was quite the handyman in his day. Am I boring you, Amanda? I don't want to drone on and on." Ben brushes her white mop out of her eyes.

"Not at all!" Amanda sits up straighter in her chair and cuddles Mason, who has fallen asleep in her arms. "We are kindred spirits now, Ben. You can tell me whatever you want, just like I can tell you." She discovers, with a sudden sadness, how very close she has become to her dying friend.

"Anyway, Grace married Butch and had a little boy they called Charlie. He was born in 1952. He's twenty-eight, now." She shakes her head, "I want to tell you about the car accident. I know what it's like to wish you had died, too."

She pauses to take a sip of tea and adjust her pillows. Amanda notices her face isn't as relaxed as it was when they were eating. The medications are wearing off. "You don't have to tell me today, Ben. We can talk again tomorrow."

"No, no. I want you to hear this. I want you to know I understand. Charlie was barely a year old. Grace and I took him with us shopping. He was in the back seat. He was a busy little guy and was down on the floor behind me, playing with some blocks of some sort. I can't quite remember. He wouldn't sit on his mother's knee and I was mad at her that he was playing in the back. Nowadays he'd be in a car seat, but back then nobody had heard of strapping your kids in. So he was on the floor where neither of us could see him. Grace tried to twist around to get his attention. The sun was in my eyes. We were bickering back and forth, probably about money. She never had any. Richard and I weren't that flush ourselves, but I always tried to prop her up because of Charlie. I missed the turnoff. It all happened so fast after that, it seemed like a dream. Grace hollered at me that I missed my turn. Instead of remaining calm and driving on, I panicked and tried to make a U-turn. I know I never even checked my mirrors and I couldn't see clearly ahead because of the sun. I acted like we were the only ones on the road." She pauses and Amanda sees her focus change—like she's watching a movie. Her eyes appear vacant and her hands shake.

"Grace never knew what hit her. When I turned, we got slammed into by a pick-up truck coming from the other direction. They hit the passenger side of my Buick head on. I passed out, I guess, from the impact, but later on I wondered if I just couldn't cope with what I knew had happened. Charlie got a broken leg." She smiles up at Amanda. "If the little guy was up front in his mother's arms as I had wanted, he'd be dead, too. Grace was killed instantly, the police said. So I know what it feels like to survive, Amanda; to wish every day it was me who died; to wish I hadn't made the stupid mistake I made."

Tears course down Ben's pale cheeks. "I couldn't stand it after I got out of the hospital. I tried for two years to face Richard's disgust with me. As for Butch, he wouldn't even let me see Charlie. My only glimpses of my grandson came if I drove down the street and saw them on the sidewalk. The Collins took care of Charlie. Existing in the same town was just plain hateful. After almost two years of torture, I ran—left and came here. Like you, I just seemed to appear out of nowhere."

Amanda still has questions, but knows it's far too late today to ask. Whatever happened to Butch and Charlie? Were the people in the truck hurt? How many people were in the truck that hit her? Has Ben been in touch with her family since she was given her diagnosis? Questions for later.

"So now we know each other's story, Amanda. We'll talk more, especially after my visit with Murdock. Tomorrow around the same time? Will there be enough pudding for tomorrow?" The exchange of secrets has ended.

"If there isn't enough pudding, I'll make more. It's almost one o'clock, Ben. We've been shooting the breeze all morning and I have a little boy who shouldn't eat just Arrowroot for lunch." She smiles down at Ben. She understands the woman wants her to leave before the pain returns, if it hasn't already. She bends down and touches her softly on the shoulder. "I'll see you tomorrow."

As Amanda returns to her apartment and goes through the ritual of feeding Mason, she worries about the process necessary to get a divorce. It will cost money they don't have, and Chester will have to know eventually. They will need to get married again—if he isn't so mad he disowns her. She's terrified of the consequences of her actions.

Chapter 16

Rose

"Call Ben and tell her I'll be by shortly after supper." Alex Gunton races past Rose's desk on his way to the hospital for late afternoon rounds.

Rose is surprised. "Okay," she replies. "I have to pick up a couple of items for her at the grocery store on my way home. I'll tell her then instead of telephoning, in case I might wake her up. She expects me after work." Her voice trails off behind her boss, as he lets the glass office door bang on his way out.

Despite it barely being the end of August, Rose shivers from the chill in the air. She's under pressure to make a decision. Even though she has a new-to-her 1979 silver Malibu, she doesn't relish a trip back to Ontario once the weather starts to turn. The days are getting shorter, and she always wears a sweater now.

In the grocery store, Ben's list isn't long. Rose wanders the aisles and searches for the familiar digestive biscuits and jars of applesauce. Amanda wants bananas so she can make more bread pudding. It's not bad. Ben shares. She grabs a half dozen of those fluffy buns Ben likes because they're fresh. The woman doesn't eat enough to keep a bird alive, whereas Rose sees herself swallowing down all her concerns by overeating at an alarming rate. Just yesterday, she tried to put on a skirt and the zipper wouldn't go up to meet the button at the waistband. She was so upset she ate peanut butter directly out of the jar.

She reaches Ben's apartment at precisely five o'clock. The door is unlocked during the day. The person with the walkie-talkie for the night also has the spare key. As is the habit of all the tenants, Rose knocks softly before she opens the door. Ben is stretched out on the couch, cocooned in pillows. She's covered in an afghan Rose knitted years ago and found stuffed in her linen cupboard; stored for no apparent purpose. Rose tip-toes over to the kitchen and starts to put the meager supply of groceries away. Ben actually looks like she could be dead.

"I hear you, you know. It's not necessary to be so quiet."

Rose tries not to react but jumps a tiny bit anyway. She tends to startle easily at the best of times. When someone who looks dead starts to talk, it can be more than a little off-putting. "Hi there, sleeping beauty. I picked up what you and Amanda asked for. The buns are fresh—still a bit warm. I can get one ready for you with a cup of tea, if you like."

"That would be great. I probably have another hour before the meds start to fade. Might as well eat."

"Alex said he wanted to come over later. Will you be okay, or do you want me here? I can pop back, no problem."

"I wish I'd known. I would have put off more drugs until later in the day. I might be in pretty rough shape by then." Ben is distressed. Even though a home visit with Dr. Gunton, especially while she's in pain, might be a good idea, the idea disturbs Rose. She sympathizes with Ben, whose primary vocation, right now, is to balance pain medication with lucidity.

"You could always take a half dose shortly before he gets here. I expect he'll be late anyway. Do you want me to come over?"

Ben's expression is hidden behind her uncombed and unkempt white mop. "Yes. Yes. I guess I need someone here as a second set of ears. I have trouble remembering all the details that are said to me. My mind wanders off like a toddler with no supervision." She smiles the now familiar watery smile up at Rose, as tea and a bun are set on the coffee table in front of her.

"No problem, old girl. I'll go spend an hour with Caesar and have a bite to eat. Then I'll come back and we can wait for Mr. Perfect together."

Alex Gunton arrives at seven-thirty. Rose thinks he's surprised to see her there, but he makes no comment. He gives Ben a cursory examination and asks her about the pain. The hydromorphone is working when she takes it, but she doesn't want to be totally out of it so still has break-through pain. The doctor tells her she must take it every four hours whether she needs to or not. He says she's built up some tolerance by now and it probably won't make her as groggy as she thinks. He writes a new prescription and hands it to Rose. "Can you get this filled for her?" He turns back to Ben. "How do you manage? You haven't been to the outpatient department at the hospital in a while. Rose, are you here most of the time when you're not at work?"

"Not at all," pipes up Ben before Rose has time to formulate an answer. "People here at The Station all chip in. And at night, I have this!" She reaches over to the end table and holds up her walkie-talkie like a prize she's just won. "Everyone shares the other one, so if I need help in the night they will come a-runnin'." She smirks at her doctor. "I haven't needed anyone yet but who knows, eh?"

"What about other stuff, Ben?"

The older woman turns to Rose. "You tell him." She must be tired, or that half dose of hydromorphone isn't enough.

Rose explains who does what and when, how they manage, and how Ben really doesn't spend all that much time alone except maybe afternoons.

"Oh no," Ben interjects. "Patrick works split shifts now and spends lots of afternoons here. We talk. I sleep. He's a great kid."

Rose turns her nose up a little in a failed attempt to conceal her feelings about Patrick and his hygiene from Dr. Gunton.

"And Cheryl has helped me with a sponge bath twice now."

Rose is shocked. She can't imagine Cheryl touching anything remotely resembling a sick and sweaty old lady.

Dr. Gunton appears impressed. He grunts as he gets up to leave. "It's working well for now, Ben, but there'll come a time when you can't stay here even with the help of neighbours. We'll admit you then, okay? Don't try to be a hero."

Ben glares up at him, determination written all over her face. "We will manage as best we can, Doctor. Thanks for the visit."

Rose can't suppress a satisfied grin. He has been summarily dismissed. She couldn't have done it better.

Once they're alone, Rose makes tea and the two women sit together munching digestive biscuits. "I guess I'd better get busy and die soon, Rose, or you'll weigh two hundred pounds!"

Rose is offended at first, but can't fault her friend for pointing out the painfully obvious. "It's not just you, Ben. I have a couple of other issues on my plate right now."

"Trouble with the new car? I thought it was pretty fancy when I saw you pull in to the front parking lot the other day."

"No! No!" interrupts Rose before Ben can continue. "The car is fabulous! Nicest possession I've ever owned. It's just that I have to get busy and make another trip to Ontario before the weather starts to get bad."

"Is your sister sick?"

Rose heaves a huge sigh. When she exhales, it's like a balloon deflating. "Maggie wants to come and live with me, Ben. I haven't told anyone. I just can't imagine how it will work out. She's been at Forest Hills Institute since she was eighteen and she's almost thirty-one! She's had every diagnosis in the book. Now they tell me—and her—that she's just mildly depressed like most people. I don't mind saying I'm very uneasy."

"Other family?" Ben tilts her head as she asks.

Rose likes to talk with Ben. Why not talk her situation over? Maybe she can work her issues through with a sounding board. She decides to share. "We didn't have a good life, Ben. I ran away when I was sixteen. Dad was a drunk and an asshole, abusive in all the ways your imagination can dream up. She got left behind—too young. I was thoughtless and I left her to deal with him. Our mother was like an empty room with the lights on—no support at all. She starved herself and was always sick. Winters were the worst. Dad took care of a trailer park and in the winter he just collected pogey, drank, and abused his family. After I left, Maggie must have had it very bad although she doesn't talk about it to me. She ran away time after time and eventually, my parents had her committed. I go see her every summer. There were times when I would travel all the way out east, sit with her for two days, and she'd never say a word! She just acted like I wasn't even there. Then I got Caesar and took him along. He broke the ice and she started to come around." Rose stops for a sip of tea and another cookie.

Ben's eyes are full of questions. "You've worked really hard to take care of yourself. It must have been scary at sixteen."

"I think back now and wonder where I got the balls to do what I did. I worked, got my GED, got trained to work in a doctor's office, and figured, if I could handle my father, I could probably work for Alex Gunton. No one else wanted the job." She laughs. "Life in Hayworth has been okay. I'm scared it will all change—that my apple cart will be toppled—if I let Maggie come here."

"Maybe all you need is a backup plan, Rose. Remember how Dr. Gunton said that if you guys can't manage to keep helping me, I can go to hospital? Well, maybe you need to find out what you can do if circumstances go sideways with you and Maggie. Maybe talk to Cheryl. She knows about these things."

"You are so wise." Rose smiles indulgently at her friend and neighbour. "I expect I'll have to drive out to get her before the end of September. Do you think Cheryl might do your mail and groceries while I'm away?"

"That won't be a problem. Joe will help, too, so you make your plans to go get Maggie but have a talk with Cheryl about options, first." She takes a last sip of tea. "I look forward to meeting Maggie! Now, I need some alone time. It's been a long day."

On her way out the door, Rose waves the prescription back at Ben. "I'll get this filled tomorrow."

****

Rose stands at her kitchen window the next afternoon, munches potato chips, and watches for Cheryl to return home after her run. The girl's habits are like clockwork and Rose knows, if she's patient, she'll be able to catch her on her way upstairs to her apartment. Work was a bitch today but she managed to go to the pharmacy to get Ben her stronger medication. It probably won't be long now. She'll start to sleep a lot more. She shakes her head with reluctant sadness and leans down to give Caesar a little pat. After she talks to Cheryl, she'll pop in to Ben's for a minute. All she really wants to do is sit down and watch the news but that'll have to wait. Here comes Cheryl in a little navy jogging outfit, perfect as usual, with just some pink in her cheeks to show she's been running; amazing, really.

Rose scoots over and opens her door just as Cheryl enters the foyer. "Hey! Glad I caught you. Got a minute?" Rose consciously attempts to appear friendly because the social worker always makes her nervous for some reason. She feels suddenly compelled to change her clothes or have a bath just to meet the girl's standards. She brushes potato chip residue from her hands across the back of her skirt.

Cheryl startles a tiny bit as she manages a smile. She takes a big breath before she responds. "Hi, Rose. What can I do for you today?"

"I need to talk to you about Ben. I have to go away for about ten days and we hoped you might take over a couple of my jobs."

Cheryl eyes the second set of stairs that lead up to her apartment. "How about I just run up and have my shower and salad? I'll come back down in less than an hour. Does that work?"

Cheryl's as good as her word and appears at Rose's door exactly forty-five minutes later. As she steps inside the apartment, her nose wrinkles ever so slightly, reminding Rose that the litter box requires attention. "Thanks for coming back down, Cheryl. Have a seat. Can I get you a drink? Tea? Coffee?"

"No thanks, Rose." Cheryl, in her yellow linen pants, sits on the edge of a dining room chair, perched like a little finch that might fly out the open kitchen window any minute. "Are you going to take another holiday?"

"Not exactly." Rose feels lumpy and dishevelled as she pulls out another chair and sits down with heavy acceptance. "I have to go back to Ontario to get my sister and we—Ben and I—need you to do Ben's mail and groceries while I'm gone. The groceries are minimal and I only go for the mail twice a week, so no problem." It all comes out in a rush.

"Sure. I don't mind at all. I can just put her chores in with mine, the same as her laundry. Happy to help." She picks an imaginary, or perhaps actual, cat hair off her perfectly pressed pants. "When do you leave?"

"Oh, shortly, I hope. I have to talk to Forest Hills Institute as well as Maggie's psychiatrist. And I have to get Dr. Gunton to give me the time. He will no doubt be wild, but I'll probably take off in a week. I'll make sure you have the post office key, and that Amanda knows you'll be doing the shopping. She tells me what Ben needs."

"What's the trouble with your sister, that she needs a psychiatrist?"

Rose is thrilled that Cheryl has picked up on her hint. Maybe Cheryl can recommend someone whom she can call if Maggie relapses. She launches into the abbreviated version. "My sister has been at Forest Hills since she was eighteen. She was diagnosed with all kinds of mental infirmities including manic depression and schizophrenia. She's thirty-one now and wants to come live with me. They expected to discharge her to a halfway house. I don't know how I will handle her. I'm a little scared, actually."

Cheryl seems calm. This must be what she's like at work. "Maybe her psychiatrist should refer her to someone here. That way, she won't be on her own. I can give you a couple of names. Does she respond better to women? There's a very reputable woman psychiatrist that comes to our hospital twice a month."

"Oh, Cheryl! Could you do that? You know, I go see her every year for a couple of days. There were whole visits when she never talked to me at all! It's just been the past few visits—since I started taking Caesar with me—that she's come around."

"Are your parents still alive? Do they visit?"

Rose can't prevent the edge from creeping into her voice. "They pay the bills. They don't visit. I doubt if they've seen her in years." She examines her hands, fidgeting in her lap. "I haven't seen my parents since I ran away when I was sixteen. I guess I was lucky. When Maggie started to run away, they locked her up." She returns her gaze to Cheryl, who's staring at her without comment "It's complicated," she adds.

Cheryl is all business. "I'll write down Dr. Wilkerson's contact information for you, Rose. When you talk to Maggie's psychiatrist, you can give it to him, her? Anyway, you can give it to whomever and they can refer the chart to Dr. Wilkerson here. Sounds like maybe Maggie might need extra support. She's been institutionalized for a long time."

Rose scrambles for a piece of paper and a pen. After Cheryl finishes writing in her perfect script, she starts to rise. "Big changes for you, Rose." *Was that scepticism in her tone?*

Later on that evening, Rose taps on Ben's door. She enters once she hears a frail "come in" floating from the back of the apartment.

"I got your prescription," Rose yells so the older woman can hear who it is.

Ben thumps out of the bathroom, supported by a cumbersome chrome contraption better known as a walker. "Where in God's name did you get that junky monstrosity?" Rose frowns at Ben, who grins in spite of her bent posture and what Rose is sure to be considerable pain.

"Patrick found it at an auction last week. It cost five dollars and he said it might help when I'm weak. What do you think? I call it the Cadillac!" She approaches her pillow nest on the couch and drops down with a muffled thud. "I must have mentioned to him I was getting a bit wobbly and this was his solution. What a kid!" Her white locks flutter as she shakes her head.

Rose feels a mixture of surprise and pleasure. Despite the walkie-talkie coverage at night, she and others have been worried that Ben could fall. This will help. "Well, good for Patrick! Now, I talked to Cheryl and she'll cover for me while I go get my sister. And, thanks to your suggestion, she's even given me a referral so Maggie will have someone to see when she gets here. She's a nice girl—weird somehow, but nice." Rose stops to take a breath. Ben's eyes are closed. "Do you need a pill, Ben? Are you okay?"

"I'm fine, Rose. Just took two an hour ago, so I'm on my way to never-never land. That's why I went to the can. Try to go before I get too groggy. You can put the new pills on my table with the other stuff." Rose notices her picnic table now holds a metal tray that supports medication bottles and stomach remedies. Constipation is an issue with the stronger pain pills so Ben has assembled a variety of stool softeners, antacids, and diarrhea remedies. "Amanda helped me put together all that stuff so I wouldn't have to truck all the way to the bathroom. Good idea, eh?" Her eyes are still closed. "When are you off to Forest Hills to get your sister?"

"Probably within the next week or two, why?"

"No reason. Your parents are still alive, right? Are they nearby? Maybe you and Maggie need to visit them—put some old ghosts to rest."

"They were horrible parents, Ben. I haven't seen them since I ran away when I was a teenager. I don't know if I could even look either one in the face."

Ben curls up on the couch and pulls up the afghan. "Monkeys on your back, Rose." Her voice starts to slur. "Monkeys on your back."

As Rose tucks the old woman in and turns toward the door, she wonders if Ben might be right. After Maggie comes to Hayworth and they see how the new living arrangement works out, then maybe she'll make an attempt to corral all those monkeys.

Chapter 17

Joe

Joe's long legs stretch across Ben's living room. His crossed ankles rest up against the base of her barn board coffee table. She's curled up on the couch, eyes closed, as one claw-like hand strokes Blanche. The cat purrs with a steady rhythm of pleasure that matches the beat of Ben's movements. Joe holds his tea mug with both hands and balances it on his barrel chest. She could be his mother, who by coincidence is exactly the same age. He hasn't heard from Chrissie again since she wrote to tell him Alice was sick, and he often catches himself pondering if he'll see his mother again before she dies. His father died quite suddenly years ago. By the time he got his sister's letter, the funeral was long over.

He knows Ben's tired. They went to the bank this afternoon and arranged for Joe to take over signing authority for her—formal power of attorney. He wanted her to have to co-sign cheques, but she insisted he start to do it all. Every week, she seems to abdicate a little more of her life's responsibilities. He guesses it's to be expected. He's organized his work so he can spend one, or maybe even two, early evenings with her. Sometimes he makes her supper, for what it's worth. Other times, he just drinks tea and she sleeps, but she says she likes the company. Today when they got home from the bank, he installed a handrail in her bathroom.

"Ever think you'll get married again, Joe?" The voice from the couch is weak and a little shaky, but certainly just as pointed as ever.

"Married? Are you kidding? I'd have to have a date first. I don't think it would be fair to count taking a client to the diner for supper when I was doing a renovation for her." He's pensive. "She's nice, though; works at the Hexagon. Cheryl gave her my name when she needed someone to look at a house before she bought it. It's been literally years since I had a relationship, Ben!" He surveys the once stunningly beautiful woman cushioned on her blue leather sofa. "Now if I could just find someone as cute as you."

Ben laughs and readjusts her hips on the couch. Blanche resettles and patiently waits for Ben to continue rubbing.

"Honestly, there are about five men for every woman as it is up here, and I'm old. No one wants a guy who's forty-five with two bad relationships under his belt. I'm a terrible risk." He takes a sip of the lukewarm tea as his eyes dance at Ben over the rim.

"You are a professional contractor, a good cook, very charming, attractive, and interesting. I think you'd be a great catch! You could always ask Cheryl out." Ben opens her eyes and squints across at him.

"You're not serious? Is she even thirty? Just what I need—a diva on my hands!"

"Don't be so judgmental. For a guy who hasn't had a date in what? Ten years? Whatever." She giggles with the effort of trying to keep track of Joe's love-life math. "She is wise beyond her years. I think if you got to know her, you'd find that you're a lot alike. And there's always Rose. She's a little closer to your age but you might run up against some family issues there. Don't ask. I'm not at liberty to say." That is obviously the end of that, much to Joe's relief. "Changing the subject, do you have any brothers and sisters? You never talk about your family."

Joe takes a breath before he wades into dangerous water. He could easily spill his guts to Ben but what would be the point? "I have two older sisters, Anita and Christine. My mother, Alice, is the same age as you. My father died a few years ago. He just dropped dead in the backyard—no slow train for the old man."

"You never visit?"

"Nope. I just left it all behind when I came out here in '66. Like I said, I'm a bad risk." He hopes he's given her enough information to satisfy her curiosity, but Ben continues to pry.

"What did your family ever do to you, Joe?"

"You're a fine one to talk, Ben. It seems to me we're in the same boat. You left family and turned up here in Hayworth before me—'55 wasn't it?"

"Yup. But our discussion is currently about you. Will you tell me what happened?"

"Aren't you tired?"

"Not at all."

"Well, I'll share if you do. What do you say?"

"You first." Ben closes her eyes again and settles in, as if she expects him to send her off to sleep with a bedtime story of some sort. Joe assumes she'll regret her request.

"My family, with the exception of my sister Chrissie, all hate me because of a tragedy that occurred when I was a kid. I was ten, for God's sake! After it happened, I walked like a drunken sailor through high school, trade school, stupid jobs, and two even stupider relationships. I was a mess. At the ripe old age of thirty-one, I got the hell out of Dodge. I figured I'd end up in jail if I didn't leave. Chrissie, she's a year older than me, always felt sorry for me and has kept in touch. That's how I know my mother isn't too well. Chrissie sends letters. I sometimes write her back but never say much. Nobody else ever writes." He knows he sounds bitter.

"What could a little boy of ten ever do to cause a family to shun him, Joe?" Ben's eyes are wide open now. They have a pain in them that doesn't seem related to her condition. "What did they think you did?"

"Do you want some tea, Ben? I'm going to make another cup." He gets up and crosses the floor to the kitchen. The faded blue back of his denim shirt faces his friend as he finishes the story. "I got fed up with my whiny five-year-old brother being uncooperative. My job was to entertain him while there was a big shindig underway for my older sister's fifteenth birthday." He turns around and meets Ben's eyes, just as the kettle begins to bubble. "By the time they found him, he'd fallen in the pond, hit his head, and drowned. He even lost his shoes." Joe's voice is quiet.

He expects a kind word from his friend—words like: "You were just a kid," but he's surprised at her response.

"It's not easy being a survivor, especially when you're to blame for the one who died. I understand, Joe. I imagine a lot of people don't."

He's puzzled. "I *was* just a kid, Ben. Everyone was kind enough and polite, as adults tend to be with someone they don't like but for some reason feel obliged to treat civilly. Of course, Anita has never said a word to me since it happened. My parents told me it wasn't my fault, but I never believed them.

I left home early. Moved in with Lisa while I was at trade school but it didn't work out. Then I was stupid enough to marry Mona. That was worse. It took a lot more to get out of it. I haven't been back in fourteen years. Chrissie's the one I keep in touch with." He's reflective as he adds, "She says my mother never asks about me. I don't even know if she and Anita are aware that I keep in touch with Christine."

"You know you need to go back." Ben is blunt. The force of her statement is a blow to the torso for Joe. He pushes himself hard and is burdened by more than enough guilt. He doesn't need someone else to jump on that bandwagon.

"So how do you know what this is like, Ben? Does it have to do with your daughter and her boy?"

Ben groans a little and leans back into the pillows while Blanche repositions her ample body against the old woman's small frame. "The whole story is pretty tedious, Joe. We all have our secrets. I was driving the car when Grace was killed—twenty-five years old, with an okay husband and a baby not yet two. She had her whole life ahead of her." Joe is uncomfortable as her eyes bore into him. "I'm just lucky I didn't kill Charlie, too. From what his father tells me, Charlie thinks his grandmother was killed in a car crash with his mother. I'd like to see him before I die but I guess he'll know me soon enough, after it's all over. He's twenty-eight now. Hard to believe he's the same age as Chester and Amanda."

She has a distant expression on her face. Joe expects she's imagining what Charlie is like now. "Can't we invite him out, Ben? I'll make all the arrangements. I'll go to the city to meet him at the airport if you want. Seems to me it would be good to meet him rather than just bequeath a bunch of cash he'll get from someone he's never met."

"I don't know, Joe. There's more to it than me driving a car in a crash that killed my daughter and gave my grandson a broken leg." She shuts her eyes and leans back again.

"What could be worse, Ben? I don't understand." Joe can sense Ben's pain and isolation as it mirrors his own. How could there be more?

"There were four other people killed, Joe!" Ben's voice has a hint of hysteria. It's obvious she hasn't talked about this in a very long time.

Joe forces himself to be soft and quiet. "Tell me what happened, Ben. I want to know."

"Grace and I were arguing and Charlie was crying. We were headed down the road toward home. The sun was right in my eyes. It was stupid. Grace yelled that I'd missed our turnoff, and I just swung the car around to make a U-turn. There was a pick-up truck coming in the other direction. I never even saw it, what with the sun in my eyes. I remembered afterward that it was red—candy-apple red. There were two couples in that truck. All four were in the front seat. They were on their way to the city to some big outdoor exhibition." Tears run down the old woman's cheeks. Joe's heart lurches as he watches her reveal long buried images of that horrific afternoon.

"Charlie screamed and screamed. There were no other sounds when I got out of the car. I just opened the door, got out, and there were five people dead plus a baby with a busted femur. How does that even happen? Anyway, I know what it's like to feel guilty. Don't you even think I don't."

"What happened then?" He wants to keep her talking if he can. She needs to tell this story at least once. Soon she'll be too full of painkillers to have conversations like this.

"I honestly don't remember a lot. Grace's funeral is a blur. Butch wouldn't let me near Charlie. My husband, Richard, hated me. He wouldn't even talk to me. Forgiveness? What's that? Once the insurance company paid everybody off, and I knew I wasn't about to go to jail, I just started to drive and ended up here—someplace nobody knew me, and where I could start over. Richard died after I came north. I've never been back. I know they all hate me. How could you not hate someone who did what I did? There's one bonus about living here in Hayworth for the last twenty-five years. I could just pack all this mess away in a box in the back of my mind, like dead stock in the antique shop. You know it's in the back room someplace covered in dust but you don't have to deal with it unless you want to." Her eyes are closed again. She must be exhausted.

"Ben, I'm so sorry and I know it's painful but I still think it would be good for your grandson to meet you before...."

"Before I die?"

"Well, I wanted to say that it would be good for him to meet you before you're done, but have it your way." He stands and turns toward the kitchen in order to put the tea paraphernalia back on the counter and tidy up.

"You're right, Joe. I'll contact Charlie if you call your mother. How's that for a deal? After all, our tears taste the same, my friend. Isn't that the saying?" Her face is without expression. *Is she daring him?*

Later on, back in his apartment with Blanche curled up in his lap, he thinks about Ben's secret. It would be a shame for her to leave her estate to this young man who doesn't even know she exists. The gesture would lose its value somehow. Maybe he'll have to hold her to her bargain.

For right now, he'll write Christine and ask her what she thinks about him calling. He pulls pen and paper out of a kitchen drawer and sits down at the Formica-topped chrome-trimmed table.

Dear Chrissie,

Thanks for writing to me about Mother. Perhaps no one but you would know I worry about her all the time. I'd like to call but don't want her to think that I'm doing it because she's dying. I don't want to upset her or make her worse.

Right now, I'm helping take care of a friend in our building. She's dying of pancreatic cancer and isn't long for this world. I've agreed to be her power of attorney and the executor of her will. Like me, she came here to Hayworth to try and outrun her past. I cannot, in good conscience, support her as she faces her demons and contacts her family, if I don't have the courage to do the same.

If you think that a call to Mother is a good idea, let me know when and I'll do the rest. If the call works out well, I might even try to visit within the next few months. My friend is very sick, Chrissie, so I don't expect it will be long.

I hope the girls are still doing well. I would love to see all of you.

As ever,

Joe

He reads the letter over and nods, satisfied that he's succeeded in conveying what he wanted to say. He folds it carefully, stuffs it in one of his business envelopes, and adds a stamp.

Chapter 18

Patrick

A small smile on Patrick's pockmarked face illustrates his pleasure as he prepares to go downstairs and spend some time with his friend, Ben. He missed her yesterday. Joe had to take her to the bank and then stuck around afterward. Today Patrick will have her all to himself, just like Matt Dillon suggested.

He likes split shifts. Up early in the morning, he walks to the diner and works through breakfast. It's busy. Once he gets Old Bertha—the dishwasher—going, he can come back to The Station until late afternoon. He's gotten into the habit of having a bite to eat—usually a sandwich made at work—before he wanders down to stay with Ben until he has to leave again. He knows he's contributed because he provided the walkie-talkies and found her a walker that she loves and uses. Now he spends extra time with her and that helps, too.

He knocks softly on the door to Number Three and opens it without making a sound. If she's asleep, he doesn't want to wake her.

"Is that you, Patrick? I'm in the can. Give me a minute."

Patrick takes stock. Amanda keeps the apartment pretty tidy. It smells like banana bread, so she must have baked this morning. Ben has stuff piled on her picnic table. There's even some kind of odd cloths stacked up. He won't ask about those. Ben appears around the corner from the bathroom and starts to wobble just as Patrick turns. He dashes over and grabs her shoulders.

"I'm okay, kid. Maybe I took my pills too soon. Today hasn't been a good day." She's dressed in a long blue robe that's much too big, and flannelette pyjamas. It seems she never gets dressed anymore.

Patrick manoeuvres himself behind Ben and keeps a light touch on her shoulders until she makes it to the couch. He balances her on one side while he positions the walker within reach and helps her ease herself down.

Her sigh of relief is huge. "Ben. You should have called me. I would have come and helped you sooner. Should you be wandering around in here by yourself?"

"When you gotta' go, you gotta' go, kid." Although pinched in pain, she grins up at him as her white hair drags across her face. "I'm glad you're here. Was it busy at the diner this morning? Did you get some lunch?"

Patrick loves this woman. Ben seems to cope better if she gets involved in everybody's business. She always says she can keep a secret and other people's problems help busy her mind—at least that's what seems to be happening. "Work was fine. Steady but fine. Do you need me to help you?"

"No, no. I'll probably doze off here shortly. You don't have to stay, but if you do you can watch TV if you want. Whatever made you decide to start with the split shifts anyway, Patrick? Did Margo ask you or did you decide on your own?"

Patrick will not leave until it's time to go back to work. Matt and Mary have been quite clear about his responsibilities. He won't let Ben down. "Margo didn't ask me. My advisers suggested it. I have a question, Ben. Can I ask you a question?" He tries to change the subject. Without waiting for an answer, he pushes forward. "Ben is a man's name. Why don't you mind when people call you Ben?" His preoccupation about being addressed by his full given name has always been an issue for him. He can't understand why Ben doesn't care that she has a male name.

Ben groans. "My given name is Benjamine—the female version of Benjamin. I guess my parents wanted a boy. I have been Ben my whole life. I like it. Now...advisers? What advisers?" His old friend gives him one of her "aren't you cute" smiles as she returns to the topic he's trying to avoid.

Ben's voice sounds more than inquisitive to Patrick. He decides he'll level with her and ignore the familiar panic he starts to feel. She would never betray him. "Matt and Mary, Ben; they advise me every day. They help me to be a good person when I might not want to be so good." He tries hard to make eye contact with Ben but knows his focus drifts up over her shoulder, as it usually does when he talks to people.

"Can you keep a secret, Ben? If you can, I'll tell you about my advisers." He acknowledges her almost imperceptible nod. "They told me to split my shifts and spend time with you. They told me to honour you and that soon you would be an adviser for me, too." He realizes Ben's eyes have gotten as round as saucers. Usually they are like slits, especially when she wrestles with her pain.

Her voice is quiet. "Who are Matt and Mary, Patrick? Did you meet them at the restaurant?"

"No. No." Patrick shakes his oily hair and laughs. "Matt Dillon and Mary Tyler Moore, Ben. I listen to them every night. Everybody else sees *Gunsmoke* and *The Mary Tyler Moore Show* but I know they talk to me. They tell me how to be a better person and live a better life." He beams from ear to ear but doesn't miss the expression of concern that Ben attempts to suppress.

She reaches up to brush her hair away from her eyes and stares directly into his. "Patrick. I want you to tell me the absolute truth. Do you hear voices? Do you have voices inside your brain that tell you what to do?"

He's afraid she's upset. "Ben, I know the voices. It's Matt and Mary. They're good people. They would never tell me to do bad stuff. I depend on them. They told me to spend time with you. They told me, Ben!" His voice sounds a little hysterical. He can hear it in his own ears. "My mother heard voices, too, but they told her to do bad stuff and that's why the nurses came to give her needles, but it didn't help. Her voices were bad. They were not like Matt and Mary."

"Tell me about your mother, Patrick. Is she still alive? Why don't you just lean back and tell me all about your family."

Ben sounds so calm, Patrick can't help but calm down, too. He settles into the chair as he watches his friend adjust her pillows and straighten out her afghan.

"I haven't seen my two younger sisters, or my father, since I left home when I was sixteen. That's nine years ago!" He can't prevent the surprise that creeps into his voice. "Natalie and Sarah were eleven and ten then. God, they were cute little girls—and nice, too!" He added this last bit as an afterthought. He didn't want Ben to think he left because of his sisters. "I sometimes think about them now and hope they haven't had problems."

"What kind of problems?" Ben doesn't close her eyes, which she usually does while he visits. He thinks about how kids in school used to treat him; about how sometimes people could be afraid if they saw a guy mumbling to himself. He wants to make sure she isn't afraid.

"Ben." His voice is soft but determined as he rests his elbows on blue-jean-clad knees and moves forward. "My mother was a schizophrenic. Nurses came once a month to give her shots. Sometimes she was good. Other times, she was pretty scary. The medication didn't help her all that much. She hung herself with an extension cord in the basement. I found her because she did it right behind my television. The cord was orange. We used it for Christmas lights. It was stored behind the furnace. I was already hearing voices, too, but never told anybody. Dad was a wreck most of the time. He worried the girls would turn out like her. They seemed fine."

Ben squirms a tiny bit in her nest on the couch. It doesn't escape Patrick's notice. "Have you ever tried medications, Patrick, or seen a professional? You don't have to go through life hearing voices, you know. It *is* 1980 after all."

"Sometimes the voices are the only friends I have, Ben. My mother's voices were bad. She got really angry and they told her to hurt herself. My voices are good. They told me to spend time with you, didn't they? I gave you my walkie-talkies and bought you a walker. I'm not a bad person, Ben. Maybe I shouldn't have told you." He presses his back into the chair and increases the distance between himself and this woman he has come to think of as a surrogate grandmother. He can't remember the last time he talked so much and now it might have been a mistake.

"Patrick, you have to live your life the best way you can. Here I am trying to die the best way I can. I'm no judge but it seems to me that getting rid of the voices would allow you to make decisions for yourself. Don't you think that might be true?"

He ignores her question. "My mother used to appear to me after she died. It would be when I watched TV. She'd just stand there with the orange cord around her neck. She never said words out loud but I could absorb her thoughts somehow. It's hard for me to explain." He answers Ben's next question before she asks it. "I don't see her anymore. I hope you'll come visit me after you die! I want us to still be friends, Ben. Don't let being dead stop you." He sees tears in Ben's eyes.

"Are you afraid to die, Ben?"

She takes a big breath before she begins. "The actual idea of death doesn't bother me so much, Patrick. The journey has its challenges."

"Like what?"

"Like pain. Like needing help and not wanting to ask. Like feeling dependent and not knowing what the next day will bring. Should I try and see my grandson before I croak? Would it be worth it? Joe thinks so, but I don't know."

She closes her eyes and this pleases Patrick. He knows she's not afraid of him. He knows she trusts him or she wouldn't close her eyes no matter how much medication she took. "Maybe you will be one of my advisers, Ben. You can help me make decisions. You can tell me what's best."

"Don't I do that now? Don't I remind you to change your clothes and eat properly? I think I'm already an adviser and you need to make use of the advice you've already gotten from me. I don't know what I'll be up to in the afterlife, but I certainly hope I don't have to come back here to remind you to take a damned bath!" While she talks, her eyes remain firmly closed but her lips are upturned slightly. "I also think you ought to call your father—or write him a letter. I could help you if you need it. Find out about your sisters." She opens her eyes wide and holds him in her gaze. "You have some business to take care of, mister. Your father and sisters have been through enough. They need to know what the hell ever happened to you. Think it over. And you don't need advisers. You're your own man. If you didn't hear the voices anymore you'd do just fine."

Patrick appreciates the pep talk but isn't so sure. The medication is probably what's loosening Ben's tongue about now. Her painkillers are kicking in. "I think you probably need a nap, Ben. I'll sit here with you until about three-thirty. Then I have to go back to work."

"No problem." Her voice starts to slur. "Cheryl will come by later. I'm good." Her eyes close completely and the muscles in her face start to sag as the medication takes her off for a couple of precious pain-free hours. Patrick sits across from her, not moving. He thinks about what she said; about that fact that she already is an adviser. He thinks about Nancy, at work. She's one, too. But what will happen when Ben's gone? Will he remember what she's told him?

The warm afternoon sun washes over the pink and green afghan and rests on Ben's scrawny legs stretched out on the couch. She seems peaceful. This is what she'll look like when it's over.

****

Patrick is preoccupied when he gets to the Hayworth Diner. He starts his shift by unloading Bertha and then he puts all the clean dishes away. Danny's doing prep work for the supper crowd. Nancy's setting tables. "Get Danny to make you some supper, Patrick. I expect we'll be busy. There's some special group in town. They've reserved three tables at the back. Fill your belly now. There'll be no time later."

"Can you make me a grilled ham and cheese, Danny, with some fries?"

Danny, an oftentimes surly man of few words, just nods a response. Patrick doesn't consider Danny a friend, or even much of an acquaintance, although they've worked in this kitchen together for more than two years. He imagines Danny just thinks he's weird. His advisers have always told him to stay away from people like Danny; to avoid potential conflict.

He sits at the staff table in the back with his fat ham and cheese sandwich cooked to perfection. The oil from the grill runs down his fingers as he picks it up. He loves the greasy texture of food and how the fries smell like fat from the grill. He remembers Ben has said more than once that he needs to eat vegetables or fruit. Maybe you don't always have to take the advice of your advisers.

"All done, Nancy." He finishes his supper and puts his dirty dishes in the plastic pan by the kitchen door.

Nancy looks up from the counter as she assembles a coffee order to go, for a guy in a plaid shirt who is waiting. She nods as Patrick pushes through the swinging doors.

Supper at the diner is busy just the way Patrick likes it. No time to think. He just focuses on the chores in front of him, determined to do a good job and keep up. Bertha helps him ensure Nancy has the right dishes at the right time. No need for clean dinner plates if what she wants is dessert plates. He can anticipate now. He knows he's good at his job. After the rush is over, he goes out into the restaurant and starts to bus tables and give her a hand. One smile from Nancy and Patrick's ready for another hour.

****

Once back at his apartment, Patrick stands in front of his television, conflicted and nervous. He can quickly turn the set on and tune in to his favourite shows. He can open his mind to the advice and support on which he's come to depend. Or he could avoid his television altogether to see what happens to the voices if they have no information to guide them.

He lies down on his wrinkled and grimy bed. Ben is right. He needs to take control. Maybe Cheryl can help him like she did before. Maybe he can take some pills. There's no guarantee he'll end up like his mother. As he tries to make a plan and sort through his options, the voices start to intrude. They tell him he's no good. They tell him he should die. They tell him no one would care. He struggles for a while. He tosses and turns as he pulls at the dirty sheets.

Take control. Make them stop! The one voice of reason eventually bubbles to the surface. Patrick gets up and turns on more lights. He goes over to his television. His hand trembles as it hovers near the power switch. Indecision only interferes for a moment. *Mary Tyler Moore* is over already but *Gunsmoke* is just starting. He'll be able to benefit from the marshal, at least. He stretches out on his couch. His heart stops racing. His dark eyes focus on the screen. Matt Dillon will tell him what's best.

Chapter 19

Cheryl

The days are getting shorter. Labour Day has come and gone. Cheryl assembles her plastic bucket of supplies as she prepares to spend the better part of her evening with Ben, whose condition is worsening like everyone knew it would. Cheryl doesn't think Ben should be alone overnight anymore. She knocks on Rose's door. Despite her reluctance, she believes it wise to have a discussion with Rose before she broaches the topic with Ben.

"Hi. Come on in." Rose seems hesitant when she sees that it's Cheryl.

Cheryl's plastic full-front apron, tied over her cotton jeans and buttoned pale blue shirt, rustles as she strides with determination through the partial opening. Her bucket contains rubber gloves, some disinfectant, and a fresh supply of incontinence pads. "We need to talk before I go over to Ben's. Is that okay?" Her voice is almost a whisper, but across the hall Ben has probably heard her anyway.

"Hi, Maggie. Have you enjoyed your first week in Hayworth?" Cheryl throws herself into social worker mode just long enough for polite discourse.

Maggie, quiet and beautiful, doesn't get off the couch. Caesar perches regally in her lap. She reminds Cheryl of some ethereal creature from a futuristic movie. Cheryl thinks the scene requires smoke wrapping around the girl's legs and crows screeching in the distance. Maggie's hair curtains parts of her face. Her lips have no lipstick but they are bright red, nonetheless. "It's lovely here. I'm just happy to be with my sister." Her smile is vacant and haunting.

Cheryl would normally ask a couple of additional questions but turns her attention back to Rose. "I don't think Ben should be alone at night anymore. Have you noticed how confused she's gotten? Amanda spends all morning and lunchtime with her. Patrick does most afternoons and Joe does supper and early evening. Do you want to rotate nights?"

Rose nods to Maggie. "Does it matter to you if I sleep across the hall a couple of nights a week, Maggie? Well, every other night actually? It won't be for long." She glances over to Cheryl for confirmation, and Cheryl nods agreement.

"I don't think she even uses the bed anymore, Rose. I'll just bring my sheets for the single bed in the office/spare room when I'm there. You can use her bed or do the same as me. I'm a pretty light sleeper so I don't think I'll have to sit up all night. What about you?"

"I'm a pretty light sleeper, too. Maggie is a night owl so she'll probably spend time over there with me. Right, Maggie?" Her sister gives Rose an imperceptible nod. Rose looks back at Cheryl with what can only be described as desperation meeting resignation.

Cheryl is all business as she focuses on the task at hand. "Okay. Now that we're settled, I have to go over there and convince Ben. I'll talk to her while I help her with her sponge bath and get her cleaned up for bed. I'll take the first turn."

She sees Rose's gaze rest on the incontinence pads in the bucket. Without waiting for any questions, Cheryl just continues on. "I stop by in the morning and get her all tidied before I get ready for work. Amanda helps her midday, and then I help later on. I'll still do that. My own schedule is so screwed up right now it doesn't seem to matter anymore." She smiles, first at Rose and then over toward Maggie. "Life is full of changes. I used to think I couldn't manage if I veered off schedule but here I am!" She spreads her arms, outstretches the bucket, and acknowledges her apron. "Must run. I have some convincing to do."

Ben is relatively alert as she waits for Cheryl. "I think I had an accident. I'm glad you're here. I didn't want anyone else to turn up." Tears slowly dribble down her hollow cheeks.

"Oh, babe, that's okay. We'll have you all pink and powdered in no time. Come on." Cheryl quickly helps Ben to her feet and supports her as they trundle to the bathroom. Cheryl works methodically and with a care and attention she developed a long time ago. Ben is cooperative and kind so the job is easy in comparison to her past experiences.

"I'm so sorry, Cheryl. You're always so perfect and now here you are, cleaning up shit and wiping me down. I'm sorry. You don't have to do this. I can go to the hospital."

Cheryl is undaunted by the tasks at hand but wants to know Ben's true feelings. "Do you want to go to the hospital, Ben? Dr. Gunton said you could be admitted any time now."

Ben's voice is soft and her words are blubbery. "I want to stay here but I don't want to burden all of you. I need to stay until my grandson comes but I don't want him to show up and find me all covered in crap." She's sobbing now.

Cheryl knows that Charlie Collins is expected, but not for at least another month. Does Ben have that long? "Let's get you cleaned up and then we'll talk." Cheryl performs the necessary rituals to get her neighbour, and now friend, ready for bed. With clean linens on the couch, a fresh pair of pyjamas, and fluffy white socks, Ben nestles down into the position that has been almost constant for the last couple of months.

"So...I don't think you should be alone anymore, Ben. Do you agree?" No point in mincing words. Ben has always appreciated her frankness in the past. The old lady doesn't respond, just peers up at Cheryl through strands of white hair. "Starting tonight, Rose and I will trade nights and stay here with you. We'll sleep while you sleep. You don't have to worry. We won't sit in the chair and stare at you all night. What do you think?"

"Will Rose have to bathe me?"

"No, just Amanda and I, as always. I'll still come down after Joe leaves and get you ready for bed. Rose will call me if you run into a problem and need me. Doesn't Patrick call Amanda if you have a problem during the day?"

"Yes. That's only happened once. I told Patrick to go get Amanda and then he went back upstairs to his own apartment. And Joe's never had to call you, so that part's worked out—except nobody in the building has any life. You just take care of me!" The tears start to flow again.

Cheryl's voice remains calm. "We're all doing fine, Ben. As long as you have what you need and aren't in any pain, everybody's happy. We'll just take it a day at a time. You stretch out and relax. I want to straighten out your medications and give your fridge and counters a bit of a wipe down. I'll run upstairs for my bed linen in a little while. I'll talk to everyone and make sure we all know what the others are doing. Tomorrow, I will get a log book so each time somebody's here they can write down what went on, when they expect to come back, and what medications you took. I still have to talk to Patrick, but we're good."

Cheryl spent the past week talking to everyone in the building except Patrick about a log book, so each would know what the other was doing for Ben. It has just been the last couple of days that Cheryl began to think overnight care would be wise, too. She silently observes Ben, with her eyes closed and white stocking feet just protruding from under that ugly, cat-hair-covered afghan. It won't be long now. Hopefully, Charlie will make it and the weather will hold into October.

Ben's voice interrupts Cheryl's reverie. "How did you ever get comfortable with helping sick people in the bathroom, Cheryl? If you don't mind my saying so, you're pretty persnickety about your surroundings. Cleaning up other people's shitty messes strikes me as behaviour you'd avoid at all costs."

Cheryl gazes across at the closed eyes. "Everybody has history, Ben. I never had a father. My mother was a drunk and spent a lot of time lying on the bathroom floor throwing up, messing her pants, and being obnoxious. I learned when I was very young, that if I wanted to survive I'd have to clean up her messes. It's easy to help you. You're sick. You brought none of this on yourself."

"You must've had a really hard childhood but you turned out okay in the long run. How did you end up in Hayworth?"

Cheryl isn't sure how much Ben remembers or even hears. She decides to remove a couple of bricks in her protective wall. Ben never gossips and it doesn't seem to matter anyway in the grand scheme of life and death. "I ended up in Hayworth trying to outrun a dead boyfriend, a baby I never met and have no idea where it is, and a mother who finally abandoned me. Any one of those crises could have been my rock bottom. How I didn't end up dead amazes me even now. You know, I lived in the back of a bus station and waited tables in their greasy spoon until I could get enough money for a bus ticket to come out west. Somebody in a shelter told me I could collect welfare if I went to school. God! I think about it now and I can't believe I ended up a relatively responsible person." She grins down at her perfectly manicured hands resting in the lap of her cotton pants. "I haven't told anybody about my background, Ben."

"Don't worry, my dear. Like they say, your secret's safe with me. Take it to the grave and all that. Have you ever tried to find your child? Do you know if it was a boy or girl?"

"I suppose I could utilize contacts through work although I guess I've never felt I deserved to know. Every day, I talk to girls who intend to give up their babies. Circumstances and society are a lot different now. You can actually keep track of your kid! Open adoption, they call it. Who knew?"

Cheryl continues. It's good to talk about yourself every once in a while. God knows, it seems to work for other people, or she wouldn't have a job! "I haven't always been so neurotic." She looks over at Ben, who has opened her eyes and watches Cheryl with an emotion akin to admiration. She's encouraged. "You call it persnickety, but I am bona fide obsessive compulsive of the highest magnitude. I crave order and can't stand objects to be dirty. I shower at least three times a day and change my clothes just as often. I moved in here because of the hot water and the fact that they would let me have my own washer and dryer—pretty pathetic, eh?"

Ben shakes her head but the movement is almost imperceptible. "You said your boyfriend died." She closes her eyes again, obviously expecting a lengthy story.

"He came back to his room one night after getting high, vomited in his sleep, and aspirated, I guess. I woke up in the morning to this terrible smell. I remember I dreamt that somebody hurled all over me. He was all grey and stone-like. His name was Jason. I knew he was dead."

"That must have been awful. What were you, fifteen or so?" Ben's voice starts to drift. "Maybe you need to try and find your kid. Now that I'm going to meet Charlie, I'm more optimistic about this whole journey. Charlie's coming to Hayworth." Her words begin to slur.

Their first night is uneventful. Cheryl just dozes. Her mind is full of images of fourteen-year-olds and what her child might be like. It makes her anxious. If she were in her own apartment, she would probably get up and clean the fridge or have a shower. Instead, she lies on her crisp white sheets, stares at the stained cream ceiling, and obsesses. She helps Ben to the bathroom once. After another pain pill, Ben sleeps through the night. Amanda arrives in enough time for Cheryl to race back upstairs, shower, change, eat, and get to work. Her rituals have actually started to interfere with her schedule. Although she feels a bit frazzled, she'll stay up later tonight and get some cleaning done—maybe even do some extra laundry—and she has to find some time to talk to Patrick.

****

At the end of her work day, Cheryl sets out for the Hayworth Diner. She hopes she can snag a minute with Patrick before his second shift starts. She finds him in the booth at the back—the one covered in copies of bills and cash register receipts—eating a mound of French fries and gravy. There's a piece of lemon pie at his elbow. His eyes meet hers as she pushes the heavy glass door open and then he immediately returns to his food.

She trots right down the long aisle and stands beside the booth. "We need to talk about Ben for a minute. When do you start your shift, Patrick? Can I sit down?"

Greasy hair, that matches a run of grease sliding down his index finger and thumb as he jams another fry in his mouth, covers one eye as he just barely makes the effort to look up. He nods, and she tries to slide into the booth without touching the table. "There's a book on Ben's counter now. Everybody who goes in and out has to make a note in it. Rose and I are taking alternate overnights with her and we'll all try not to let her be alone for more than a few minutes. We hope to be able to keep her in her apartment until Charlie comes. Can you write in the book?"

His eyes haven't left his plate since she sat down. "What do I write?"

"Jot down how she is; if she takes any pills; if you call anybody because she needs bathroom help."

"I help her to the bathroom."

"What? Have you really?" Cheryl is more than slightly surprised that this unusual young man would be so hands-on.

"Well, just to pee. I help her. She's never pooped herself when I'm around but I know she might. I'd help her. It's okay." He finally permits his eyes to meet Cheryl's across the cluttered booth. They're as black as onyx.

"I'm impressed, Patrick. Where did you learn to be so helpful?"

His eyes drop back down to his plate. "My mother was sick a lot. She took pills and sometimes needed help. I helped."

"Good for me to know." She's all business. "I have to go. I want to try and have a run today. Rose has night duty and I think Joe is there now."

She starts to wiggle her way out as she continues her efforts to avoid the table.

"Can I ask you a question?"

"Sure, Patrick; ask away." She's pauses with one leg swung out as if poised to gallop for the door.

"If I wanted to see somebody, like a doctor, say—somebody who could decide if I need to take pills to settle my mind—do you know anybody? Anybody I could talk to?"

Cheryl controls her face so no expression of surprise filters through. She leans over closer to her neighbour and former client. "Do you want to see a psychiatrist, Patrick? Is that what you think you need?"

He returns his gaze to his plate. "Ben says I need to try and live my life without my advisers, Cheryl. She says I have lots of people to help me and that I don't need them—that I can get rid of them with pills. I'm not sure she's right. It didn't work very well for my mother but I think I should try—for Ben." His voice is barely a whisper. Cheryl has to lean over and face the smell of greasy fries in order to hear him and protect his privacy.

"Call me at the office tomorrow, Patrick, and I'll give you the information you need. You'll have to see a doctor to get the referral made but I can help with that, too. A little piece of advice?" She reaches out and forces herself to touch the soiled shoulder of his jean jacket. "You have to do this for yourself and not for Ben, but I think it's a wise decision."

She stands up, mercifully away from the messy booth and the overwhelming smell of the food. He graces her with a full-faced smile that exposes the now-familiar gap. "I'll call," he says and then starts to shovel pie into his mouth.

Cheryl walks back to The Station, anxious to have a shower and go for her run before darkness settles on the little town.

Chapter 20

Ben

What day is it? Friday? Saturday? Ben knows that it's Thanksgiving. Charlie will be here on Thanksgiving weekend, but she can't quite figure out what day it is today. Will he be here today?

She dozes on crisp, cool sheets in a hospital bed in the middle of her apartment. She feels clean so someone has done her bath. Her blue leather couch is pushed up against the wall over by the picnic table. Cheryl borrowed this bed from the hospital. She said she and Amanda were getting sore backs from bending over the couch. She was right. The bed is better but doesn't do much for the décor.

She opens her eyes just a sliver and sees Amanda at the kitchen counter. Mason isn't here. His wooden playpen sits empty. It must be Saturday so Chester's minding Mason.

"Hi, Amanda. What day is it?" She finds it hard to push the words out of her face and across the room.

Amanda wipes her hands on a tea towel as she dashes over to Ben's bedside. "Hi, Ben. You're awake! You had your bath. I changed your pad, got you into a fresh nightie, and you never opened your eyes!"

"I was asleep, I guess. What day is it?"

"One day before Charlie gets here. Joe left for the city this morning to pick him up at the airport. It'll be a long day. I expect Joe will have him at the hotel, downtown, by midnight tonight. He'll be here for the day tomorrow. We're all organized. Are you excited?" Amanda tucks in the now-ratty afghan and tidies the edge of the bed as she talks.

Ben's voice is raspy and weak. She tries to lift her head so the distance between them is smaller. "I just don't want to die before he gets here, that's all. I want to have my wits about me. I don't want to sleep through his visit."

Amanda pats her hand. "Cheryl will be here all night and will get you all spiffed up before Joe brings him over. Joe will make lunch and call me or Cheryl if you need some special attention."

Ben's breath comes out of her in uneven bubbles. Any topic of conversation seems to make her emotional. The last couple of weeks have been like this— every time she talks, it seems as if it's goodbye. She assumes that means she doesn't have much time. "You have been a good friend and a good nurse, Amanda. I think you missed your calling." Her hand, just skin and bone, is tender as it pats Amanda on the wrist.

"I'm glad you woke up before anybody else gets here. I wanted to tell you a little secret." She grins, and Ben suspects she knows what Amanda will say. "I met with Murdock Blackney. He thinks he can manage a divorce on the QT if Jeremy hasn't divorced me already. He said he'll find out as many details as he can. All because of you, Ben. He told me you already made sure he'd be paid."

"It's the least I could do for one of my nurses. Don't forget, you promised to tell Chester the whole story after Murdock figures out your status."

"I know. I know. It might mean I get another wedding day!" Her excitement is suddenly tempered. Ben knows what she's thinking.

"No—I won't be there to dance at your wedding, but take a minute to think about me and I'll be there in spirit I'm sure." She sees tears in the girl's eyes.

Patrick arrives just after lunch to spell off Amanda. He has a sandwich from the diner in a brown paper bag. Ben doesn't eat much anymore—just the odd spoonful of applesauce or some juice. Her teeth are now too big for her shrunken mouth. She still relishes a cup of tea but someone has to help her. She can't reliably hold the cup anymore, even if it's only half full. "Call me if Ben needs any special help, Patrick. I can come in a minute." Since Amanda and Cheryl began to mop her up after accidents and change the incontinence pads on her bed, they started to refer to it as special help and personal care in order to spare her feelings. It's nice. Respectful. Ben cannot find words to express how grateful she is.

He saunters over to the bed and pats Ben on the wrist. His hands are the only reliably clean part of him. He hates rubber gloves, so those hands must touch scalding hot dishes all the time. It's remarkable, really.

"Hi, Ben. Tomorrow's the big day, eh? Your grandson comes tomorrow, right?"

Ben nods. Talking is such an effort. She spends most of her time thinking about her answers while she struggles to find a way to get the words to propel themselves out of her face. A smile, of some fashion, is almost always her "go-to" option.

Patrick waits until Amanda says good bye and then settles into the chair across from Ben. She likes it when people sit there because her eyes can rest on them without the need to turn her head. They're close enough for her to see them properly. The less she has to twist the better. He pulls his sandwich out of the bag. It's wrapped in wax paper to protect the toasted bacon-lettuce-tomato creation. Mayonnaise oozes out the sides. Miraculously, Patrick produces a napkin. All she can smell is toast. She hasn't had toast in a long time because it's too hard to swallow. Even a cookie can be a problem if she doesn't hold it in her mouth until it gets really mushy. The smell will do today.

The boy grins at her. "Want a bite?" He stretches a blue-jean-jacket clad arm across the space between them.

"No, thanks," she rasps. "Enjoy yourself."

"I have some news I want to tell you, Ben." He chews and talks. A word or two emerges between bites. "I spoke to Cheryl and she told me about some lady psychiatrist that visits here every so often. Dr. Gunton made me a referral and I'm scheduled to see her in two weeks. What do you think of that?"

He sounds so satisfied with himself and proud. "What's her name?"

"Dr. Wilkerson. She's here at the hospital every couple of weeks. Cheryl says she's nice. Can't hurt, eh?"

That's the same doctor that Maggie sees, and Rose already told Ben that her sessions were going really well. Maggie continues to hold her own.

"You'll have to tell me what you think after you meet with her." Ben can hardly get the words out. Patrick has to lean over a bit to catch them. Ben shuts her eyes. This is the signal to all her different care givers that she can't talk anymore. She has a lot of medication in her system all the time now so sleep is her major occupation.

It isn't actually sleeping. It's more like drifting. Ben imagines she's in a big swimming pool. She floats just under the surface of the water. She can hear most of what's going on around her but voices are blurry and muffled. As the pills start to wear off, alertness returns. In order to interact at any level, she must embrace the pain. As another dose of medication starts to take effect, she returns to floating and listening, dozing and dreaming. She imagines this might be the moment of no return.

It must be a couple of hours later because she can hear Rose and Maggie in conversation. She senses pressure—a warm object against her leg—and knows that Caesar has stopped by for a visit. In her own way, Ben is alert to her surroundings. She knows Rose and Maggie are here this afternoon because Joe is on his way to Edmonton to pick up Charlie. Her heart swells.

"Hey, sleepyhead. Do you need anything?" Rose fusses over sheets and pats both Ben and the cat at the same time.

"I'm okay. What time is it?"

Maggie responds. "It's just past three and we thought we'd make tea. May I make you tea, Ben?"

"Sure, but you have to help me." Ben forces the words. Maggie is a sweet girl. For some reason, she acts like she's about eighteen instead of thirty-plus. Rose treats her like a daughter or niece instead of a sister only a few years younger than her. It's like time stopped when the girl entered Forest Hills Institute.

Medical types speak of inputs and outputs. There isn't much of either anymore. Ben is well aware that the end is fast approaching. Maggie cranks the bed up a little higher and then hauls Ben into a semi-sitting position. She holds the half mug of lukewarm chamomile tea to Ben's lips. Ben gives it a try. Smells aren't particularly interesting and this tea is no exception. She manages a small sip and then shakes her white hair at Maggie. She leans into the back of the bed for support. Enough of that. "Thanks," she croaks to the girl.

"Maggie and I want to tell you some news, Ben." Rose repositions herself, smoothes her denim skirt, and takes a sip of tea. "We plan to go to Ontario this spring to see our parents. Dr. Wilkerson says that the act of confrontation is unfinished business for us and we need to do it in order to get on with our lives." She finishes with a flourish.

Maggie examines her lap. She reaches for Caesar and pulls the cat toward her. It seems that stroking Caesar calms her. Ben suspects the decision to go to see Abner and Ruth Woodward may not have been entirely unanimous.

Rose continues. "We'll make the same trip I make every year except this time it will be a bit earlier and Maggie will be with me!" She leans over and gives Maggie a little pat on the hand. "It will be a sisters' road trip. Seeing the folks will be the hard part, but once that's behind us we will have a fabulous adventure!"

Does she sound a little too enthusiastic? Ben lets her eyes rest on Maggie, who still hasn't looked up. To Ben's knowledge, Maggie hasn't been any real trouble for Rose. She seems to just sit in the house all day with Caesar. She's never wandered across the hall to visit with Ben when Rose is at work. She would certainly be welcome and has been issued an invitation more than once. All she does is attend her scheduled appointments with her psychiatrist and go with Rose to shop for groceries. Ben thinks this can't continue forever. The girl has to get her life back somehow. Maybe Dr. Wilkerson believes that seeing her parents after all these years—confronting them directly— will help both women move on. Ben wishes she could stick around for the outcome but knows she can't.

A crisp little tap on the door announces Cheryl's arrival. She has brought her supper and a bucket full of paraphernalia. Ben relaxes. Cheryl has become her friend throughout this journey and that has been a real gift.

Rose and Maggie get ready to return to their own apartment. They talk a bit about tomorrow's schedule, Charlie's visit, and Rose's turn to stay the night. Caesar is presented for a final pat of the day and off they go. Ben doesn't miss Cheryl's expression of distaste as the big tortoiseshell cat is carried across the threshold and out into the corridor.

"Never mind the cat, Cheryl. I like cats," Ben rasps at Cheryl's back as she carefully sets her supper on the island and her bucket on the floor.

She turns toward Ben. "You are at risk for all manner of diseases in your condition. A cat could contaminate your whole bed! Not to mention the hair. God!" She immediately starts to tidy even though little of her services are actually required.

Ben taps the side of the bed to catch Cheryl's attention. She motions for the girl to come closer. As Cheryl bends over near her face, Ben whispers "Sit down and visit with me. Have your supper. I'm okay right now but a bath in the morning before Charlie gets here would be wonderful."

"Of course. Whatever you want. What about supper? Do you want to try some soup, maybe?"

"No, I'm good. I'll probably need more meds in an hour or so and then I won't be much company." Ben can see Cheryl start to calm down. She goes over to the sink and lets the water run until steam rises from the faucet. She washes her hands for what seems like five minutes. She returns to the chair across from Ben.

"I finally got up the nerve to fill out the paperwork, Ben. He or she is fourteen so it might be a few years before I get a response, if it even happens, but at least I've made a start." She smiles a soft, sad smile. "You inspired me when you contacted Charlie and asked to meet him and now tomorrow he'll be here."

Ben is alerted to the familiar pain that starts to prickle at the edges of her body. It hasn't gotten bad yet, but this is when she's supposed to take more pills. There's one more subject to discuss first. "Cheryl." She holds up a frail hand and motions for the girl to come closer. Cheryl obliges and leans in toward Ben once again. "What about your mother?"

"You never quit, do you? I'm still struggling. I don't want her in my life, Ben. I've decided I'm selfish. I've worked hard to get this life and I don't want there to be any chance she'll ruin it. I'll tell you what I'd like. I'd like to find out where she is and what she's up to. I'd like to just stand across the street and watch her—get a peek at her, that's all. I'd like to have one more look at the woman who permitted her daughter to be abused and then abandoned her so she could run away with some guy. I'm just not prepared to talk to her. Not yet."

She reaches for the pain pills and jug of water on the table. She fills the glass and brings two pills for Ben. In as intimate a gesture as any action Ben can imagine, Cheryl swings her hip on to the side of the bed, wraps her arm around Ben, and drops the pills on her dry and coated tongue. Then she lifts the glass to Ben's lips. She knows exactly when to pull back and when to tip forward. Swallowing is difficult. Ben silently worries about what will happen if she lives long enough to be unable to swallow anymore. Ben absorbs love from the arm wrapped around her.

****

The next morning, Cheryl gives Ben a full bed bath that includes washing her hair in a dishpan she places on a straight chair by the bed. It's no small feat and some serious mopping up is required when all is said and done. It's Thanksgiving Sunday. Cheryl will stay until Joe shows up with Charlie. Joe will call her or Amanda if Ben needs any special attention during the visit.

Her care isn't as challenging as it used to be, now that she doesn't eat and hardly drinks anymore. They have her pills all planned so she'll be awake for a couple of hours. Ben's nervous. Charlie is twenty-eight and, until a few weeks ago, he considered her dead. He's married. His wife couldn't come with him as she's due to have her first child near Christmas. Ben is doubtful she'll be around then. This visit has become an emergency.

Ben recognizes Joe's rap on the door. All this is happening because of her bargain with Joe. Ben thinks he'll be able to go back to Nova Scotia after the holiday. Cheryl opens the door to reveal Charlie and Joe. "Come in. Come in." She gestures toward the bed. "We're all ready for company."

Joe approaches Ben and lifts her hand into his. "Ben, I'd like you to meet Charlie Collins. He has been beside himself with anticipation as he waited to see you." Joe grins and gently transfers Ben's fragile, nearly weightless, hand into Charlie's.

Ben gazes upon what she can only comprehend as the male version of her daughter's face. It takes her breath away—the almond brown eyes, the soft auburn straight hair. He's tall, like Grace, who took after her father. She doesn't know what to say. She just stares at him like he's a mirage. She knows she probably looks like an idiot but doesn't care.

Joe interrupts her open-mouthed reverie. "I told Charlie the whole story on the drive back in the truck yesterday—just as you asked. He knows all the details, Ben, including about the estate."

"Where are the pictures?" Ben wants Charlie to have some photos of her with Grace, and some of her before she got sick. She is well aware of her sunken cheeks and how she is now merely a skeleton with skin and hair. Before Cheryl leaves, she opens a drawer in Ben's desk and brings the pictures to them. Charlie has pulled the straight-back chair near the bed and continues to hold Ben's hand. He hasn't said a word. He just stares at the woman in the bed with her mouth gaped open and smiling at him. Ben feels pure joy.

Charlie spends the day. Joe goes in and out. He prepares lunch for the two men. They have a visit in the hall while Cheryl returns to attend to Ben. Her pain increases and Cheryl gives her some more medication. Rose and Maggie arrive around supper time. Joe will take Charlie back to the city, and the airport, tomorrow.

Ben doesn't feel the need to say much. She just wants to lay her eyes on this lovely man who is her grandson. She manages to tell him a couple of stories about Grace, and to impress upon him just how much he resembles his mother. He tells her about his life and work as a physical education teacher and football coach. He tells her how excited he is about the coming baby and shows her pictures of his wedding. Her eyes can't open any wider as she tries to drink him in. The day goes by faster than any day in a long time. When Charlie hugs her and says good bye, she knows she has tied all of her loose ends. She's happy.

****

Early in December, the pain changes. Her condition gets worse. She needs more medication and she spends most of her time floating just under the surface of the water that is her consciousness. She drifts like a leaf on the river. She thinks about Charlie. Someone is washing her hands and face. She senses the feather touch of long hair and thinks it must be Amanda. The girl should be with Mason and Chester, not washing an old woman. She hears the wind rattle the windows. The weather must be fierce. The lamp by her bed seems to always be on. It glows orange through her eyelids. Didn't it used to be in the other room? Is it Christmas yet?

What's happening? Alex Gunton's irritating voice crashes around the bed. He's talking—to her? He's been here before. Was it lately? Has he been here often? Not remembering is frustrating. She feels the prick of a needle and the pain starts to recede. She'd like to thank him but just can't seem to make her mouth move even as she opens her eyes. It must be time to go to sleep. Someone holds her hand. That is so good—like an anchor while she floats.

Chapter 21

Joe

It's a big funeral. It seems to Joe like almost everyone in town turns out for the celebration, as Joe and Ben named it when they planned the affair before her death. People talk about her. They drink buckets of wine and tea. They eat plates of cookies. Joe's a little overwhelmed at how many people fill the Hayworth Arts Centre. Antique shop customers stand up before everyone and tell their personal stories about how a piece of furniture, purchased long ago from Ben, holds pride of place in their home or office and reminds them of her every day. Others talk about how they caught the collecting bug from Ben. Patrick, of all people, plunks himself beside the mahogany urn that holds her ashes, strokes it softly with one hand, and speaks with surprising eloquence about his friend. Joe is stunned, and by the expressions on the faces of his neighbours, everyone else is, too. What has come over Patrick?

Joe works with Murdock Blackney to execute Ben's estate. The will has to be probated, and progresses as expected. Joe has taken over estate finances and paid any bills. He and Ben prepaid the rent through March before she died so he could work as time permitted, to empty her apartment and to sell or give away her possessions. He has spent a lot of time sitting on the blue leather sofa. He has thought about Ben and how she influenced his life. He has made reservations to fly back to Nova Scotia in early March. They had a bargain and he will honour his commitment.

As the celebration winds down, he makes an effort to speak to each person in turn.

"Thank you for coming."

"Yes, she was a fine lady."

"No, we won't be auctioning her possessions. Most of them are spoken for."

"Yes, she had family. They were here before she died."

As much as everyone seems to know Ben, most people didn't really *know* her at all. They're all in the same boat as her neighbours were before they began to take care of her. She is mysterious to them. Joe and the other residents at The Station have chosen to keep her secrets.

Before long only Rose, Maggie, Patrick, the Wolskis, and Cheryl remain. They all sit at a table together and have one last cup of tea to honour their friend. "Christmas is coming," Joe begins. He permits his gaze to travel from one person to the next. "How about I cook Christmas dinner for everyone and we have it in my apartment?"

Amanda silently confers with Chester before she comments, "We're expected at Chester's brother's house for Christmas Eve, but are available on Christmas Day."

Cheryl pipes up that she has a commitment to deliver dinners for shut-ins at noon, but is around after that. Patrick nods, and says the diner will be closed but he can get a mincemeat pie the day before. Rose and Maggie offer to help Joe in any way he needs.

"It's settled, then. We will have Christmas dinner together, at about five o'clock, and anybody can come whenever they like. Blanche and I will 'receive' any time after three." He stands up, scraping the wooden chair across the hardwood floor in the process, and makes a little bow. "Thank you all for your gifts of so much help to Ben, and to me, through all of this. I think it's time to get out of here."

"What about Ben's ashes, Joe?" Patrick's voice is soft. Everyone stops moving their chairs in order to hear the answer.

"The funeral home will ship Ben's ashes to Charlie. They'll be buried beside Grace. It was what she wanted."

Patrick gives a nod of approval.

✳✳✳✳

Christmas dinner is a resounding success. Joe has a tree in the corner, trimmed with antique ornaments Ben gave to him before she died. Under the tree are parcels from Ben. When she closed her shop, she set aside a gift for each of her neighbours. Her original intention was to have some sort of party to get to know everyone better. When it became clear that wasn't going to happen, she enlisted Joe's help to ensure each one got to the right person.

After supper, when everyone feels stuffed and mellow, Joe distributes the gifts on Ben's behalf.

"This is for Mason, but you can help him open it." He places the gift gently into Amanda's hands. They open the parcel together. She peels away the soft tissue paper inside the bag to reveal a clear ball with a Santa and a reindeer inside. As the ornament is shaken, it snows. A little note tells Amanda that the snow globe was made around 1920. Mason, in bright red coveralls, squeals with delight as Amanda carefully upends Santa time after time.

Joe turns his attention to Patrick. "Ben told me you always admired this in the shop but could never save enough money to afford it. It was stashed in the back room the whole morning we helped her clean the place out. This is for you." He presents a box, wrapped in tinfoil, to the kid.

Patrick's eyes widen and sparkle. He folds back the foil to expose an original box. The surprise on his face reveals his utter disbelief. It holds a Lehmann Limo wind-up tin toy. There is a message in Ben's handwriting. It says the toy was made between 1929 and 1935. He scans the group. "I would go in the store and look at this before she closed up. It's worth more than I make in a month!"

Everyone asks to have a peek, and he gingerly extends the car in one hand and the box in the other so that each of his neighbours can make a closer inspection.

Joe continues to present Ben's gifts. He reaches over and places a brown paper parcel, big enough to be supported by both Rose and Maggie, on their knees. "I'm supposed to tell you it matches your apartment."

The sisters gasp as the paper falls away to reveal a turquoise, yellow, and cream quilt with a note pinned to the corner. It says the textile was handmade locally at the turn of the century. For once, Rose is obviously at a loss for words, and Maggie, who is the quietest of anyone, makes the connection. "Rose gave Ben the pink and green afghan she originally knitted for me when I was at Forest Hills. Isn't it funny how she chose this gift way back last spring when she closed her shop?"

There is a collective nod. Joe thinks everyone must feel very close to Ben right now. "She didn't leave you two out," he says as he picks up a small package shaped like a box and gives it to Chester to do the honours. Amanda's eyes are on her husband as he unwraps a small oil painting, not more than five by seven inches in size, depicting wheat fields and a little building, weathered grey and drooping with age. The note says the artist is local and the painting was done in 1910. It also says it will be up to them to discover their relationship to the work. Joe points out the signature just barely visible in the bottom right hand corner. It says D. Wolski, 1910.

"I've never heard of any artists in our family." Chester looks at Amanda and then at the group in general. "I need to have a serious chat with my dad." He smiles while his eyes overflow with curiosity.

Joe turns to Cheryl. "Now, Ben didn't know you very well when she closed the shop last May, but you became a close friend. She wanted you to have this." He sets a small blue jewellery box in her lap. Cheryl opens the box containing an antique cameo brooch—an art deco design with smooth edges and minimal trim. The base is cream with the white shadow of a woman, hair done in an extravagant up-style. "Ben was well aware that you are not a fan of antiques, but since this belonged to her and we had it cleaned at the jeweller's, she hoped you wouldn't object too much." He grins as he teases her with Ben's words, but Cheryl's expression says it all.

She turns her face to Joe as tears puddle her eyes. "I miss her more than I thought I ever could. Oh my, this is so beautiful."

With this portion of his executorship tasks out of the way, Joe turns to his kitchen. "Shall we all have tea, now?"

****

Just before his trip east, the estate finally clears probate and Joe is able to distribute the last of Ben's possessions. The blue leather sofa goes to Patrick. Joe will have the coffee table and the inverted helmet bowl that has always adorned it. Cheryl, Rose, Maggie, Amanda, and Patrick choose whatever they want. Chester sells her truck. The remaining items go to Segue House, the local women's shelter, and the final cheque goes to Charlie. His work for his friend has come to an end.

****

Rose will take good care of Blanche. Joe would have loved to have her company if he had decided to drive across country, but February is a time to avoid the blizzards and whiteouts on prairie highways, not to mention the inevitable challenges that present themselves around Lake Superior and northern Ontario. He is on his way to the city to catch his flight to Halifax. Christine will meet him. His plans are to stay at Chrissie's for three days while he visits with their mother and any other family members willing to endure his company. Will he actually see Anita?

As Joe speeds south toward the Edmonton airport, on treacherous roads without adequate sand, he realizes it's not the highway conditions that are making him nervous. It's been fourteen years. Christine is anxious to see him and that's his saving grace. He's excited to meet her kids again. His stomach is in knots. He hasn't flown since his honeymoon in 1963, so his insides have lots of excuses for churning the way they do.

"Don't put it off," Ben said. "The situation turned out fine with Charlie, in the end. It was my fault we never had a relationship. I should have pushed for it but I let the past stand in the way. Don't do that, Joe." Her words rattle around in his brain as he navigates his truck into the long-term parking lot at the airport. If Ben could do it, so could he. He was just a kid! Surely his mother will see him. Christine says she will but he has his doubts.

For February, the flight to Toronto is uneventful. The wait to change planes is almost more exhausting. Joe comes to the realization that he is truly a northerner when he discovers how overwhelmed he is with the activity, the rushing, the fancy clothes, and the sheer vastness of the place. Suddenly, the Hayworth Diner and The Station are very old-fashioned and shabby—just the way he likes it, he decides with a tiny grin as he lines up to board his flight to Halifax.

Christine is waiting for him as he glides down the escalator to airport reception. She's tall. Her faded blond hair is streaked with a shade of silver. It shimmers under the airport lights. She's dressed in blue jeans and looks just like the pictures she's sent. He would know her anywhere. She races toward him and wraps her arms around his neck. "Welcome home, kid brother," she whispers in his ear. "Let's go get your suitcase. We still have a two-hour drive, and they've predicted a snowstorm for tonight."

As they load her elderly Corolla, she continues to chatter. "The girls are both home and, hopefully, making us supper. Brooke has reading week. I was so happy you could come when she's here. Mom expects us tomorrow. We'll take her lunch. There's a girl who comes everyday to make sure she has a bath and that supper is ready. She gets short of breath so easily; she can't do much for herself anymore. Her mind is sharp as a tack but her heart's running out of steam." All this rolls out of Christine's mouth and across the front seat to Joe. He imagines the words as marbles and he's having trouble collecting them all. Must be reverse jet lag.

"Mitch won't be home when we get there. He'll be at the hockey arena. Wait. Maybe it's curling tonight. He makes ice for both places, so I can't remember." She darts a quick glance over at Joe. "He'll get home probably about ten. Late for me, but not too late for you, eh? Still on Alberta time."

Joe finally blurts what's on his mind. "Do you think Mom really wants to see me, Chrissie?"

"She's so excited, Joe. She told me yesterday that she thinks you blame her for Adam's death. After all these years, and since Dad's gone, she wants to talk to you about it." Christine has her eyes on the road. It's starting to get dark. Joe's happy she can't see his face.

"Why in hell would I blame her for what I did?" He can hardly force the words out of his mouth.

"I don't know, Joe. I don't know that it was anybody's fault. It was a long time ago. She seems to need to talk to you about it. You will talk about it with her, won't you?" She takes her eyes from the wheel just long enough to cast a sideways glance. "She's dying, Joe. Let her say her piece, no matter how hard, okay?"

He changes focus. "What about Anita? Have you talked to her? What does she think about my arrival and the fact that you and I stayed in touch?"

"Anita's a hard person. She likely hates all of us, but she has to stick around because her husband has such a successful business. I can't imagine why he stays with her. She's tough. She did say, though, that they would come to a family dinner at my place the night before you leave—just family. At least Anita likes the girls. Mom will be there. It'll be good." She reaches over and pats Joe's hand.

Joe discovers he's a little shy around his two grown-up nieces. Brooke was four and Josie was two when he left. If it weren't for the pictures, he would not have known either of them when he and his sister finally piled through the back door of the nondescript family bungalow. They, on the other hand, treat him as if he just lives down the road and has stopped in for a brew after work. They're both tall like their mother. They're funny and beautiful. Brooke favours Chrissie when she was that age. Josie has her father's high cheek bones and heavier build. They are fabulous and Joe is charmed by them both.

****

As they pull into the dooryard of the old farmhouse, he's slammed backward to his childhood. It's hard to imagine that there have been no changes, but the place looks exactly the same. The front steps still sag to the left. The living room curtains are still that ugly faded green. The driveway seems to have turned mostly to grass from lack of use. From the outside, that's the only difference. When Joe opens the back door, it squeaks in exactly the same way it did the night Adam died and so many people were tramping in and out.

Chrissie jumps ahead of Joe. She carries a basket full of containers identified as lunch-on-the-go. Joe stands for a moment and smells the familiar smells of old wood and linoleum. His eyes fall on the farmer-made cupboards and the kitchen table with all the knife marks and stains. His heart thumps as he eyes the door to the sitting room.

"She's in through there, Joe. Go see her. Chrissie sweeps her hand toward the door. I'll get lunch organized."

He takes a tentative step into the darkened corridor that leads through to the front room. "Mom, it's me. How are ya'?" His hands won't stop shaking. By the time he turns the corner, Alice is perched on the edge of her recliner, arms outstretched, and tears coursing down her surprisingly wrinkle-free cheeks. *Don't start to cry!*

He takes two steps across the room and bends down, allowing her to put her frail, sweater-clad arms around his neck. She weeps openly now. "I didn't believe you would come, Joe. I didn't believe you would come." Her breath escapes in short gasps.

Joe glances around the room. Her bed is there, as well as a toilet chair. This is her headquarters, it appears. The television, the radio, and a pile of books all have pride of place. "Let me stand back and have a look at you, Mom." He turns and grabs a wooden chair that he places across from her, but close enough so that he can reach out and touch her hand. His mind flits quickly to Ben and back. This space, like Ben's living room, is operation central.

They have lunch and they talk. Joe tells his mother about his work and where he lives. The truth comes out when he realizes Chrissie has shared her letters over all these years. "But you never tried to get in touch with me, Mom." Joe tries to avoid the familiar sting of rejection and anger, not spoken but always loitering on the edges of consciousness, poisoning any possible sense of well-being.

"I always thought you blamed me for Adam's death," his mother responds. "I didn't want to overstep the bounds."

"Blame you! Why in God's name would I blame you for the fact that I left Adam in the woods! It was my fault. I was just a kid, but all the same, it was still my fault. Everybody blamed me. I felt it. I knew it." He can hear his voice escalate. He takes a deep breath.

"Nobody blamed you, Joe—except maybe Anita because her party got ruined. You didn't leave Adam in the woods. Adam came home and told me you were behind him somewhere. I just assumed you were out in the yard at the edge of the trees. I told him to run and fetch you. You came in and he never did." She stares straight into Joe's eyes as tears start to fall once again. "You must have known it was me who sent him into the woods, not you that left him there! Joe! You must have known!"

His eyes well up as he returns his mother's gaze. He can't talk. The words won't come. "Everybody said it wasn't your fault, Joe. You mean to say you never believed that?" Alice's eyes are locked with his, now.

Finally, he forces the words. "I felt everyone blamed me; that they just tried to spare my feelings." He turns from his mother's horrified eyes and directs a quizzical brow wrinkle toward his sister.

"Nobody knew for sure, Mom." Chrissie is standing beside her brother now. You and Dad never talked about it again." Her voice is gentle. The soft pressure of her hand lingers on Joe's shoulder.

His mother's regret moans out of her as she leans back into the oversized cushions of her recliner. "Adam's death ruined all our lives. Anita turned into a hard rock. Your father likely stopped loving me that night, and you have borne this burden for thirty-five years. Can we forgive ourselves and each other, now? I'll be gone soon. I want my three remaining children to put the past behind them before I go."

****

Dinner on his last night becomes a true family affair. Joe corrals Anita the minute she steps into Christine's back porch, and shuffles her down the hall until they reach the linen cupboard at the end. "I'll start by apologizing for ruining your birthday party in 1945. Adam's death was almost more than any family could bear. I always thought it was my fault. Maybe you thought so, too. I don't want to be your enemy, Anita."

"I'm here, aren't I? Give me some credit. I talked to Mom. She finally told the truth. No one would ever tell me what really happened. It was like Mom and Dad refused to ever discuss it again. My biggest problem with this family is nobody tells the truth."

The tension in Anita's face, a lifelong picture she has presented to the family she resents, begins to soften. For an instant so brief that Joe can't be certain he really saw it, her lower lip seems to tremble. Just as suddenly, decades of habit kick in and she's once more in control. "So, level with me. Will you ever get married again? Chrissie says you live with a cat named Blanche. She's kidding, right?"

Chapter 22

Amanda

"Hello?" Amanda answers the phone while she keeps one eye on Mason, who attempts yet again, to haul himself up by the couch cushions.

"Hi, Amanda, it's Murdock Blackney. How are you today?"

"Good. Good." She reaches across to Mason and holds his hand so he won't tip backwards. "What can I do for you this morning, Mr. Blackney?"

"More like what I can do for you, Amanda. First, call me Murdock. Second, can you come down to the office later on this afternoon? I have the results from my research. It's taken almost three months, but I think I have some answers and we can formulate a plan."

"Is it good news?" Amanda prays Jeremy went ahead and divorced her before she married Chester.

"There's good news and bad news, I'm afraid. Come to the office about three this afternoon, and I'll go over the details with you."

"Okay. See you later." She signs off, and sits down on the couch with her son. As she wiggles a stuffed puppy in front of clapping hands and listens to Mason's gurgles, she manages to push back the fear that nibbles away at her senses.

Amanda takes the remainder of the morning to complete her chores. As she methodically drags her broom across each of the apartment building stairs, her eyes keep returning to rest on the door of Number Three. She misses Ben. She would like to have just another half hour with her friend. She frets as she thinks about her possibly illegal marriage. Ben was the only person who knew until they shared her tale with Murdock.

Just as she's about to bundle up Mason in his stroller and manhandle the contraption back out and down the steps, Maggie appears from behind the door of Number Two. Caesar wiggles between her feet, marches across the foyer, and presents his head to Mason for stroking. The child sputters with delight. "Hi, Maggie, what are you up to today?" The girl still makes Amanda a wee bit nervous. She hardly ever says more than hello and Amanda can't remember ever having a conversation with her alone before.

"Hi. Is it okay if Caesar visits with Mason? Do you mind? I'm sure he gets tired of just me all day. We used to visit with Ben after Rose got home from work. I miss her. I bet you do, too."

That was a lot more than Amanda has ever heard her say before. "Caesar's fine. And, yes. We miss Ben a lot."

"I'm going for a job interview today! I just had to tell someone and I heard you in the hall. The phone at Dr. Gunton's office is busy so I can't tell Rose." She laughs and claps her hands together like a little kid.

Amanda is more than a tiny bit curious. "Where's your interview? That sounds exciting."

"At the women's shelter. They need a bookkeeper. It's three days a week and better than being stuck here all the time."

"I didn't know you could keep books." Amanda is suspicious this might all be fabrication of some sort.

"Oh, I took courses when I was at the institute. They insisted I study and I've always been a whiz at math, so here we are. What should I wear? I've never been on a job interview before."

"Wear clothes that are neat and tidy. I don't think the staff at the shelter would insist on formal work dress, but no jeans."

"Can I show you what I've picked out?" She opens the apartment door further and dashes inside before Amanda can answer. She returns a second or two later with a pair of black slacks and a grey patterned sweater-set on a hanger. "What do you think?"

"I think that's perfect." As she starts to wedge the stroller out to the step, she turns back toward the young woman, who's bending down to steer Caesar inside the apartment. "Good luck, Maggie. Let me know how it goes." Will wonders never cease? The girl seems quite different when Rose isn't around.

****

Murdock Blackney's office looks like it belongs in a detective novel. His secretary, an older woman with a bun and sensible shoes, sits in an anteroom behind a small wooden desk that supports a typewriter, telephone, notepad, and basket of papers. There's a potted plant of some sort on top of the lone metal file cabinet. It droops like it has lost all hope. The secretary peers at her over dark-rimmed reading glasses, when Amanda pushes open the heavy wooden door with the frosted glass insert bearing the lawyer's name.

"Hi. I'm Amanda Wolski. Mr. Blackney asked me to come in today."

"He'll just be a minute, Mrs. Wolski." She glances at the light on the telephone. "He's still on the phone."

Amanda moves over to one of the three wooden straight-backed chairs that line the opposite wall in the drab office. Mason is behaving, having devoured a cookie, and is now rolling a truck back and forth across his stroller travel-tray. She bends over and loosens his clothes. Dressing a baby for this weather is hard, but she decides to disturb him long enough to get him out of the snowsuit or he won't have patience to last through their meeting. She just has time to get her coat and his outer clothes piled on another chair when her lawyer lumbers through the door of his office.

"No more calls, Flora. We'll be about half an hour."

Flora nods at her boss. She is obviously a woman of few words.

Murdock holds the door for Amanda so she can push the stroller inside. Mason squeals with delight to be moving again. She sits in the chair indicated by the lawyer. It's across from his desk but, rather than taking his place behind it, he sits in the other client's chair right beside her. He's a big and burly man. He fills the room. "I have good news and bad news, Amanda. Sorry it's taken so long to find out. The mail can be a bitch but there you have it. The good news is that you are, in fact, divorced. Apparently, the Bradway family tried to get their son an annulment but that didn't work, so they started divorce proceedings exactly three years after you left. You were divorced in absentia so get no settlement."

"I never wanted their money, Mr. Blackney." She can't help but feel relieved though she knows there's more to be revealed. "You said there was bad news, too?"

"Afraid so. Call me Murdock. According to the date the divorce was made final, you got married beforehand. Therefore, you're not really legally married now."

"Is what I did illegal?" Amanda feels her face flush. Perhaps she's a bigamist and will have to go to jail.

Murdock laughs—a big round laugh that shakes the belly he attempts to cover with a pinstriped waistcoat. "That will be our little secret, Amanda. Ben asked me to determine your status and I did that. Your first marriage is done and finished. The only task you have now, is to convince Chester you want to get married again."

The walk home is colder. The wind has picked up. She wraps the cover crocheted by Rose, around Mason's face. He loves the stroller and starts to drift off to sleep regardless of the elements. Amanda walks with a brisk step. She wishes she could talk over with Ben what she will say to Chester once she gets home. She decides to put off telling him until tomorrow.

****

The next day—the one that could potentially change her life forever—dawns crisp and clear. Will it ever warm up? There is more snow predicted for later on in the day. After Chester leaves for work, she bustles through her chores. She plans to fix a special dinner for them—a baked chicken with all the trimmings—Sunday dinner in the middle of the week.

While in the foyer of the building sweeping down the stairs as she does every morning, Maggie pops out to say hello. Amanda is reluctant to ask if she got the job but Maggie solves the mystery. "I start work on Monday! Can you believe it? I got the job!"

Amanda is happy for her new friend. She sets aside her broom and moves into Maggie's space to give her a quick hug. The girl tenses up a bit but accepts the show of affection. "I am so excited for you. That was fast! You must be very proud of yourself."

"I know I probably got the job because I was abused but everybody has to start somewhere. I think Rose and I are going to have everybody in for a little get-together this weekend. You and Chester will have to come." She leans over to touch Mason on the top of his head. "And Mason too, of course."

"Just let us know when and we'll be there. Congratulations!" Amanda resumes sweeping as Maggie skips back into Number Two. It sounds like she's humming under her breath!

Amanda fusses the day away. She cooks. She cleans. She gets Mason all ready for bed and ensures every detail is perfect for her evening with Chester. She wants him to be able to survey his surroundings and appreciate how great their life is. She wants him to ignore the fact that she has lied to him for over three years. She's scared to death as she obsesses about what his reaction might be. She can't even think about what his parents will say. She is beside herself by the time he walks through the door, wearing a tired expression on his handsome face.

"Man, supper smells good. Is this a special occasion I've forgotten? It's not your birthday, or Mason's, or mine for that matter. It's not our anniversary. What gives?" He wraps her in a bear hug and nuzzles her masses of curls.

"I wanted us to have a nice supper and a little talk."

His response shows alarm mixed with curiosity. "You're not pregnant again, are you?" He rebounds in just a split second with, "That's okay, honey. We'll manage, if you are. Don't worry."

"No, Chester. We're not pregnant—at least not yet." She forces a smile. "Why don't you put your son to bed while I finish getting dinner ready and then we can talk?"

All the time he's in Mason's room, she runs through her speech in her mind. *Tell him the facts. Keep it simple. It was nobody's fault.* She loves him so much.

He encourages her when he returns. "Okay, love. Spill the beans. What has got you so hyper? I'm starting to worry."

"Chester. I have to tell you a story. Some of it you know and some of it you don't. Mostly all of it has been resolved already, so don't get upset. Promise?"

"My God, Amanda. Did you kill somebody? You look like a scared rabbit. It's okay if you did—kill somebody, I mean. We'll go on the lam." He grins at her in an obvious attempt to calm her down.

"When we met, I told you all about how my parents died in a car crash and how I was in foster care and worked at a resort before I came out here."

"Yes. Yes." He nods. That's good. "You want to have your own restaurant someday and I want that, too."

She nods acknowledgement as she continues. "What I didn't tell you is that I was married when I came here." She sees a dark cloud she can't quite interpret travel across his beautiful face. She gulps for air and continues. "It all happened in a whirlwind. He was very rich. I didn't know how to manage, really. Anyway, it wasn't long before he was involved with someone else and I just left. I travelled west and ended up at the camp. Then, when it closed down I came here."

"Did you get a divorce?" His voice is quiet. She hopes it means he intends to reserve judgement.

"Well," she borrows Murdock's line, "The good news is I'm divorced. Apparently, Jeremy's family secured that eventually."

"The bad news?" He still hasn't moved from his chair at the table, and her feet are glued to the floor in front of the stove. She stirs gravy and watches her husband as closely as she is able.

"The bad news is that the divorce was made final after our wedding date. Murdock Blackney says we aren't legally married. On the upside, the Justice of the Peace could do that in about five minutes." She holds her breath and waits for his response. When he continues to stare at her without talking, she adds, "Before she died, Ben hired Murdock to help me fix this. I had to talk to someone. I didn't know what to do!" She hears the slightest twinge of desperation push out between the words.

Chester gets up and goes into Mason's room. He's gone for what seems like a very long time. Amanda is beginning to think she should go in and get him when he re-emerges with their sleeping little boy in his arms. "We are a family," he whispers to her over their child's tiny sweet-smelling body. "Will you marry me? Again?" He's smiling.

Amanda tiptoes over to her husband and son. She leans against Chester's shoulder as she attempts to avoid disturbing the baby. "I love you, Chester. What will we tell your parents?"

After Chester returns Mason to his crib, they sit down to discuss a plan. At first, Amanda describes how she came to tell Ben about her secret. "Ben told me about the tragedy in her life and how she intended to try and right some wrongs by contacting her grandson. I saw how it all worked out and I just wanted to get rid of my secret, too."

"You could have talked to me, you know. That's the part that upsets me. You were reluctant to come to me." His face is sad.

"That wasn't it, Chester. We don't have the money to hire lawyers. When Ben offered, I just had to take the chance."

"Okay. So do you want me to tell the folks?"

"I don't know. We could always just get married now and never let on."

She grins across the table at him, as she tries to present a mischievous option that would serve to paper over the whole situation. His reaction surprises her.

"Okay. How's this. We'll have a little wedding here at The Station. It's not as if the tenants don't all have secrets of their own. There's Joe, flying east to see his mother for the first time in years, and Rose turning up here with Maggie. God knows what else is bubbling just under the surface at this place. I think they can all keep a secret. We'll have a little Victoria Day potluck and wedding. We can swear everybody to secrecy. But...there's one condition."

She continues to watch her husband but now with considerably less trepidation. "What's that, Chester?"

"On the twentieth anniversary of our first wedding, we have another party, and we tell everybody the truth! Can we do that?"

"I think they call that 'kicking the can down the road', don't they? But that's fine with me. I like the idea of a secret potluck wedding. My concern would be how to get the J.P. to keep it to himself; and who knows who'll be living in Number Three by then. We still have another few weeks before the lease is up."

"The J.P. drives a Ford, so I can take care of that angle. You'll be able to size up whoever moves in to Number Three. We'll be fine. Supper is great, by the way." He pours more gravy on his chicken. "I guess we'll be in new dress territory?"

"We'll see. Depends on the budget. You didn't seem too worried when you guessed we might be having another baby." She catches Chester's eye and grins.

Chapter 23

Patrick

Patrick squirms, reluctant and shy, as he sits on a black vinyl stacking chair near the front door of the Hayworth Community Hospital. It feels like he's been here for hours even though he knows it's only been minutes. He doesn't like to be mixed up with the wheelchair-riding old lady who emits periodic moans, as she waits for an X-ray after a fall; with the snotty-nosed toddler who roars around unsupervised, and screams at the toys he's thrown on the floor; or with the sallow-faced gentleman in the hundred-year-old suit, who appears to have death lurking on his shoulder. Patrick's not sick. He has an appointment to meet with Dr. Wilkerson. This is his fourth visit since before Christmas but he still isn't comfortable in the hospital waiting area.

"Patrick Hollinger." The chubby-faced receptionist peeks around the corner of her cubicle and stares straight at him. "You can go in now. The doctor is ready to see you." At least they don't use Dr. Wilkerson's name. If they did, everybody within earshot would know he's here to see the psychiatrist that comes to the hospital every two weeks.

The office seems sterile—devoid of personal touches. It's used by many different travelling professionals who spend certain days at the hospital. To Patrick, Rachel Wilkerson is the only accessory required in this uninspired place. He thinks she's beautiful. She is tall and thin. She has long, thick brown hair she wears loose around her shoulders. She always dresses in straight skirts, blouses tucked in, and blazers she sometimes wears and sometimes hangs on the back of her chair. He admires her skin. It is so smooth and seems to have a perpetual tan. She wears a huge watch on her left wrist. Patrick thinks it's a man's watch with its big, roman-numeral face and shiny gold links. Patrick is smitten but knows he will never reveal to her what an absolutely perfect human being he thinks she is.

"Hi, Patrick. Come in. Come in." She waits at the door of the office as she usually does, shakes his hand, and motions him to one of the two upholstered bucket chairs by the window. Her desk is separated from the sitting area by a coffee table. She only retreats to the desk to write a prescription, make a call, or jot down an important date or fact in his chart. She sits across from him, smoothes her skirt, crosses her legs, and gives him what he considers to be her undivided attention. "So...tell me about the last couple of weeks. Do you continue to take your pills? Have we successfully wrestled those voices into the back cupboard, Patrick?" She leans forward, seemingly interested and engaged.

Patrick is always anxious to respond to her—to please her. "I take the pills just like I'm supposed to. They don't make me sick. I've got one hand, my left, that trembles a bit but it isn't too bad. It doesn't bother me at work. It's not bad enough to make me drop dishes or spill stuff."

"Let me see." She holds both her hands out at arm's length toward Patrick. "Do this so I can assess."

Patrick mimics her. His left hand has a slight tremor.

"Is it worse if you get anxious or upset?" She lowers her own hands back into her lap and Patrick follows suit.

"I try hard not to get anxious or upset, Doc." He attempts to appear confident and brushes a greasy strand of hair out of his eyes. "But to be honest, it's worse if I find myself almost late for work or if the diner get busy. I can still do my job." He reinforces his previous remark. It would be really bad if she didn't want him to take the pills anymore. He's just started to change. He thinks he's more comfortable; normal somehow. "The worst part is the dry mouth. God, I drink all the time!"

"Do you follow my instructions and drink water, not pop?"

He nods. This part has been hard, but he's cut way back on the sugar and greasy food since he began seeing Dr. Wilkerson regularly. Margo and Nancy, at the restaurant, say it's more expensive to feed him now because he asks for meatloaf, mashed potatoes, and salad instead of fries and gravy. He laughs and reminds them that he doesn't drink as much soda, so that should help.

"I drink all the time, but mostly water just like you said. I'm a lot better."

"Well you appear healthier and sound better, too, Patrick. Do you plan to ask your boss if you can do a few shifts waiting tables?" He hesitates before he answers, and she jumps in. "I can give you a mild anti-tremor medication if that would help. It's really common to have tremors and this stuff will stop them cold." Her perfect white teeth seem to sparkle when she smiles.

"That would be good. I think Margo would give me shifts if I asked, but the shaking worried me."

"Good. That's settled. Let's talk about the voices and watching television."

"The voices are still gone, Dr. Wilkerson. I can just sit down and watch *Gunsmoke* for the story. I think about my friend Ben a lot now. Not that I hear her voice." He's anxious to make that clear to his doctor. "But she helped me before she died. She said I needed to focus on real advisers and not TV voices. She was right."

Rachel Wilkerson settles back in her chair. "I think we can start to talk about your family more now, Patrick. Are you okay with the idea of exploring your mother's death and your reaction, as well as how it might have affected the rest of your family?"

Patrick's stomach lurches. He must be on the road to recovery. She said they wouldn't start to talk about Mom until after he got on medication and showed real improvement. "I'd like to call my dad soon, Dr. Wilkerson. Do you think that's a good idea?"

She leans slightly forward in her chair once more. "I think calling your father is a fine plan, Patrick. We'll take a couple of sessions to talk about your parents and then you'll be all ready to make the next move."

****

There's a spring in Patrick's step as he locks the door to Number Six and trots down the two flights of stairs to the foyer. Amanda is sweeping. He gives her a broad, toothy grin. She looks at him in a kind of puzzled way—surprised, but not at seeing him exactly. "Patrick, you're different. Let me see!" She steps closer, leans against her broom, and peers at his face.

Patrick lights up. "It's pretty normal, right?" He needs more than the opinion of the denturist before he makes his pitch at work. "Natural?" His new front tooth sparkles as he favours Mason with another huge smile.

"It's better than pretty good, Patrick. You are very handsome." Amanda gives him a flirty little head tilt. "You'll have to beat the girls off with a stick. Did you decide to turn over a new leaf?"

Patrick doesn't share every detail. He knows he has to work on trust but he likes Amanda a lot. "Ben always wanted me to get a tooth. She said she'd pay but I didn't want to accept charity. She left me enough money to get it done. Joe paid the bill out of her estate." A sudden wave of loss overwhelms him. "She was a great lady. I really miss our afternoon talks even though she was so sick and all."

"I miss her, too, Patrick. Well, you look quite fabulous and Ben was absolutely right as usual."

Patrick continues on to work, buoyed by Amanda's flattery. He intends to ask Margo, today, if he can have a few shifts waiting tables. Lately, he's been helping both the owner and Nancy bus tables when it gets busy and they seem to appreciate it. They have even begun sharing their tips with him so that's significant. Now that he has his tooth and he doesn't hear the voices, he wants to get out of the kitchen and work with customers. He knows he can do it, but Margo has to give him a chance.

He gets to the diner just as the breakfast crowd starts to thin out. He stashes his jacket in the back, nods to Danny, and returns to the front, dishpan in hand. He cleans empty tables while Margo is at the cash, ringing out four government workers who gather here for breakfast every Thursday. She glances over at him as the bell above the door tinkles the group's departure. "Good morning, Patrick. I'm glad you're here. Breakfast was busy and I have two group reservations for lunch. I said I would take a shift since Nancy wanted the day off but I had to call her in."

"I could do it."

"No, Patrick. I appreciate the help with clearing tables but...you know."

Patrick sets the dishpan down on the booth table and walks, with purpose, over to the counter. Margo has her back to him as she pours coffee for a couple who just settled up at the front near the door. "Margo." He whispers so that the couple can't hear him. "See, Margo. What do you think?" He shows off his new smile and then worries that the shock might make her drop the cups.

"My God! Aren't you the movie star! But you didn't want a plate in your mouth. Didn't you say you figured it would give you problems, Patrick?" She leans closer to him and lowers her voice. "Let me take this order and we'll talk."

After the tables are cleaned, old Bertha is humming, and the couple have their bacon and eggs, Margo and Patrick sit together in the staff booth at the back. He makes his pitch. "I started seeing a doctor a couple of months ago, Margo. I like her. I take the pills she prescribed and I'm better. I follow Ben's advice, too." He gives her a shy smirk, in an attempt to indicate to Margo that he is fully aware of her concerns and he's addressed them. "I take better care of myself, too." He hopes she notices his clothes are clean and his hair isn't greasy—or hanging in his eyes, for that matter. "Give Nancy the day off. Let me help you and then decide."

"What about the dishes?" He thinks she's considering.

"If we both clear tables, I can handle Bertha for today. Of course...," he leans back in the booth, gives his boss a brazen stare, and grins again. "If you like my work, you might have to find yourself a part-time dishwasher."

"All right, mister. Your tooth is great and you don't smell bad, so what have I got to lose—except a few customers, right? Let Danny know what we're up to and I'll call Nancy. She'll be thrilled. Her niece has a recital at school. She'll owe you one."

Patrick gets up to go find Danny, who is probably out back having a smoke. This is his chance. He can hardly wait to tell Dr. Wilkerson.

The day flies by. It's busy, just like Margo said it would be, but Patrick is confident and as good as his word. He takes orders, keeps them straight, delivers them hot, and clears his tables. He does exactly what's necessary with the old dishwasher to ensure they don't run out of what they need, and stacks the excess to run through when it quiets down in the afternoon. He makes tips—and pretty good ones. He'll go home today with an extra twenty dollars in his pocket.

By early afternoon, the rush starts to wind down and he notices Margo behind the counter with a clean, empty mayonnaise jar. She tapes a piece of paper to the side. When he gets closer, he discovers it says: "Patrick's Tips". "I cleared some tables that were yours and needed a place to put your tips. I saw you drop money into my jar so I figured you might want one of your own."

"Does this mean you want me to stay around for supper?" He empties his pockets and drops the change and bills into his new tips jar.

"Whoa! You cleaned up! I gather the customers like your style, Patrick. And yes, I want you to stick around tonight. I will also schedule you into most of my shifts so I can pay more attention to my real job. Know any dishwashers who are out of work?"

****

"Alystair Pontiac Buick. We deal in only the best. How can I help you?"

Patrick is propelled back years into his childhood as he listens to the familiar singsong voice, with its slight hint of a twang. "Raymond Hollinger, please." He's rehearsed this a thousand times but he's twitchy with butterflies, nonetheless.

"Raymond Hollinger, Sales Manager. May I help you?"

He's the sales manager now, but he sounds exactly the same as he always did. "Hi, Dad. It's me. Patrick. How are you?"

"Patrick?" The voice is quiet on the other end. "Let me close my door." The phone hits what sounds like the surface of the desk but for just a second, and then Raymond returns. "Where are you, son? Are you okay? Can I come and get you?"

Patrick fights not to cry. He wishes he were across the street from the car dealership and could just put down the phone, trot over, and open the plate glass door. He makes an attempt to laugh though the tears catch in his burning throat. "No, Dad. I'm fine. I'm in Hayworth. It's in northern Alberta, about five hours north of Edmonton. I've been here for over three years now. How are the girls?"

"The girls are good, Patrick. They're both in university. Where have you been? What have you been doing? We found your note. You said not to try and find you but we did anyway. We were heartbroken, Patrick."

"I just bummed around for a long time, Dad. When I came up north to Hayworth, I met some good people. I'm better. I have a nice job and a nice place to live. You don't have to worry about me."

They talk for a long time. Raymond wants to come to Hayworth. He wants to see his son. He wants Patrick to come home and visit with his sisters. He wants Patrick to come back.

"I can't come back, Dad, at least not yet. Too much stuff there." As a sudden afterthought, he adds. "But you can come visit me here in Hayworth. You fly to Edmonton and then take the bus—or maybe my friend Joe would take me into the city to meet you. I don't have a car. Don't make that kind of money." He's embarrassed.

"I'll come to Hayworth." Raymond Hollinger says in a solemn voice. "I need to see you, son. I'll set aside the week of May that includes Victoria Day. Would that work for you?"

"I'll make it work, Dad." Patrick provides his phone number—another extravagance he's permitted himself since Ben got sick. His father will call with details and maybe call him some weekend when the girls are both there.

Patrick hangs up the phone and goes over to stretch out on the big blue down-filled leather sofa bequeathed to him by Ben. He wishes he could tell her about the progress he's made, thanks to her. He realizes, with pleasure, that he can think about her and miss her without voices creeping through his brain, distorting his thoughts, and making him dependent on anyone besides himself.

Chapter 24

Cheryl

Cheryl sits at her glass-topped dining table staring at a blank sheet of paper. With ruler and pen at the ready, she drinks her second cup of coffee on this early Saturday morning in late March. The address is to The Department of Social Services in Nova Scotia. After a few subtle inquiries at work, she has determined that the Catholic Home for Unwed Mothers in Sydney recently closed and all their files were turned over to the provincial government. She pens a carefully constructed letter requesting information regarding the birth of her child,

To whom it may concern:

My name is Cheryl Nadler.
My date of birth is September 10, 1951.

On September 30, 1966, I gave birth to a child at Sydney Memorial Hospital after residing at the Catholic Home for Unwed Mothers for three months. To my knowledge, the child was adopted and I have no further details.

If it is the practice of your department, I would appreciate my contact information be kept on file in case this adopted child ever wishes to locate his/her birth mother. I sincerely hope it may be your policy to forward my particulars to the adoptive parents in the event they support their child's future meeting with a birth parent.

She adds her mailing address, her residential address, and both her home and work phone numbers. She silently reads it one last time. Her hands tremble just a little, as she carefully folds the single sheet of paper and tucks it into the white business envelope. She will stop at the post office on Monday. With the first step taken, all she can do is wait for a reply. Ben would be so proud of her. She gets up to wash her hands and polish the fingerprints off the table.

The next chore won't be quite as easy. Her reservations are in place. She plans to fly to Halifax to see if she might find any trace of her mother. Her research to date has yielded less than stellar results. Elsie Nadler moved to Halifax in the fall of 1966 with some guy. Cheryl is hard-pressed to remember if she ever knew his identity—just another one of her mother's men. There were so many. Maybe she's married to him now but after fourteen years, who would know that history anymore?

She's used her social work contacts as best as she could and obtained a list of hostels and soup kitchens, as well as women's shelters in the area. She plans to visit each of them and show anyone who will have a look, the one picture of her mother in her possession. She also intends to visit the police station and the library. If her mother is dead, maybe there's an obituary. If she was ever arrested, maybe they will tell her.

****

The trip from Edmonton to Halifax in early April is long and uneventful. Cheryl retrieves her luggage and turns to the Rent-A-Car stall. She chooses a compact, nondescript Ford for her week in town. She's booked into a small motel just off the main thoroughfare and her one wish, at this point, is to have a shower. She will start her search tomorrow.

Cheryl's night is restless. The motel, of course, isn't up to her standards. During most of the sleepless hours, she imagines bugs crawling up her arms and gnats cocooning in her hair. By six that morning, she's had three showers. After breakfast at a local family restaurant that Cheryl assumes probably hosts some decidedly non-family types during its overnight operations, she sets out for the Steward Women's Shelter. It doesn't advertise and isn't in the phone book. She only knows about it thanks to the women's shelter in Hayworth. The administrator expects her.

"I want you to know I've done some of the legwork for you." Phoebe Tucker is seated behind a dilapidated government surplus desk. She peers at Cheryl through heavy glasses constantly sliding down a nose that has clearly been broken more than once. Phoebe is thin and angular. Her clothes don't suit her. They obviously once belonged to someone else. There isn't an item in the place that doesn't look like it once belonged to someone else. "I even talked to the previous manager, and she was here in 1966. We've never heard of Elsie Nadler. I'm sorry, but fourteen years is a long time."

Cheryl accepts the woman's apologetic smile and is reconciled to going away empty-handed, when Phoebe adds, "On the upside, I called Feed the Lambs, a soup kitchen down by the waterfront. I talked to Harley—he's been there for over twenty years. He said he would talk to you after they served lunch today. I think he might have information, but of course, he wouldn't share details with me." She nudges her glasses up her face for the umpteenth time.

Cheryl rises and shakes Phoebe's hand. "I appreciate all you've done. I am probably on a wild goose chase, but the deathbed advice from a very dear friend was to make the effort or I would regret it." She nods to the shelter manager and smiles ruefully. "So here I find myself accepting favours from complete strangers."

After leaving the shelter, Cheryl parks her car in a lot near the waterfront, dons the running shoes she brought with her, and starts to trek along the boardwalk. Because she grew up in Cape Breton, and relocated directly to Alberta as soon as she could, Cheryl never really learned much about this beautiful port city on the south coast of Nova Scotia. As the April wind whips her short dark hair about, she soaks in the sights and sounds of tugboats, fishing vessels, souvenir shops just starting to ramp up for the tourist season, and workers on break seeking a sheltered spot to eat a sandwich and stare at the sea.

She finally retreats from the wind to a tiny restaurant just around the corner from a government wharf. It's not quite noon so she can find a table for one, order a lobster roll, and stare out the window at passersby. What will this Harley have to tell her? It sounds as if he might remember her mother or know where she could be. After her lunch, she goes for another quick walk and then makes her way to Feed the Lambs.

The place is located down an alleyway just off Water Street. She knows she's in the right place because there's still a short lineup of men and women standing outside and patiently waiting their turn. She is about to return to her car and wait another hour, when a voice booms from the doorway. "Are you Cheryl from Alberta? I'm Harley. Come on in. Let her through, folks. She's not here for lunch; she's come to see me." He says this last part with a bit of a lecherous grin, and the men at the front of the line whistle and laugh.

Cheryl isn't sure what to do, so she simply follows Harley's finger as he points out his office.

"Make yourself at home there, Cheryl. I'll just be a minute. We're busier today than I anticipated. You're not in a hurry are you?"

She shakes her head as she glances back at him.

"She's not much of a talker," she overhears him say to the lineup. There's some muffled laughter but Cheryl doesn't get the impression they're being mean. She's shy and she knows it. If she worked here, it would be a different story. When she can put on her social worker personality, she's fine.

It's twenty minutes before he returns. "So...glad Phoebe called and told you to come down. You're Elsie Nadler's daughter, right?"

"Yes, Mr...," she replies, as she fumbles in her bag for the picture of her mother.

"Just Harley. I gave up on last names a long time ago." He reaches for the picture. "That's her all right. I've been here so long I guess I know everybody. She and some guy used to eat here almost every day for about a year—late sixties." He reaches for a slip of paper on his desk. "Back then, if people got more than two meals a week, we asked them to register. I dug up the old list." He hands a photocopied piece of paper over to Cheryl. "You can keep that copy but have a look at the book, too. They might have been in off and on after that; hard to say."

"Thank you, Harley." Cheryl takes the paper and stares at it for a moment. Harley has carefully blacked out all the other names on her copy with marker, leaving only her mother's and a man's name she doesn't recognize—Dugan Gill.

Before she looks up, Harley adds, "I probably should have blacked out Dugan's name but if they ever got married, Elsie might have changed her name to Gill. Finding someone after fourteen years is tough at the best of times but don't show that paper around. I don't want anybody accusing me of not keeping secrets. You understand?"

"I'm a social worker, Harley. I understand confidentiality. Rest assured no one will know where I got the information." She stands up and reaches out to shake his hand.

****

Cheryl spends the next three days in the library reading obituaries in old Nova Scotia newspapers preserved on microfilm. Each night, her eyes feel like they will pop out of her head by the time she returns to her motel room.

Her search is not without its rewards. She finds a tiny obituary for Dugan Gill in a Cape Breton newspaper. He had two sons. He died in hospital in Sydney following a long-standing battle with lung disease, in 1975. There was no mention of Elsie Nadler.

With a couple of days remaining before she has to return to Alberta, Cheryl contacts the Halifax Police Service—Community Outreach Division. She makes an appointment to meet with Constable Donovan Martin. She tells him on the phone exactly what her search entails, and he doesn't refuse to see her so maybe he will actually be of some assistance. Perhaps Elsie's in jail. The concept is disquieting. She hasn't totally worked through the idea of actually talking to her mother. For now, she would be happy to simply locate her.

****

"How do you do? Please be seated." Cheryl has been shown to an office on the second floor of the busy downtown Halifax headquarters of the local police. Donovan Martin is in uniform and standing behind his desk. He leans over and offers his hand. He has a nice smile—kind but not patronizing. Cheryl always worries that the police will patronize her, like they used to when they would bring her mother home in the middle of the night.

"Good afternoon. I'm Cheryl Nadler. We spoke on the phone."

He nods and motions for her to be seated. He has a file in front of him. It's closed. She can't see the name on the tab. "You told me on the phone that you're trying to find information about your mother, an Elsie Nadler?"

"Yes. Yes, but she may have been married to a man by the name of Dugan Gill. She might have gone by Elsie Gill by the time she crossed your path, if she ever did." Cheryl's anxious to know what's in the file but Constable

Martin appears to be in no hurry.

"Miss Nadler, do you have any proof that Elsie Nadler was your mother?"

His use of the past tense does not escape her notice. Cheryl's prepared and has brought with her the old picture taken when she was ten, sitting with Elsie. She also has her birth certificate which clearly identifies Elsie Nadler as her birth mother and her father as unknown. She opens the top of her portfolio-like handbag and produces them. "Here you go," she states as she extends her hand to the policeman.

"Thank you, Miss Nadler. I'm sure you appreciate that we have to be sure we are speaking with the correct person before we divulge confidential information."

Cheryl nods, and can't help but glance in the direction of the file as it sits like a prized possession on the desk between them.

He hands her back her picture and identification. He opens the file and removes a type-written letter which he carefully places on the folder, now closed once again. His big square hands rest together on the paper and he looks Cheryl straight in the eye. "Miss Nadler, I am sorry to inform you that your mother passed away on or about March 7, 1976. I have a statement to give to you. In it you will find the circumstances of her death and the results of our investigation. Take a few moments to read the letter and then I will answer any questions you might have."

Cheryl takes the letter from Constable Martin.

> *Elsie Nadler, born May 5, 1931, in Sydney, Nova Scotia, was found deceased in an alley off Water Street in Halifax on March 8, 1976. Autopsy results indicate she had been dead for about twenty-four hours when found. Cause of death was strangulation by person or persons unknown. The likely motive was theft of drugs or alcohol. Elsie Nadler was drinking heavily prior to her death.*
>
> *The victim was cremated and her remains interred in the Halifax Public Cemetery. Her possessions, of which there were few, were destroyed after three years.*
>
> *If there is a request to visit the cemetery, documentation on file with the Clerk of Police Service will describe the location of the unmarked grave plot.*
>
> *The Halifax Police Department expresses its heartfelt condolences.*

Constable Donovan Martin
Police Community Outreach Division
Halifax, Nova Scotia

With all her strength, she wills herself not to cry as that would be ridiculous after all these years. She finally meets Constable Donovan's gaze. "May I keep this?"

"Absolutely. It is part of our protocol to provide family with documentation. You and your mother were separated for a long time."

The statement isn't said as a question, but Cheryl gets the distinct impression the Constable would like some history she is reluctant to share. "We lost touch a long time ago. Thank you for your time and all you've done." Cheryl stands up and smoothes the front of her linen trousers. "I'm on my way back to Edmonton tonight." She reaches out to shake his hand. He walks her down the stairs and sees her out the main door but never says another word.

She could go to the cemetery before she drives to the airport but what would be the point? An unmarked grave in a field of unmarked graves is easy enough to imagine. She points the little Ford toward the airport.

****

Cheryl is dog-tired, and more than a little grimy from travelling all night and half the day. She parks her 1978 Toyota Celica in her regular space at the front of The Station. She hurries inside and up the stairs to unlock her apartment door. Then she turns on her heel and races back down to haul her suitcase out of the trunk. Up she flies again. All she thought of on the way home was laundry, a healthy meal, a hot shower, a fresh nightgown, and a clean bed.

She leaves her suitcase in the middle of the floor and turns to lock her door. She suddenly realizes she has no milk and no produce. There's frozen bread to make toast, some raspberry jam, and tea. After she slots the bread in the toaster, she sits down and surveys her apartment. It's perfect. It smells good. The place is so neat—except for the suitcase in the middle of the floor. She's surprised to discover that she doesn't feel compelled to unpack it immediately and do laundry right away.

She sits on the couch, munches on toast, and sips her tea. Crumbs drop on the floor. Her mother is dead. She finishes her snack, puts the dirty dishes in the sink, strips off her travel clothes—which she leaves unceremoniously on the bedroom floor—and, in her bra and panties, crawls into bed.

It's four-thirty in the afternoon and Cheryl sleeps for fourteen hours.

Chapter 25

Rose

Rose hopes against hope that this pilgrimage, for that is how she has come to think of it, during the first week of May won't be complicated by bad roads. Surely to God the snow has stopped for a while.

She runs her finger down her checklist. They leave tomorrow. The routine will be the same as every year she went to visit Maggie. Three days to get to Ontario, two days at their destination, and three days to return. They are each away from work for two weeks so there should be time to spare. Joe will take care of Caesar this time around. She helped him out with Blanche when he went back to Nova Scotia in February so he could hardly refuse. She doesn't want to have to worry about the cat. Maggie will be worry enough, thank you very much.

"Maggie, are you all packed? Don't take too much. Comfy clothes for the car, a sweater, and a jacket. I don't imagine Ruth and Abner will offer to take us out for dinner, so don't waste the space with fancy stuff." She's yelling in an attempt to be heard through the walls, but is suddenly aware of Maggie standing in the doorway to the bedroom. "Oh, I didn't know you were right behind me. God, you can be quiet sometimes! Are you packed?"

Maggie nods. As is her custom, her long straight dark hair is pulled back in a ponytail at the nape of her neck. She often uses a brightly coloured bow wrapped around it, now. Rose thinks this is a positive development. She's wearing a tie-dyed skirt and a baggy blue sweater. Her feet are bare. "I'm all ready, Rose. You're sure you want to do this? You seem so anxious and upset.

We don't have to go see our folks on my account. I could happily live the rest of my life without ever seeing them again. They're awful people, Rose."

Rose expels a gust of air. They've had this conversation on numerous occasions since Ben died. Rose has repeated to Maggie that they need to visit their parents at least once, to make it known that the couple didn't manage to totally ruin the lives of both their daughters. "Like I've said before, Maggie, I think we need to show them we're okay. I'd like to charge them with abuse and neglect but that ship has sailed. I just want to see them once and get their reaction. That's all."

Maggie shrugs—that way she has of flipping her shoulders when she wants you to think she doesn't give a rat's ass. She cares. She could stay home if she wanted to. She has to take ten days off without pay from her new job in order to make the trip. "Anyway, I'm all packed. Just don't leave me there. I don't have enough money to get back by myself." She tries to smile while she says it, but Rose suddenly realizes the problem.

"Maggie—I would not leave you alone with Ruth and Abner ever again! Please don't even think that! This trip is just to finish with them. I have to do this in order to move forward. I want them to feel terrible that they could have two wonderful daughters like us in their lives and instead they have no one at all. I want to walk out their door and know they will miss us a lot more than we'll miss them. I don't want to make up with them, Maggie, even though that's what Ben advised us to do. I want to finish with them!" By the end of this soliloquy, Rose is shaky and tearful. She plunks down on the corner of the bed, and her gathered skirt billows out around her waist like one of those inflatable tires kids wear when they're swimming.

Maggie moves into the room and pats her on the shoulder which, with the exception of rare occasions, is about as affectionate as she gets with anyone other than the cat. She actually hugs Caesar and kisses the top of his velvety head. "We'll go. We'll show them what they're missing and that they couldn't keep us down, and then we'll come home. What time do you want to leave in the morning? Early? I can go up and tell Joe when we plan to leave so he'll know."

Rose covers Maggie's hand, still resting on her shoulder, with her own "You go tell Joe...and don't forget your medication, Maggie."

Her sister turns back before she fully escapes Rose's bedroom. "Not a chance, sis."

****

The excursion to Whitney is stressful and boring at the same time. Maggie still hasn't gotten a driver's licence, so Rose is behind the wheel for the entire trip just like always. She thinks they might have managed in two days if Maggie could have helped with the driving, but her sister still seems afraid.

Now they are just a few hours from Whitney, the small suburb of seniors' trailer park housing where Abner and Ruth Woodward have made their home for the past number of years. Maggie and Rose are booked in to the Aurora Inn located in Penny Falls, their old home town and only about five kilometers from their parents. Rose decided when she planned the trip that familiarity might be an asset. She knows the inn and the restaurant. She knows herself well enough to realize she might need that comfort.

Maggie has very little to say. She hasn't talked much the whole trip so Rose experiences the same sort of solitude she did when she travelled by herself so many times before. Of course, she had chats with Caesar when she was in the car with only him for company. She takes yet another stab at conversation. "Are you nervous about seeing them, Maggie?"

Curled up in the seat, Maggie focuses on her hands. Her long hair hangs loose today and obscures the side of her face. Rose can't gauge her mood. She mumbles that she'll be okay. She just wants to get it over with.

Rose is suspicious but she's not sure why. "Maggie, do you remember the last time they came to see you at the institute?"

"Yes," comes the soft reply.

"Will you tell me about that?" They stopped visiting after they moved to Whitney. The little community isn't that far from Forest Hills Institute. Rose has always suspected there was an incident of some sort.

"I hated their visits! I told them to never come again." She turns toward Rose, who can only take her eyes off the road for a moment to glance over at her sister. "I hate them, Rose. I'm not sure I can go see them. Can I stay at the inn or at least just sit in the car? I'm so scared they'll try to put me away again!" Her voice starts to shake. Rose knows her sister will begin to cry soon. It's happened before.

"You don't have to come in if you don't want to. Who knows, Maggie? Maybe they won't even be around. After all, this is a surprise attack and they could be away for all we know." She takes a breath. "All I want to do is confront them in person, tell them they were horrible parents, show them how well we survived, and let them see how much they missed. That's all. I just want to say my piece."

"If Ben wasn't dead, would you want to do this?" Her tone holds a challenge somehow, and Rose has to think fast.

"I would have come to this eventually, on my own. My experiences lately with you have changed me. I think Ben just pointed out the obvious and got me to this place a little sooner. Her death illustrated the urgency. People die. Tidy situations up when you can, that's all."

It's mid-afternoon when they finally arrive at the Aurora Inn. Penny Falls is the same as it always has been. They check in and go for a walk together before supper. Afterward, they drive to Whitney—just to get the lay of the land. The address was in the phone book so there was no need even to enquire as to their parents' whereabouts. Whitney is like almost all trailer parks, with street names like Sunset Drive and Rainbow Road. They cruise up and down the streets. All of the house trailers are perched on narrow lots, slightly angled to the road, each with a large window facing out. They all have little wooden decks and short driveways to accommodate a single car. Many are decorated with planters, garden gnomes, or trellises that wait patiently for a vine of some sort to poke its way out of the cool ground and start climbing. There are macramé hangers between curtain panels, supporting pots with spider plants and trailing vines. There are stained glass ornaments stuck to windows with suction cups. They locate 28 Autumn Lane without much difficulty and cruise by without stopping. There's an ageing Chrysler in the driveway and two cases of empty beer bottles stacked on the deck. It will be easy to find the Woodwards in the morning.

Rose and Maggie don't sleep much that night. They watch a movie although Rose is pretty sure Maggie isn't paying it any attention, either.

"Maybe Mom and Dad will want us to stay for supper. Maybe they'll want us to meet their friends."

"Maggie, have you decided to knock on their door with me? I'd be very grateful not to have to do this alone, but don't get your hopes up. You saw the beer bottles at the door the same as I did. I don't think much has changed."

"I'll come with you." She says this while she gnaws like a hamster on her knuckle, and stares at the television.

****

The next morning, the women enjoy a hearty breakfast in the hotel restaurant and then go for another walk around Penny Falls. They return to their hotel room and dress with care. For some reason, Rose needs to present her very best self. Maggie follows her lead. Their intention is to be at 28 Autumn Lane in Whitney by mid-morning.

Rose parks her almost new silver Malibu out in front of the trailer they are confident belongs to their estranged parents. The Chrysler is still in the same position in the driveway. There is a third case of empty beer bottles at the side door. Maggie points out the trim in the picture window—plastic poinsettia lights still hang like it's Christmas.

They walk up the wooden steps together and ring the doorbell. There's a curtain that covers the window so they can't tell who approaches. Ruth Woodward swings back the door with a ready expression of welcome on her face, obviously expecting someone else. "You're early! I thought you said you'd be here at eleven." Her face turns a mottled grey and red almost instantly.

Maggie is the first to speak. "Hi, Mom! I bet you're surprised to see us!" She sounds like a little kid instead of a thirty-one-year old woman who was abused and institutionalized for most of her life.

"Hi, Ruth. Maggie and I decided it was time to get in touch. You look well." Rose can't bring herself to address her mother by anything but her given name. She's not as thin as she used to be. "I see you're not starving yourself to death any more. Is Abner around? We hoped, if we stopped by in the morning, he might be sober." Try as she might, she can't keep the sarcasm and disdain out of her voice.

"Who's at the door? I though the Rogers weren't here 'til later." Abner Woodward emerges from the back of the trailer. Always a short man and heavy set, age does not appear to have served him well. He practically kicks his sagging beer gut in front of him as he looms out of the shadows and pushes his way in front of Ruth. She quietly steps back without another word. "What the hell is this?" He glares out at them both, like he just discovered two rodents on the porch.

Maggie, surprisingly, jumps in again. "We wanted to come and see you! It's been years. How have you been?" She sounds like a long-lost cousin instead of their daughter. Rose suddenly realizes Maggie is trying to maintain some sort of decorum, but Rose can tell by the fiery hate in her father's eyes that it won't work.

Rose catches her mother's attention. "Can we come in for a few minutes? We just wanted to see you. We leave to go back out west tomorrow. Maggie and I both have jobs to get back to." She tries to make it sound as if they are successful and busy—wasn't that the plan?

Abner blocks the door. Rose isn't sure he will let them in at all. She sees Ruth touch him on the arm and he moves out of the way. "Come in," she says. "We expect company for coffee in about half an hour, though."

So they are summarily dismissed already.

The house trailer opens directly into the kitchen. All the walls are wood panelling and subdued. There is some kind of disgusting green carpet on the kitchen floor. Cheryl pops into Rose's mind. She would be appalled. The living room is to the right and, except for the absence of a tree, is still decorated for Christmas with the plastic poinsettia lights trimming the front window as Maggie observed on the way in. More plastic poinsettias are stuffed into corners everywhere. There is a woven blanket hanging on the wall above the mottled brown sofa. It depicts two bears at a stream ripping apart a big salmon. The cushions on the couch have pictures of dead deer hanging from trees and there's an actual deer head mounted on the side wall. The carpet on the floor of this room is mottled brown, just like the sofa, and in a similar condition as the one in the kitchen. They are not invited to sit. As her mind flits to Cheryl again, Rose feels this might be a blessing.

She takes a deep breath and begins. "We wanted you to know that Maggie is doing well with me in Alberta." They both agreed not to reveal their exact location until they assessed their reception. Rose has already decided she doesn't want them to know where they live. "She has a job as a bookkeeper and I am a medical secretary. We live together and have a lovely apartment."

"And a cat named Caesar. Our friend Joe is taking care of him!" Maggie seems anxious to contribute. "I'm not sick anymore."

"Well, whoop-de-doo!" Abner sneers at both of them in turn. Ruth starts to open her mouth and he gives her a glare that would stop a train.

"Listen!" Rose continues, but now she knows there will be no fence-mending today. "You ruined our childhood, you son of a bitch! And Ruth, you just stood by and tried to starve yourself to death! You were evil, horrible parents. The reason we came here today was to tell you it didn't work. We're neither dead nor destitute, no thanks to you!" She stops to catch her breath and glances at Maggie, who is now focused on the floor. Her hair conceals her reaction.

"We tell people we don't have kids!" Abner shouts. "That might give you some idea of how little we care. I don't give a damn if you're the Queen of Sheba. You two don't exist to us. We never wanted kids to begin with. Stupid here," he eyes Ruth, "made a couple of mistakes in that department. Man, are we done? The Rogers will be here any minute. Did you get all your crap off your chest? I hope so. Don't let the door hit you in the ass on the way out!"

Rose and Maggie turn to leave. They nod "hello" to the Rogers as they pass on the stairs leading up to the deck.

"Who was that?" Mrs. Rogers asks as Abner opens the door.

"Oh, just a couple of Jehovah Witnesses. Nobody important." Rose thinks he manages to say this just a bit louder than necessary.

****

She expects the three-day journey back to Hayworth to be quiet. She anticipates Maggie's withdrawal. As for herself, she's shell-shocked and oddly disappointed. Maybe she needs to face the fact that, in her heart of hearts, she wanted her parents not to be the people she remembered.

Maggie proves Rose wrong. The first surprise comes just after they leave Penny Falls. "When we get back to Hayworth, will you teach me how to drive?"

"What? You? Drive? What brought this on?"

"I was just thinking. There are other trips we could take. Have you ever been to the west coast? I haven't. I haven't been to the east coast, for that matter. Cheryl and Joe are from down east. If I learn to drive, we could take trips in the car or go by plane, and rent a car. I could help with the driving! Good idea?" She's antsy in the seat, excited, and vibrant.

Rose laughs in spite of herself. "Sounds like you have it all worked out."

"Well, the way I see it, we just have one another, and our friends of course; so let's make the best of it. I'm so glad you let me come to live with you. You won't be sorry, I promise."

"I'm not sorry, Maggie. You, my dear, have changed my life for the better.

We are okay!" She squares her shoulders and focuses on the road.

"Will you teach me how to knit, too?"

Chapter 26

Ronny

Veronica Étang unfolds her five foot eight inch self out of her confining seat on the bus. She reaches into the overhead bin for her duffel bag, slings her hobo purse on her shoulder, and makes her way to the front to disembark. The bus from Edmonton, after having stopped and started through every little Wild West town along its route for the past eight hours, has finally arrived at the Hayworth Diner in Hayworth, Alberta on this beautiful May 14, 1981. She bends over slightly to get a better view of the roadside restaurant, as she negotiates the steps into a new community and what she sincerely hopes will be a new life.

She seems young for her forty years. Her naturally curly hair, dyed almost white-blond, is cropped short and twists around her brow and ears. She's making a valiant attempt to get used to it. She wore her dark hair long all her life—pulled back with elastics, raked behind her ears, and generally in a state of disarray. She loved her wild and crazy hair. She isn't all that happy with this short, blindingly bright version but she doesn't want to resemble herself—and she most certainly does not.

From her telephone conversation with Amanda Wolski, the building manager of a place called The Station, she knows she's in the right place. Her instructions are to have a cup of tea in the local diner and wait for Chester Wolski to pick her up at five o'clock to take her to her new home. She will be the replacement tenant in Number Three. Amanda also told her that another resident, Patrick Hollinger, would be working a shift that afternoon at the diner, and for her to introduce herself.

Ronny unceremoniously opens the glass entrance door by nudging her big blue duffel ahead of her with her foot. She meets the gaze of a young guy behind the long service counter and soda fountain. She thinks this place is a relic from the 1950s, and all this guy needs is a jaunty little hat to transform him into the quintessential soda-jerk. He looks up and gives her an ear-to-ear grin.

"You must be Veronica Étang. Did I pronounce that right? Tea or coffee?" He continues to wipe down the long counter as he talks. "You can just leave your duffel by the door. No one will bother it. Amanda told me you'd be on the bus. Her husband, Chester, will pick you up after work. I'm not off 'til eight, or I'd lug your bag back to The Station for you."

"Tea, please. And call me Ronny." She shoves the big bag into the corner by the coat tree and moves over to sit on one of the empty stools. There are many. The place is bereft of customers except for a teenage couple down in a back booth. At this time of day, the coffee crowd has vacated and the diner staff can only wait for the supper rush to begin.

"I'm Patrick. I live at The Station—up in the nosebleed section in Number Six. Nobody shortens my name—I prefer Patrick. So what brings you to Hayworth, Ronny?" He pours hot water into a little metal teapot containing a teabag. With practised precision, he places it, along with a heavy china cup and saucer, a spoon, and a napkin, carefully in front of her. "Are you hungry? We could do an early supper for you while you wait for Chester."

Ronny appreciates the attention but she's impatient to see the apartment. She will go grocery shopping after she gets rid of her bag. Amanda said the store is within walking distance of the building. It appears most of the town is within walking distance, even the place she'll be working. Damn good thing since the last expense she needs right now is a car. "No thanks, Patrick. I want to get some supplies after I meet Amanda and unload my stuff."

"No problem. You're going to rent Number Three. You'll be happy to know Ben had us leave the big kitchen peninsula, the picnic table, and the spare room bed. At least you won't have to stand at the counter to eat or sleep on the floor. I slept on a camp cot for ages before I got a bed."

"Amanda said there was some furniture, but...a picnic table?"

"Yeah! Neat, eh? Ben was great. Some queer ideas but a fine lady. She was an antique dealer here in town for years." By now, Patrick is methodically arranging clean glasses and cups on open shelves behind the counter. He turns toward her as he adds, "She was a great friend to me; helped me a lot."

"Did she move away? Ben is an interesting name for a woman."

"Your name is Ronny. How is that different? And, no, she didn't move away. She died just before Christmas. We all took care of her—everybody in the building."

Ronny's glad Patrick's back is turned so her new neighbour can't see her face. She lacks the courage to ask if this Ben person actually died in the apartment—or in the bed she expects to sleep in.

They continue to chat—about the town, The Station, and Patrick, himself. He seems to be a very outgoing guy, originally from Ontario. He's all excited because his father will arrive from Edmonton on the very same bus tomorrow. It seems it will be the first time the kid has seen his father in ages. He says Ronny will meet him over the weekend at some sort of party happening on Victoria Day at The Station—just for residents. He's sure Amanda will include her.

Chester shows up. He fills the restaurant with his swagger and his good looks. "I'm supposed to meet a Veronica Étang." There's nobody there but Patrick and Ronny so he's looking right at her when he asks, "Did I pronounce that right?" She nods and smiles.

Maybe she should have given more consideration to the last name she chose. She wanted it to be easy for her to remember—Veronica Lake from the movies to Veronica (Ronny) Étang—French for pond. Too late now. She's made her bed. Speaking of which, it will be nice to get to the apartment and see what she's gotten into.

****

Chester drags her duffel bag out of the back of his old pick-up and sets it down in front of Number Three. Just as he's about to go around to his own apartment to get Amanda, she appears, walking slowly and leading a little boy by the hand.

"Hello, you must be Veronica. I'm Amanda. I have your keys as well as the lease for you to sign. This is Mason, who has just recently decided he no longer needs his stroller. It slows me down but when I can, I let him walk if he wants to." She opens the door to the apartment and they all manoeuvre inside. Chester and the cumbersome bag bring up the rear.

Ronny assesses the big space and the peninsula with the marble top. The picnic table is huge and rough but in a funky way she thinks she likes. "Just call me Ronny, Amanda." She bends over to address Mason. "And it's very nice to meet you, little man."

He grins up at her and offers a bite of his cookie.

"If you need anything to get by until you're organized, just let me know."

"Thanks, Amanda. I have the basics—cup, plate, bowl, set of silverware, pot, and frying pan—in the bag, along with bed linens. I'll take a quick trip to the grocery store and that should get me through for a couple of days. I start work on Tuesday."

Chester picks up Mason and takes him back to their apartment while the two women finish their conversation. Ronny hears them jabbering away to one another as they leave via the front door. The Wolskis must have an outside entrance someplace else.

"Can you keep a secret, Ronny?"

"Why yes I believe I can, Amanda. I'm to be the counsellor at the women's shelter. I'd better be able to keep a secret!" She smiles although she thinks it's probably more indulgent than necessary.

"There will be a little wedding here on Monday afternoon. The only people who know about it are the residents. Patrick's father will be visiting, so he's invited, too."

"Who's to be married and why is it a secret?"

"Chester and I will be the bride and groom. The reason it's a secret is a long story. I'll tell you some time. We were actually married over three years ago. Let's just say, we need to get married again and we want family to continue to think we were married the first time. It's complicated."

Ronny is very happy to be included. "I love weddings! The fact that you'll marry one another again means you must have gotten it right. Don't worry, I have no one to tell so your secret's safe with me."

Amanda seems sad. "That's what Ben used to say—'Your secret's safe with me. Take it to the grave'—she took a lot of secrets to her grave. Sorry. I didn't mean to sound so maudlin, Ronny." She shakes her red hair just a little. "Welcome to The Station. I'm sure you will love it here. If you need help, just come and get me. Until you get a phone, we're around the back."

****

They must have listened for Amanda to finish up and leave because the tenants across the hall open their apartment door just as the building manager goes down the front steps. Ronny barely has her door closed before the tap-tap bids her to open it again.

"Hi. We're Rose and Maggie," says the older one. "We would very much like to invite you to supper." They act anxious but festive somehow, in knitted sweater sets and gathered skirts—very spring-like. The one with the long hair holds a kitten. A full-grown tortoiseshell version meanders across the hall and into Ronny's apartment. "I hope you like cats. Caesar, there, makes himself at home. He was good friends with the former tenant."

"I'm Maggie," says the younger one. "This is Caramel. We just got him last week. Isn't he sweet?" She holds the kitten out to be inspected.

Ronny nods her agreement. "I'm Veronica Étang, but you can call me Ronny."

"We'll be working at the same place!" Maggie almost jumps up and down, she's so excited. "I work at the shelter three days a week. I'm the bookkeeper! We'll be able to walk to work together!"

Ronny isn't so sure about this child-like creature who must be thirty, if she's a day. It's almost as if she has the mind maturity of a teenager. "Nice to meet you both and I appreciate the invitation, but I really have to go get some groceries—pick up staples. You understand."

"All figured out," Rose replies, as if she's had this planned for ages. "You don't want to carry groceries home by yourself so we'll go in my car. Maggie will finish making supper while we're gone. It will be perfect!" She claps her hands for effect.

Ronny silently admits defeat—she's out of her league. These two, especially Rose, seem to have her life figured out. Little do they know! "Okay. Okay. Give me five minutes to wash my face and we'll hit the grocery store. I made a list when I was on the bus."

****

Supper proves intriguing. They sit at a dining room table Rose tells her came from Ben's antique shop many years ago. Maggie doesn't talk much but then suddenly bursts forth with a cascade of sentences, one bumping into the other.

"How did you two come to live in Hayworth? You're not from here, are you?"

"Rose came here years ago. Then she came to the institute and got me. We don't have any other family—well we do really, but they say they don't have kids, so I guess that means we don't have parents. Right, Rose?"

Rose gives her sister the look of indulgence you would give an overly enthusiastic child and then turns her attention back to Ronny. "We're estranged from our parents. It's a long story. We'll tell you all about it some time."

Ronny expects to hear a lot of stories over the next few months. She gives them her prepared backstory. She was a lay-counsellor at a shelter in Montreal. Because she doesn't speak French very well they couldn't keep her on so she applied for the job here. Yes, her last name is French. Her father was French but they never spoke the language at home, and she went to English school just like he had as a child. Politics are changing in Quebec and she needed to move on. No, she's never been married. She was an only child, her parents are deceased, and she is alone in the world. The scar on her neck? Why, that's from an old car accident. No big deal.

They talk. Rose and Ronny drink wine. Maggie abstains. She says she takes pills so she shouldn't drink. They discuss the upcoming nuptials on Monday. Ronny thinks it's a good start to a neighbourly friendship. She decides working with Maggie will likely be fine.

She crawls into her hand-me-down bed, between clean sheets bundled with her across the country, comforted in the knowledge that there is food in the cupboards, a good job starting Tuesday, interesting people around her, and a plan for a safe future. She's happy and secure for the first time in a long time.

****

Everyone said attire would be casual, so Ronny chooses to wear crisp ivory cotton pants and a turquoise sweater to the afternoon wedding. She fluffs her hair up and adds blue crystal drop earrings. As she gazes at herself in the bathroom mirror, she's still uncomfortable with the new version. She wants to let her hair grow again but knows she can't give in.

Chester, Amanda, and Mason are too cute. The Justice of the Peace says all the right words and the whole process is over in no-time flat. He departs right after the ceremony and the residents of The Station begin to party in earnest.

The first new person Ronny meets is Cheryl. She is a small woman with short dark hair. She's in excellent physical shape and extraordinarily pretty. Today, she's decked out in a floral dress with a deep v-neck. The dress accentuates her curves. Everybody tells her how gorgeous she looks and they're right. She talks to them all in turn, shows off a picture, and receives oohs and aahs in the process. Eventually, she approaches Ronny.

"Hi. I wanted to formally introduce myself. I'm Cheryl Nadler, your upstairs neighbour in Number Five. I'm a social worker at the provincial government services offices. I hear we're in the same kind of work. Is that right?"

"Why yes, it is. News travels fast." Ronny is still not certain she can trust these people regardless of how nice they are. "At the women's shelter. I start tomorrow. I don't mean to be nosey but you've been showing everybody a picture." She doesn't come right out and ask to see it.

Cheryl holds out a snapshot and Ronny takes a quick peek. It's of a young girl, perhaps twelve or thirteen. "A relative, Cheryl?"

"Not exactly; well, maybe. This is the first picture I've ever seen of my daughter. She's fourteen now." Ronny is quiet. She just stares at the photo and then back at Cheryl. "I wrote the Department of Social Services in Nova Scotia shortly after Ben—she's the lady who used to live in your apartment— died. She'd really encouraged me to try and find my child. Apparently, the adoptive parents had an alert in the file to say that if either birth parent asked questions, to contact them. Social Services sent me this picture along with a letter to say that when Amy—that's her name—is sixteen, they will let us get in touch if that's what Amy wants. It's a start. I'll tell you the whole grisly story sometime. It will take a couple of pots of tea, or a bottle of wine, but it's not a secret anymore." She grins. Cheryl can't seem to wipe that expression of pure joy off her face and Ronny figures she'll hear the tale before long.

"Let's go introduce you to Joe. He built the marble-topped peninsula in your kitchen, you know. He lives across from me in Number Four. He's a nice man and a good cook. He always brings a great dish to these little gatherings we have. He has lots of family down east. I hear his two sisters plan to come here for a week this summer."

As Veronica and Cheryl approach Joe, Ronny overhears the conversation underway between Joe and Patrick's father, Ray. "Yes, that's right! I surprised him with the car. It's not much. He expected me on the bus, Saturday, but I'd made arrangements to meet an old friend at one of the Pontiac dealers in Edmonton. I thought the kid was going to piss his pants when I got out of that Acadian in the parking lot. He figured I rented it to drive up instead of taking the bus!" Raymond Hollinger throws back his head and laughs the laugh of a barrel-shaped man, deep and rollicking. His Buick belt buckle pitches and rolls in response. "It's a demonstrator, and I could get it wholesale 'cause I'm in the 'biz', if you know what I mean." He leans a little closer, winks at Joe, and then glances over at Joe's big blue monster. "If you need a new truck, I can put you on to my friend. He'll help you out. Give you a good deal."

Ronny smiles politely as she and Cheryl interrupt the men. Joe seems grateful. Introductions occur all around. Ronny learns this is the first time Ray has seen his son in over four years. She also learns that Joe's sisters have never been to Hayworth and he just saw them for the first time in fourteen years, a couple of months ago. It seems she may not be the only one with a complicated past.

****

The following day, Maggie and Ronny walk to Segue House together. It's a beautiful mid-May morning and the trip takes a mere fifteen minutes. Segue House is a nondescript boxlike building. It looks like a simple 1950s red brick apartment building housing six apartments, two per floor. The security tells another story. When they approach the front door, Maggie rings a bell. In a moment, a crackling intercom springs to life.

"Can I help you?"

 Maggie stands on her toes so her mouth is quite close to the metal speaker embedded in the wall. "Hi. It's Maggie Woodward. Security number 1981-49. I have Ronny Étang with me. She starts today."

"I'll have to see identification. Hold on."

Ronny holds her breath. The plan was that the director of Segue House would be there this morning. She's the only one who knows Ronny's true identity. A buzzer sounds and the women open the heavy, solid steel door in order to enter a vestibule with a second locked door. This one is glass. It's a double-buzzed entry system. Obviously, they have experienced some issues. Ronny is nervous.

Ava Burrway appears from around the corner. Maggie stands quietly. Ronny watches the woman approach the glass door. She is tall and shapely, in that middle-aged way women have of filling out in all the right places. She's not particularly striking, with short brown hair and prominent features beginning to sag—the telltale first sign of a person nibbling at the corners of fifty. She's wearing a navy pant suit along with sensible shoes. She nods to Ronny, who holds up her Ontario driver's licence against the window. It has her picture and clearly refers to her as Janine Taylor from Sudbury, Ontario. Ava examines the document, nods slightly as she casts a glance toward Maggie, and presses the buzzer. This permits them entrance into the hallway. The door on the left is closed. The door on the right opens to the apartment that houses offices and the general meeting room. The stairs are at the back of the hall and lead to two apartments on the second floor, as well as another two on the third.

"Maggie, I left some paperwork on your desk. After the long weekend, there's a lot to do. Veronica, we can go right into my office and get down to business. Follow me."

"I'll see you at break time, Ronny. We can have coffee in the kitchen whenever you're ready."

Ronny nods at Maggie and follows her new boss into what must once have been the master bedroom. Ava closes the door. "Sit down, Veronica. Or do you prefer Ronny?"

Ronny nods. She sits in a straight-backed chair across from Ava's desk. There are footfalls above. It sounds like there are children in the upstairs apartment.

Ava casts her eyes toward the ceiling. "I have a mother, and her three children under the age of five, in the apartment above us. They've been here a week. She could use someone to talk to and I'm very happy you're here. Let's get a few basics out of the way. Are you happy with the name Veronica Étang, Ronny? If so, Murdock Blackney, our lawyer, will do a legal name change for you. I think that's important before your ex-husband gets out of jail. What do you think?"

"I need to start somewhere, Ms. Burrway."

The straight hair flutters quickly. "No. No. We are all very informal here. Call me Ava." She adds by way of an apology, "I know I appear like a bit of a stick in the mud. The older I get, the more I seem to channel my uncommonly rigid mother, but I assure you, Ava is fine.

"Now, Maggie is the other person besides me who needs to know the truth. Maggie has to process the paperwork and ensure you get paid. The girl who works nights will know you as Ronny. We can keep a secret. By the time this guy is out on the street, it will be like Janine Taylor never existed. You'll see."

About the Author

L. P. Suzanne Atkinson was born in New Brunswick, Canada and lived in both Alberta and Quebec before settling in Nova Scotia in 1991. She has a BA in Psychology from Mount Allison University, a Bachelor of Social Work from McGill University, and an MA in Sociology from Acadia University. Suzanne spent her professional career in the fields of mental health and home care as both a therapist and trainer. She also owned and operated, with her husband, both an antique business and a construction business for more than twenty-five years.

Her philosophy of life is based on two qualities for which she continually strives. They are her benchmarks. First: there is no better descriptor than to be called a kind person and good friend. Second: a lesson learned and not shared is information squandered.

Suzanne writes about the challenges inherent in aging and about the unavoidable consequences of relationships. She uses her life and work experiences to weave timeless stories that cross many boundaries. She and her husband, David Weintraub, continue to make Nova Scotia their home.

Email – lpsa.books@eastlink.ca
Website – http://lpsabooks.wix.com/lpsabooks#
Facebook – L. P. Suzanne Atkinson – Author

Watch for:

Segue House Connection: Regarding Hayworth Book III

Coming in the summer of 2017